THE MAGPIE TREE

By Katherine Stansfield

Falling Creatures
The Magpie Tree

THE MAGPIE TRÈE

KATHERINE STANSFIELD

Allison & Busby Limited
12 Fitzroy Mews
London W1T 6DW
allisonandbusby.com

First published in Great Britain by Allison & Busby in 2018.

A CIP catalogue record for this book is available from
the British Library.

First Edition

ISBN 978-0-7490-2171-9

Typeset in 12/16.25 pt Adobe Garamond Pro by
Allison & Busby Ltd.

The paper used for this Allison & Busby publication
has been produced from trees that have been legally sourced
from well-managed and credibly certified forests.

Printed and bound by
CPI Group (UK) Ltd, Croydon, CR0 4YY

For Tay, my Miss Wolffs, i.m.

ONE

The day I went to Jamaica Inn was the day I saw a man hanged.

The hanging was at the gaol, in Bodmin, and it was done early, before the sun had time to rise higher than the walls where the gallows stood. By evening, I was in Jamaica, and the hanged man in the ground, dropped in a pit behind the walls they'd hanged him from. He'd never escape. His bones would soften into the soil and he'd become that wretched place, feed it as he faded, while I was free to leave the moor, go on with the rest of my life. That's what I told myself as the cart rattled up the high road to Jamaica Inn.

But it was a lie. I would never be free of what had been done.

The inn was full of bodies and all of them men, save for me and Mrs Williams. That was not her name, of course. Not her true name, at any rate. She had told me she was called Anna Drake. I didn't know if I should believe her.

She'd asked me to work with her. I didn't know if I should believe *that* either but I had nowhere to go after the hanging was done but to Jamaica Inn, where she was going. I'd lost my work on the farm because of meeting her. This woman calling herself Anna Drake.

This woman now asking the man behind the bar the price of rooms.

Paying was her concern for I had nothing to my name, not a ha'penny, and so I looked about me at this place she'd taken me to.

Jamaica Inn was like all inns – white walls yellowed, slate flags dirtied with mud and candle wax. A thin dog gnawed a bone in the corner. The crowding made everyone too close, forced people to whisper. Pipe smoke curled at the ceiling, as if the fog had crept in from the moor beyond. The smoke didn't deaden whispers, though, as fog would. Instead it moved them about the room so that the air seethed with the secrets of the men gathered in that place, and there were many that came to Jamaica Inn. It brought them up from the south and took them north, for the inn stood on a good road. The coaches stopped there. You could get far away from Bodmin Moor if you called at Jamaica.

I knew another way to leave that inn, that inn thick with the smell of meat cooking and of men. To leave the whole world behind. To forget the sight of my friend jerking at the end of a rope.

Anna caught me, of course, and stayed my hand. She didn't care for thieving. I said to myself, later, Shilly. You'll have it later.

'One room, you're wanting?' the barman said.

'Yes,' I said.

'We'll take two.' Anna counted out the money.

'Better you're in together,' the barman said in a low voice. 'Ladies on their own in this place . . . Well. You're safer with a friend.'

That was my thinking too, but Anna was of a different mind.

'Two rooms will suit *us* better,' she said.

The barman said he was away to fetch the keys and I was left in no doubt about Anna and me. Though I'd had her in my arms the night before, her flesh against mine, her wetness in my hands, she'd had her fill of me.

A group of men, huddled nearest the cold hearth, had taken her fancy now. She half-turned to listen to them talking.

'Coal,' said one of the men. 'That's what them wicked women done. Turned him into a lump of coal.'

'A little boy?' said his friend. 'They turned him to coal?'

'You heard me.' He was old, this one speaking of coal. Wrinkled as a summer apple forgotten at the bottom of a winter barrel.

'You know him?' Anna whispered to me.

'Why would I? We're ten miles from the farm.'

'That's hardly far, Shilly.'

But ten miles could take you a long way on Bodmin Moor. Into a world of strangers. Into a marsh and so to your end. Anna didn't understand such a place.

The wrinkled man's two friends were each a little younger than him, but not by many years. I had the sense they were often to be found so seated. It was the drink. They reeked of it.

'Them women lured the child into their cottage,' one of the friends was saying now. 'Tricked him.'

'And when the cottage door was locked on him,' the wrinkled man said, 'them creatures said their Devil words and the boy was changed.'

'And then they burnt him!' one of the friends said.

'And then the boy was ash!' said the other. 'They put him in the tea tin and stirred it up so his mother and father didn't know he was in there, and then his mother—'

'She boiled him up and drank him.' The wrinkled man took a long swig of beer and the others screeched with laughter. His lips were shiny with drink. I thought about pressing my own lips against his, flicking my tongue across them for the drops, to have them slip down my throat.

''Tis wickedness, though,' the friend said.

'Something should be done,' said the other.

'Oh, it will,' the wrinkled man said. 'You mark my words. The squire there, he's offered a reward to see the women hanged.'

A chill passed over me though the day was warm for it was late August by then. I thought again of my friend. Matthew Weeks. Anna and I had failed him. May God have mercy on his soul, and hers too. Charlotte. She they said he'd killed. Oh God, for a sup—

'Here we are, then,' the barman said, and my heart stopped with the fright of him coming back so sudden. He handed us each a key.

'A jug of beer,' Anna said, and then my heart was loud in its rejoicing. Though we were but lately met she knew me well. Too well, I sometimes feared.

'I'll bring it up,' the barman said. 'Rooms are at the top of the stairs, end of the passage there.'

'I'll take it here, in the bar,' Anna said. 'Just one glass. My friends by the hearth only need topping up.'

The barman turned to me. 'And you, miss?'

'She'll inspect the rooms,' Anna said. And then without looking up from counting the money she said quietly, 'Not a drop, Shilly. You hear me?'

She took the jug of beer to the men by the hearth.

'Gentlemen. Your glasses are low. Allow me. You were speaking of two women turning a child to coal. Where are these fiends to be found?'

I took the keys and left the bar. She would keep me lonely even as she kept me by her side.

'Trethevy,' she said when she came to take her key. If she had drunk any beer then she held it well for she didn't sway or pitch. Perhaps she *could* hold her drinking. I knew so little about her and yet I'd thrown in my lot with hers.

She sat down on the edge of my bed, as far from me as she could without being on the floor. Her bony lightness barely made the cover ruck.

'What's Trethevy?' I said.

'A hamlet.' She took out her pipe. 'That's where they're living, in a wooded valley haunted by a saint, apparently.'

'Who's living there?' I said.

'The witches. The pair said to have turned a child to coal.'

I moaned and covered my face with my hands. 'I can't. Not again. Not after Charlotte . . .'

'You needn't upset yourself, Shilly. I don't believe those women are witches any more than I am, but what I *would* like to believe is this talk of a reward. It's being offered by the gentry there, Sir Vivian Orton, and we must be quick if we're the ones to gain it. We cannot live on air alone.'

'Sharing a room would've saved money.'

'We need to start earning if we're to establish the agency,' she said, as if I hadn't spoken.

'Agency?'

'You're right. That is too grand a name to start with. A business, then, for private cases. This disappearance of a child is an excellent start. Finding him will be our next investigation.'

She sounded pleased a boy had been turned to coal. She was cruel, and I could be cruel likewise. In that we were a good pair.

'You've given up, then?' I said.

She pursed her thin, bloodless lips and looked down her thin, bloodless nose at me. 'If you're referring to my attempts to join the men at Scotland Yard, then yes, Shilly, I have given up, because I don't need them. Far better to work for myself. A new opportunity presented itself in the bar this evening. You're keen on portents. Don't you think hearing of the lost boy is a sign I'm right to find my own way?'

'And what am I doing in all this, aside from knowing what are signs and what aren't? You said we'd be equals, Anna, if I came with you. You said you'd take me to London.'

She got up and went to the door. 'Equals, yes. Taking you to London – I don't believe I ever promised that. You must have imagined that part of the conversation, perhaps when you were dr—'

'Are we going, then, to the saint's place?'

'I've paid for seats in the Boscastle coach,' she said.

'Boscastle . . .' The corners of the room fluttered and I had no breath. That place. Not that place.

'Shilly, are you listening? I said we're not going so far as that. Trethevy is on the *way* to Boscastle, so my friends downstairs tell me. We leave at eight. I'll come and dress you before then. You can't keep wearing her clothes.'

And she was gone.

I lay down on the cover. It was hot in the room for the day had been hot and there was no wind to send it away. Sweat prickled like gorse under my arms, at the back of my neck, and I knew I should take off my dress, let the air reach my flesh. But it was the last of Charlotte Dymond left to me. I ran my damp hands across the green silk that she had worn when I first met her. It had been a good dress once, for she had liked good things. But now the silk was thin in places, and there was a tear at the waist. I slipped my hands across my breasts, under my backside, to feel the wear of it.

We were to catch a coach going to Boscastle, Anna had said. That was where Charlotte had come from. My girl. Oh, my girl in this green silk dress. Oh, my girl. This silk that had touched her, as it now touched me. I rucked the skirt up round my waist and made believe my hands were hers seeking me, helping me.

When I was finished, I was hotter than ever, and damp now all over, but still I couldn't take off Charlotte's dress because it clung between my thighs and that was a good thing. There were few of those in the world.

I opened the window wide as it would go. I leant out and breathed the moor to cool myself, breathed all its dank, dark air – the aching, lonely miles of it that spread across the land and made Jamaica Inn a small place, a nothing place, and me a nothing soul inside it.

TWO

Anna said I stank. I knew it, but I didn't care. I wanted her to smell me, to want me as I wanted her. I'd had her once. I'd have her again, but it meant doing as she asked, so I took off Charlotte's dress and folded it best I was able. I was never neat with such things and the dress was wilful. That was Charlotte, still making the world do as it didn't ought to. I gave up and stuffed the dress in Anna's travelling case.

Anna snatched the dress back out. 'It's time you gave her up, Shilly.'

'But—'

'You know I'm right. A new start, after today. Charlotte Dymond is gone. Just as Matthew is.'

If only it was that easy.

There was no fire lit so there was no burning the dress. Instead, Anna took a pair of scissors from a pocket of the case, one sewn into the lining, and cut the dress to ribbons. I lay down in the nest of them on the floor and wept, of course I did, but I couldn't put the dress on again, couldn't put *her* on again and that was right. That was needed. Anna, I needed. More than I cared her to know.

She pulled me from the floor and set me in a chair, then she gathered the green silk slips and threw them in the grate. I turned the chair so that I couldn't see them.

'Now, who will you be, Shilly?'

'I . . . I would be myself.'

She waved away such a foolish notion. 'I got rid of your farm clothes. You don't need them now that you're a detective assistant.'

She was dressed in red, a deep red that made me think of blood. There had been too much of that spilt on the moor, and it was good that we were leaving. Her short yellow hair was hidden beneath a wig of black knotted at the nape of her neck. It lent her meekness she didn't truly have. If I could have picked a wig for her to wear it would have been the long red curls, and that she would *be* the woman who had such lovely ringlets.

She was rummaging in the case. 'We're presenting ourselves to the squire of Trethevy. You can't very well go as a milkmaid. Ah! *This* might do.' She pulled out a dress of palest blue, a dress cut from the summer sky that waited beyond the window. 'This will suit your dark hair. It might even make you look less . . .'

'Less what?'

'You could use more colour in your cheeks, that's all.'

'Well,' I said, 'if it's more colour I need then *this* would be better.'

I pulled from the case the purple mourning dress that belonged to a great friend of mine. She was a false self, I knew. Another that Anna put on for show. But all the same, I liked her.

Mrs Williams.

Oh, how I'd missed her! The curves her special padding gave to Anna's narrow body. The neatness of her waist. The trim fur hat atop her false red curls, and the plumpness of her painted lips. I knew such things were tricks, of course. But that didn't mean I didn't like them. Sometimes I was all for being tricked.

Anna was looking me up and down as I clutched the dress.

'She shouldn't be a bad fit. But remember, Shilly. Mrs Williams is more than just the dress and the hat and all of that. She's a widow and she knows her own mind. The latter won't be a problem for you.'

'Anything else?' I said, quickly stepping into the dress before Anna could change her mind.

'Mrs Williams was originally from Clerkenwell, but your accent won't carry that. It's time she was refreshed anyway. Who do *you* think she is?'

I wriggled my hips and pulled up the dress. The padding Anna had sewn inside felt strange, like my body had broken out in lumps, grown bones where they didn't ought to be.

'Don't yank it like that – you'll tear the stitching. Let me do it.'

She slapped my hands from trying to smooth the lumps. With some little tugs and shifting the cloth so that the dress hung more squarely, the padding fell into place. I put my hands on my new hips and turned to face her, but she had moved away, to rummage in the case.

'Now, where is it? Ah . . . I think it will work.'

She held a bag, drawn closed with fine string. She opened it, reached inside and pulled out a pad of red fur that looked like a kitten, curled and sleeping. The bag slipped to the floor, Anna shook the kitten and lengths of hair were all at once dangling, bouncing.

Mrs Williams's long red curls.

I grabbed the wig from Anna and put it on. It was scratchy and terrible from the first but I told myself discomfort was worth it for such loveliness.

'One last thing,' Anna said.

She had found a little pot and wiped whatever was in it across my lips. I felt the slickness of the paint. Felt her finger pressing, smoothing. Moving into my mouth. I licked her.

She jerked away and went back to the wretched case.

'So,' she said without turning round. 'Who is she?'

I thought a moment, watching her.

'She writes books,' I said. 'She's with the Temperance. And she killed her husband with a poker for his drinking.'

Anna faced me, grinned. 'I should think we'll get on famously, Mrs Williams. Now, one last touch.'

She took my hand in hers.

'You can't be a widow without a wedding ring,' she said. 'Unless you've come to grief and had to pawn it?'

I shook my head. 'Things aren't so bad as that.'

She slipped it on, that thick band of shine, and it fit so well, like it had been made for me. Like *she* had made it for me, to make me hers, as men make women theirs before God and all the rest of it. There was none but us there that morning to witness our joining together but joined we were, in a bedroom of Jamaica Inn in August 1844. Did the ring mean anything to Anna? Anything more than a trick? I didn't know. The ring was heavy and I feared I should bang it against things, doors and the like. I'd never worn jewellery in my life until that moment.

Something else was weighing me down besides the ring. Something I'd carried from the moor.

'If I'm Mrs Williams,' I said, 'going to see about this boy turned to coal, who does that make you?'

'I'm Anna Drake.'

'That's the name you'll be using? That I'm to call you when others are about?'

'Yes,' she said. 'Why?'

'Well, you had different names on the moor, didn't you? Why are you using your true name now, for this case?'

She shrugged and set Mrs Williams's fur hat on my new red curls. 'Does it matter?'

'Of course it matters! It's who you are.'

'Names are just letters. You know that better than most, Shilly. Or would you prefer it if I called you by *your* real name?'

'But Anna Drake isn't your name, is it?' I said, and felt like taking off my ring and throwing it at her. 'That's why you'll use it. You promised you'd be honest with me, Anna. That's why I said I'd come with you.'

'"Anna". See? You have it. What more needs saying?'

'A great deal more,' I muttered, but she wasn't listening, whoever she might be. If there were ever to be answers, she'd make me wait for them.

She said we should each take a few things, and that she would send for her case once we knew where we'd be staying.

'Will the case be safe here?' I said.

She locked it with the little key she kept on a thin chain round her neck. 'I've paid handsomely to ensure it.'

'More spending.'

'Time we were earning, then,' she said. 'Come on. The coach will be leaving soon.'

That cost us dear too, for Anna had paid for seats inside the coach when we could have saved and sat outside. It was such a warm day I didn't see why she'd wasted the money and I told her so.

She hushed me, glancing at the others squashed in the coach with us. 'It wouldn't do to arrive in Trethevy looking too poor to ride inside. We're seeing a squire, remember.'

'But we *are* too poor, aren't we?'

She wouldn't answer. I wondered if there was more money tucked about her person than she let on. If there was, then it would be gone soon enough if she was in charge of it. I'd have to have my wages regular and keep them myself or I'd be in the poorhouse before too long. My wedding ring might have to be pawned after all.

The coach was full on leaving – six of us inside and the wise souls riding with the driver. We stopped many times as we crossed the moor and the faces changed, but not the smell of sweat and not the lurching that made me regret the eggs I'd eaten before we left Jamaica Inn. After Camelford there was only three of us – Anna and me and a young man who slept, his mouth fallen open and spittle sliding down his chin.

He woke with a start when the driver shouted Bossiney! Bossiney! and the coach tumbled to a stop. The spittle man got out and in his place came a young woman with a braggaty face. The marks weren't the pox. They were the mottles people were born with. A misfortune. I had to look out the window to keep from staring. And I was glad I did look out, for not long after we left Bossiney's narrow streets I saw the finest sight of my short life. It was the sea.

I had seen it before but only from the high reaches of the moor where it had the shine of a new sixpence, and the thinness of a sixpence too. A scratch of light on the edge of the world the sea had been to me then, a small thing, but now I saw it was a great slipping shakeabout of the sky's blue and slate and gorse colours. I wondered if the sea was bigger even than the moor itself, and as I was so wondering I heard a strange noise, a grindy-clack like the black cat at the farm had made when she watched birds on the barn's roof. But I was the black cat in the coach that day, grindy-clacking my teeth at the sight of so great a thing as the sea. I wished to eat it – to have it in my mouth and keep it for myself. Know it better.

Anna was likewise bewitched, and leant across me to have a better view, almost lying in my lap so I had two things to enjoy.

'I'd happily never go back to London if it meant seeing this view every day,' Anna said.

'Quite lovely,' said the young woman sitting across from us. She fiddled with her cuffs. She liked Mrs Williams, that was me, better than the sea. I could see it in her soft smile and the tilt of her chin.

Then the sea was gone for we were jouncing downhill, fields and their walls getting between me and the blue greatness, but I had no time to feel the loss sorely for we went over a bridge with a lurch that threw Anna to the floor. I helped Anna up and the coach climbed the hill beyond. On the other side of the road to the sea was now a thick bank of trees that kept pace with us.

I didn't like this. The trees were very close together, all higgledy-piggledy trying to peer round their brethren, peering at the coach as we passed. I didn't know there could be so many trees in one place. On the moor, the ground had been thick with stone and that had kept trees sparse, stopped their roots, and the wind had kept short and twisted what did find a way to grow. The trees in this part of the world were tall and so broad I couldn't see beyond the wall they'd made. I hoped we'd soon pass their darkness but before we had outrun them the coach stopped and the driver shouted Trethevy.

'This is it,' Anna said, opening the door.

'I think it was back a way, where the sea—'

'Get out if you're getting!' yelled the driver, readying to crack his whip and be off again.

Anna hauled me from the coach and then the driver was away, taking with him the woman. She watched me from the coach's window, her braggaty face growing smaller, and so more beautiful, and then winking out.

Before us was a wide house with many chimneys. More of the thickety trees were crowded nearby, flanking the house on two sides. They creaked their knees in the bare breeze, a great spread of them, stretching how far I didn't know. A prickle crept up my neck as I thought to myself, there could be anyone watching me in there. They'd be able to see *me* without *me* seeing *them*. That gave all the knowing to the trees and their hidden watchers. I was weak and ready to run.

But Anna wasn't having that.

'Time to go to work, Shilly. Let's see if we can't put a stop to this nonsense of witches.'

She pulled the rope and set the bell clanking because we were business callers now, not hiding our true purpose like when we ferreted in the places the moor kept its secrets. The door opened.

'Yes?' said a sour-faced woman with a sour voice.

Anna told her we wanted the reward. She didn't say it quite so bold as that, of course, but that was the bones of it. The money.

'Is the squire at home?' Anna said.

'He is,' the sour-face said, 'and I'm to admit callers about them women in the woods.' This fact seemed to rankle with her, but she let us into the hall.

'Have you had many calling about the reward?' Anna said, and I could hear the worry in her voice.

'You're the first,' the sour-face said. She looked us up and down all sneering. 'But I don't suppose you'll be the last.'

And with that rudeness she led us down a passage wide as the whole house I had lately left.

Her clothes were plain as mine had been before Anna dressed me better, though not as worn as mine from working on the farm. This woman had decent fastenings on her dark-blue dress and wore a clean apron over it, which I had never had about me. She clumped along, a grumbling step, and I thought her to be fifty or so and likely a housekeeper.

Anna spoke low to me. 'We must have cards made, once we're established.'

'Cards?'

'To announce ourselves. It doesn't make a good first impression if we can only give our names verbally on arrival.'

Would my name go on such a card? Even if she said it was there, I would have to trust she wasn't lying, and she was good at that. I needed to learn my letters. Then I could be more certain about the things Anna Drake said.

The sour-face took us to a room and shut us in. The room was awash with sickly light for the walls were green, the rugs too. The place was filled with chairs and small tables, as if a party was thought to come but each person would be made to eat alone. Anna took a chair by the window and bade me sit next to her and stop fretting, but the window gave on to the trees outside and they were still very darkly gathered. I moved to the other side of the room, the corners of tables catching at me as I went.

'Must you roam like that?' Anna said.

'I'm looking at the pictures,' I said, seeing the frames and fixing on them to hide my being ill at ease.

But that was a poor choice and no mistake, for the frames were made of wood and they held nothing but more woods still! Every painting in that room was of trees – boldly alone or clumped together as if whispering. I peered for signs of life beneath the branches. People taking charge of the tallness gave me comfort, but such comfort was thin. It was as if the woods had come inside the house. And what did they want from us?

Something dropped into the fireplace with a rustle. I scurried to sit with Anna and pressed myself against her.

'What was that?' I whispered.

'I don't know – a twig, dropped by a bird? Does it matter? Shilly, you're pinching me.'

'We must be careful. The woods are watching—'

'Hush!' Anna said. 'We're trying to get rid of witches, not be mistaken for them ourselves.'

'You said you didn't believe they *were* witches.'

'I . . . I'm reserving judgement on that matter.'

I sat back in my chair. She had come closer to my way of thinking about such things as witches and curses and other parts of life that were strange troubling. And she needed me for all of that business. She'd have to keep me close.

Anna twisted so that our hips were not so snug together. 'A child is missing, Shilly. That's the matter at hand. I'd ask that you—'

A woman screamed outside the door.

THREE

There was the slap-dash-slap of soft shoes in the passage. And then silence. I got up and opened the door a crack. There was no sign of anyone but shouts reached us. I strained to catch the word that sounded so vexatious to the shouter.

'What is that she's saying, Shilly?'

'Fidge-un,' I said, trying to give the shout some letters.

'Which means?'

'How should I know?'

I went and sat beside her again, and then the door was thrown open and a wide man was bearing down on us.

'My sincere apologies,' he shouted.

He got hold of Anna's small hand and it was lost inside his meaty one, and then my own hand was being crushed.

'You've had no tea!' he roared, and was back out in the passage thundering. When he seemed satisfied someone had likely heard him, he dragged a chair across the floor, hauling it through the rucks it made in the rugs, and thumped it in front of Anna and me.

Now I had a chance to look at him, and there was a good lot to look at. He wasn't tall but he was broad – his neck especially so. It was the same width as his reddened face and that was no thin bit of him. I thought him to be somewhere between thirty and forty. His eyes were grey, one of them lazy.

'Thank you for seeing us, Squire Orton,' Anna said.

He waved her words away. 'We don't stand on formality here in Trethevy. Call me Sir Vivian.'

Anna gave a good attempt at a smile. 'How kind. Sir Vivian, my name is Miss Drake, and this is Mrs Williams. We offer a service which I gather you might need.'

As much as he was able, given the tightness of his chair, Sir Vivian leant towards us. The chair creaked like the trees beyond the house. With his bad eye not able to move freely, he had one for each of us as he said, 'You get rid of witches?'

I said yes as Anna said no.

'Which is to say,' Anna said quickly, 'we will ascertain if the problem thought to be supernatural can be explained more rationally. We use the methods of Scotland Yard. You might have heard of the new branch there. The detectives?'

'They've taken a child, you know,' Sir Vivian said. 'These women. Taken a boy. From right here in Trethevy. From *my* land!'

'I gather there's a reward offered for the boy's safe return,' Anna said.

'And for the discovery of who took him. I'm on the bench, you see. Much as my tenants would like to string these wretches from the nearest tree, you have to hang with due process if you're a magistrate.'

On hearing this from Sir Vivian I wished to spit, for I had no love for magistrates.

'Why not just turn these witches out?' I asked him. My family had been turned out more times than I cared to remember. It was an easy way to be rid of poor people. 'If they're on your land—'

'Ah, but they're not, Mrs Williams. The women are cunning, as you'll soon discover.' The squire fixed me with both his eyes – the good and the bad. 'They've taken up residence in a cottage across the river, on land belonging to my neighbour Trunkett, and they've chosen well in that regard for Trunkett will not be moved to action.'

'You've asked him to remove them?' Anna said.

Sir Vivian's already red face now went redder still and he puffed and blew like a fretful child. 'I have! Went down to his estate myself, all the way to Truro. Beseeched him in person. The man won't take action.'

'And what reason did he give?'

'That *my* reasons weren't good enough,' Sir Vivian said, fussing with a loose thread on his chair's cushion. 'Trunkett says the women have done nothing wrong, that he won't be party to persecution on the basis of superstitious nonsense. Thinks himself greatly learnt does *Mister* Trunkett.'

'Forgive me, Sir Vivian,' Anna said, 'but your neighbour might be right. These women may be as worldly as you or I, but even . . . even if they are of the . . . What I mean to say is—'

'If they're witches,' I said.

Anna swallowed, then went on quickly, 'Yes, even if they are such, they may be innocent of the charge laid against them. It does no good to presume guilt.'

'Whether they be witches or no,' Sir Vivian said, 'I *must* have the means to be rid of them before they strike again.'

I heard more shouting from the passage. That same strange word as before. *Fidge-un. Fidge-un.* And then the sound of pans falling. Sir Vivian paid no heed to the row. He was asking Anna for letters to recommend us.

'We're without them at the present moment,' Anna said, 'having come to Trethevy as soon as we finished our previous case.'

'Ah. That is a pity.'

'But not a problem, I'm sure. I would be pleased to write to our last client and ask for a letter to confirm our services.'

25

Write it out herself, she meant. Such was the trouble we found ourselves in.

The door opened then and a girl came in with a tray of fine teacups and a shining pot. She set the tray on the littlest table nearest us and then scurried to be gone, but before she could close the door again a beast had barged past her and come stalking into the room.

'Oh no you don't, you blighter!' Sir Vivian shouted, charging at the creature.

I saw then that it was a cat, but I didn't trust my eyes for it was a huge thing, all hulking shoulders.

The cat hissed and wrapped its limbs around the girl's ankles. The claws must have found their mark because she screamed, and screamed louder still when Sir Vivian tried to drag the beast away.

'Pigeon! You rogue!'

Free of the cat's attack, the girl rushed from the room, but the cat leapt from Sir Vivian's clutch and raced after her. The squire quickly shut the door and sat down again. A scratch on the inside of his wrist was wetly red.

Anna cleared her throat. 'A spirited animal.'

'Is it the witches' doing?' I asked. 'Such people can make beasts do as they didn't ought to. I have seen it.'

Anna tapped the arm of the chair but said nothing. The tapping I knew to be a sign of her disquiet at such talk of witching, but the not saying so was a sign of change.

Sir Vivian dabbed at his bloodied wrist with a handkerchief. 'I wish that were the case, Mrs Williams, and that you could rid Pigeon of his tempers when you rid me of those wretched women. But Pigeon was a fiend long before they set up home in the woods. He's my wife's pet, and she will indulge him. He plagues poor Lucy and is forever chasing her.' He looked mournfully towards the door. 'She might have stayed to pour the tea.'

'I'll do it,' I said, and set to stirring. It did no good to be idle when people were offering something for free. As well as the tea, the tray bore a plate of neat mouthfuls of cake I thought fine. 'Strange,' I said, 'for a cat to be called after a bird when one would be so afraid of the other.'

'My wife has a talent for such surprising notions.' Sir Vivian took the cup I offered. 'Her list of infant names contains not a few unusual choices.'

'Expecting then, is she?' I said.

The squire gave a funny cough and took to staring at his teacup, and Anna, well. I'd seen that look from her before and knew I'd said something I shouldn't. Well-to-do people didn't like to talk of babies coming.

The squire coughed again. 'There is some . . . urgency, one might say, in having these women gone. That is . . .'

'I understand,' Anna said. 'Given the nature of the crime, a child being taken, your fear is quite personal in nature, if I'm not mistaken?'

'You are not, Miss Drake,' he said, and beamed with what looked like relief. 'That is why I must be rid of these women in the woods as soon as possible, but you must work with stealth as well as haste. If the pair should know that you are in my pay, well. Let us say, there may be consequences.'

'For us or them?' I said.

'Why, for everyone, Mrs Williams. The future of Trethevy depends on it.' Here his voice hardened. 'You must help me be rid of them.'

'You mean that we must find the boy,' Anna said, 'and find out who has taken him.'

'Whoever that might be,' I added, for Anna had been right to talk of suspicions. They had led many a good soul to the gallows.

'Yes, yes. Quite so,' the squire said.

'And his name?' Anna said.

The squire squinted. We waited.

'The boy's name,' I said, to help. 'Him that's lost.'

'Ah. It's Haskell. One of the Haskell boys. Now, we must discuss terms. Find the boy and rid me of the women, if they're the ones – and I don't doubt they are! Do this and the reward of thirty pounds will be yours.'

I thought we should slip from the room to decide the bargain between us, but Anna told the squire we would take what he offered. My voice was not to be heard. She'd lied when she said we'd be equals.

'Splendid!' Sir Vivian said. 'As to your accommodation, I cannot offer you lodgings here as Lady Phoebe must not be disturbed on any account. I am only following medical advice, you understand. The doctor says that as long as my wife enjoys undisturbed rest, our prayers will be answered.'

'We shall be covert in our investigations, Sir Vivian,' Anna said. 'I propose to pass as an artist visiting Trethevy's famous waterfall.'

And me? Her bag-carrier, no doubt.

Sir Vivian waggled a finger at Anna. 'You're a clever little thing, Miss Drake. I have a summer house I can put at your disposal. Haven't had much chance to use it since it was built last year. I had hoped my wife and I would spend some afternoons there this summer. It gives very dramatic views over the waterfall.'

'Too dramatic for Lady Phoebe?' I said.

'One tries not to blunder, Mrs Williams. One tries. It will be good to have someone in there, keep out damp and itinerants, though I'm afraid you'll find it sparsely equipped for staying overnight. I shall ask Mrs Carne to provide you with such things as you might need.'

He charged to the door, wrenched it open as if the house were on fire and bellowed for this Mrs Carne, who I guessed to be the sour-face who'd shown us in. Anna and I followed the squire into the passage and then to the hall, where another voice sounded, a soft voice, but it brought him up short as though he'd been struck.

'Vivian . . .' the voice called.

I gasped. There was a ghost at the top of the stairs.

FOUR

Her skin was milk-pale, her hair whitish yellow, like scalded cream. She was wrapped in layers of white ruffling cloth and lace and shawls, as if to better nest the swell at her middle. At her feet sat Pigeon, licking what might have been the squire's blood from his claws.

'My dear!' Sir Vivian called up. 'What are you doing out of bed?'

'The noise . . .'

'I instructed Mrs Carne that no one was to disturb you in the east wing. If my own servants won't—'

'Do we have visitors?'

'Oh, my dear, you are troubled, I can see it. It's the women. *These* women, I should say.' He pushed Anna and me closer to the stairs. 'Miss Drake and Mrs Williams are going to rid us of that which has so sorely troubled us and I'm afraid my excitement got the better of me. They are *investigators!*'

The pale woman put a pale hand to her breast. 'Investigators?'

'You see how she fears them?' Sir Vivian said to us quietly. 'I couldn't tell her of my offering a reward. Just the mention of the wretches weakens her so, and she is already the most fragile of souls. You haven't come a moment too soon. Now, if you will wait here for Mrs Carne, I must see to my dear wife.'

He bounded up the stairs, making certain to avoid the fiendish Pigeon, and gathered up Lady Phoebe as gently as if he worried her middle would stave in, like she was made of eggshell.

'For all his noise, the squire is a fearful soul,' I said to Anna, once they were out of sight.

'Isn't he? Ah, our cheerful housekeeper has returned.'

Mrs Carne's scowl was coming for us. In her arms were blankets, with candle ends perched on top. Anna and I relieved her of her burden – that she felt it *was* a burden to aid us was clear, for when I asked her the way to the summer house she gave us no help.

'Ask the Haskells. They ought to be doing more for their living.'

'They've lost a child,' I said, quite stunned by the cruelty of Mrs Carne's words.

'Well, they should've taken better care of him, shouldn't they? And I'll thank you not to go upsetting her ladyship about it. All this talk that *her* child will be taken and coal left in her belly in its place, it's enough to bring things on early again. Lord knows we none of us wish for that.'

'Have there been many losses?' Anna said, stuffing the candle ends into the large black bag she carried everywhere.

Mrs Carne sniffed loudly. 'Not for me to say, is it?'

'Your discretion becomes you, Mrs Carne. And what do you make of these strangers in the woods? Do you believe they've taken the boy?'

The housekeeper gave either a sneer or a smile, I couldn't be sure which, her face being so worn and mean.

'Like as not he's hiding somewhere, not wanting to go to the quarry and do an honest day's work.'

'I take it the quarry belongs to Sir Vivian?' Anna said.

'It does. And he's losing money with every day that passes. Captain's been up here time and again, what with them downing tools to look for the boy. It's my wages they're taking if the orders aren't filled, and all for a lazy scoundrel who'll turn up when he's hungry.'

'The squire clearly thinks the matter more serious,' Anna said.

Mrs Carne gave a low laugh. 'That he does. No more sense than his father before him. I been here long enough to know the ways of the people in these woods. Sly, the lot of them.'

'That key for us?' I said.

Mrs Carne handed it to me. 'Don't trust them,' she said. 'None of them in the woods.'

Two paths led from the house. One back to the road, and so to the sea and light and room to breathe and think. The other to the trees, and so to their watching, their waiting.

A burst of white and black flashed from the roof into the air, making my heart leap. A magpie, swooping off to the trees. Anna followed as if the bird was showing the way we were to go.

'I'd like to reach the summer house before the light goes,' Anna called back. 'But if you'd prefer to spend the night in the woods then by all means take your time, Shilly-shally.'

I sprang after her. Shilly-shally, the name they'd given me at the farm for all my lateness. The name that took the one my mother had given me.

We were close to the trees now, and my uneasiness was great.

'Don't you feel it?' I said.

'Feel what?'

'The trees. There's something not right about them.'

'The only thing I can feel is your boots clipping my heels, Shilly. Why must you crowd me? I know it must be hard for you,' she said, and passed beneath the branches, 'without the drink, but if we're to . . .' Her voice grew faint. The trees swallowed her sound.

I dithered, looking back at the manor house. The roof was pinked in the last of the sun. A soft blush warmed the sky above. I took a deep breath, to hold the light inside me, and went into the trees.

All at once the bit of breeze there'd been dropped away and that was a strange thing, for on the moor it had always been windy. Even on a day that wasn't windy proper there had always been a *bit* of wind drifting around, stirring the gorse. We were never without it. There was no gorse here but plenty of moss spreading damply across the tree trunks, across the rocks all tumbled about. And ferns and brambles and blind nettles. The whole world had gone green, but for Anna.

There was her red dress ahead, weaving through the trees as she followed the path that had grown muddy now we were beneath the branches. The trees' limbs grew so thick overhead that I almost felt I was indoors, save for where the last of the day's light found a way to break through and spot the mud with sun. A smell lay thickly on the air, but wasn't bad. It made me think of the last of the hay store – the summer's cutting was there, but as staleness, almost forgotten.

I heard water tumble close by but I had no sight of it yet. The river was somewhere in these woods, and across it the pair of women who gave Sir Vivian so much worry. If they'd taken a child, what might they do to us trying to prove their crime? There was still time to make Anna see that getting rid of these strangers was a poor notion, that we should try to find some other work, for if this dark place should be the last that I should see—

I couldn't see Anna.

I called her, called her by the names I'd known her by before – Mr Williams, Mrs Williams. I could barely hear my voice, couldn't be sure my tongue was making noise. I hurried along the path and stumbled on a root thrown out to catch me. A prickling thing reached out and snagged my skirt. I grazed my palm on a tree's skin sharp as glass. A flash of something at the wall of my eye – faster than I could see but I knew there had been movement there. Something had leapt. I ran and ran.

And then there she was. She had found the light.

But the earth had broken open at her feet.

FIVE

It was a pit, fifty feet wide, I guessed, and half so deep. It was a shock to me there, in the close press of the trees, that such ground could be clawed back, but there it was, and there were the bodies working it. I couldn't tell if they were men or women for they'd been made loose grey shapes by the dust that covered them. Slate dust, I guessed, catching sight of a huge dark block being hauled to the surface. The hauling was done by means of a rope that passed over a wheel set atop a wooden contraption. This was on the bank opposite us, where the trees had been stripped away. In their place had grown a shed with a tin roof.

'What do you know of quarrying?' Anna said, peering into the pit. 'Are there likely to be tunnels?'

I got hold of her arm to make sure she didn't fall, then looked down likewise. The pit's sides were uneven, like a loaf with the middle ripped out. People perched on the scattered ledges and the air rang chink-chink-chink from their tools. If I hadn't seen them I would have thought the sound a strange Trethevy bird. There might still be some such creature yet to show itself amongst the magpies.

'Tunnels to lose a child in?' I said.

'Or to hide one. I wonder if they're much like mineshafts?'

The slab being hauled to the surface rose slowly in the air, and spun a circle, just as slow, the rope creaking, creaking. The grey shapes that were people passed beneath it, never looking up. The creaking stopped, the slab hung in the air. Loud in my head was this thought – the horse causing that wheel to turn, that rope to pull, dear God let its heart keep beating. Let its breath come deep and full. Let the beast not shy and bolt, send that wheel crashing down.

I pulled Anna back onto the path.

'I don't know about any tunnels or mineshafts,' I said, 'but I *do* know the quarry will still be here tomorrow. We need to find where we're staying.'

Anna seemed to notice the light going then, and quivered into the collar of her dress. 'I hope it's not far. Mrs Carne could hardly be described as helpful. I wonder at her reluctance to help the squire's cause.'

'Mrs Carne might be a witch as well,' I said as we set to walking and the trees closed over us again. The water sounded closer now but still all I could see were trees and trees and trees.

'I'd ask that you keep an open mind in this case, Shilly. Just because what happened on the moor was . . . was what it was, it doesn't mean that every claim of witchcraft will have merit. Such cases must be very rare, and I haven't yet heard anything that suggests the women on the other side of the river aren't simply spinsters who—my word!'

We had come to a clearing with a dozen or so squat cottages. The one nearest us was cluttered up with stuff, the window ledge crowded with glass bottles. My spirits leapt at the sight. Anna went up to the front door, which had things hanging off it, held fast by nails. She poked them, while I took one of the bottles and sniffed it.

My curse made Anna look over.

'Trethevy's brewing not to your taste, Shilly?'

'It's piss!'

'If you're saying that for my benefit, then it's not necessary. Far better to just keep away from it in the first place.'

'You don't understand. It really *is* piss in here, not drink.' As I put the bottle back I heard a tinkly sound inside it. Holding my breath so as not to get another draught of the stench, I put my eye as close to the neck as I dared and jiggled the bottle. 'Piss and pins.'

'For what purpose?'

I shrugged.

'And these?' Anna said, running a hand over the things hanging on the door. 'Who has need for more than one knocker on a single door?'

I went to her side, careful not to upset the other bottles that stood close to the doorway. Stones they were, on the door – all different colours and sizes. Each had a hole through it and hung from a nail by way of a bit of rope passed through the hole. I cupped a stone in my hand. It was the colour of rust and pitted with shiny white flecks, and the hole was smooth, such as water might make over time. The whole door was covered with the roped stones, top to bottom. I pulled one so that the rope was taut, then let it go. It knocked the door, and set all the other stones rattling.

No sound came from within. I looked at the other cottages, likewise cluttered with bottles and hanging stones as this one was. Some looked so thick with the clutter that I thought it would be hard to get inside at all. There was no sign of anyone about. No smoke came from the chimneys. No washing was airing. There was no one to ask the way to the summer house.

And then there was.

She came hurrying towards us from the trees beyond the cottages, but her hurrying wasn't fast at all, for she was hobbling, and as she drew closer I saw the skin of her face was papery from being old. Her old face and her hands were the only parts of her body to be seen, for she was covered by a black shawl that looked so large as to be wrapped around her many times over. It was as if she'd clothed herself in the shadows that hung between the trees.

'You've news?' she said. 'Tell me you've news.'

She clutched at me and I feared it was to stop herself from falling down, such were her tremors.

'We're looking for the summer house belonging to Sir Vivian Orton,' Anna said.

'The summer house . . . Not Paul?'

'I'm afraid not.'

This made the woman's tremors worse so I set her down on a stone bench nearby, which thank goodness had no stinking bottles on it. The black shawl looked so tight about her throat that I thought it might be causing her breathlessness, but when I went to ease the tightness she quickly pushed my hand away and was at once more steady.

'Can I fetch someone to help you?' I said.

The woman shook her head. 'There's no one here, my sweet. Those the quarry can spare are looking for Paul. He's been taken. I thought that's why you'd come. Thought you'd been searching. I'll be all right.'

'The missing boy – you're a relation?' Anna said.

'Paul's my grandson.'

'Ah,' Anna said. 'It's Mrs Haskell, then.'

So raggedy the skin of her hands was, like it had been badly torn and not healed well. She caught me looking and tugged the cuffs of her dress to further cover her hands.

'Come to see the waterfall, have you?' she said.

'I've heard it's spectacular,' Anna said.

'You drawing, then, or are you poets?'

'We're artists, yes.'

'That's what the others said they was doing here. Them furriners.' Her voice was hard now. Harder than the slate being split in the quarry. It was hard as moor stone.

'You mean the women who've come?' I said. 'Across the river?'

But she caught sight of something behind me and struggled to her feet. 'You been in the water again?' she shouted.

I turned to see a boy of around eight making his slow way down the

38

path towards us. He was dragging a spade, which left a furrow in the mud. When he drew close I could see he had been doing as Mrs Haskell feared for he was shivering and dripping.

'Peter! What *have* I told you!'

The boy hung his head and let his spade fall to the ground. 'I only been in the shallows. Not deep. I han't found him.'

He fell to scritching then and Mrs Haskell was all sorrowful. 'Oh, my bird, my sweet. Come here.' She wrapped him in the folds of her black shawl. Over his head she spoke quietly to us. 'Twins they are, Peter and Paul. My nestle-birds. Their closeness makes it worse for the boy.'

'Nestle-birds?' Anna said.

'Family's youngest,' I said.

Mrs Haskell nodded and there were tears from her then, as well as the boy, and I thought how bad it must be for them all, losing the child.

'How long is it since you last saw Paul?' I said.

'Days now. I . . . We've barely slept. It's too long. He'll be—'

The boy with her, the brother, began to scritch again at these words and the woman tried to be more cheery.

'Come on now, my bird. We'll sit by the fire and have you dry before your mother comes home. How about that then, eh?'

She turned to lead him to one of the other cottages.

'Please,' I said, putting a hand on her arm to stop her. She flinched. 'Can you tell us the way to the summer house?'

'Oh, I was forgetting. Of course, my sweet. Of course. You're not far. Go on past the cottages here, where Peter's just come, and then at the fallen oak you must bear left. Go on a little way further and you'll come to the monks' wall. Keep that on your left and go a step or two more and you'll come out on the river. Go upstream, climbing then, and you'll see the squire's summer house. White and black it is.'

'The monks' wall?' Anna said. 'There was a monastery here?'

'So they say,' the old woman said. 'For serving Saint Nectan.'

At these words the boy began to shiver violently.

39

'Now, Peter, don't go fretting. 'Tis only the saint I'm speaking of. Not them others.' She tucked a lock of the boy's hair behind his ear. 'The saint is good to us, we know that, don't we? Go in and stir up the fire now.' When he'd gone inside she turned to Anna and me and her face was riven with worry.

'You must be careful, my birds. You've come at a bad time, and no mistake. The woods are troubled.'

'The bottles, the stones on the doors,' I said, 'they're protecting you from the woods?'

'Oh no. The bottles and the hag stones are to keep away them furriners on the other side. There's nothing to keep the woods from what they're wont to do.'

'Which is?' Anna said.

'Ah, you'll see, you'll see. Or if *you* won't . . .'

She took a step towards me and the wind was all at once whirling past me and the river was crashing its way closer.

'. . . I think this one will.'

And then so soft I thought she must be speaking only inside my head, her voice like embers sifting the last of their warmth . . .

You feel it already, don't you, my bird? Feel how they've been peaceful, so peaceful for so long. And now they're wakened. It's hate does that, brings the strangeness to the woods again.

'Whose hatred?' I managed to whisper.

But the embers were ash, were gone.

It was Anna's voice brought me back to the path and the mud and the wretched trees.

'Come on, Shilly, while we've the last of the light.'

The door to the cottage was closed.

SIX

We went on as Mrs Haskell had told us. Each cottage we passed had piss bottles before the doors and windows, and hag stones on the doors themselves. There being no one about gave an uncommon feeling to the place. A brooding, a waiting. Or maybe that was the woods, the strangeness Mrs Haskell had told me of. Brought by hate.

'What did Mrs Haskell mean when she called the women furriners?' Anna said.

The word sounded so odd in Anna's mouth, her trying to speak like someone from my part of the world.

'That the women don't belong here,' I said.

'Oh. She meant *foreigners*.'

'That's what Mrs Haskell said.'

'In a manner of speaking, I suppose she did. Oh!'

Anna fell. A root snaking for her, I thought, then saw she'd tripped over a spade. The one the boy had dropped. I helped her up.

'Perhaps Peter thinks his brother might be in a tunnel, like you do,' I said.

'But he told his grandmother he'd been in the water. Why would anyone dig in a river?'

'The woods, maybe – sending everyone mad.'

Anna leant the spade against the wall of the last cottage and then we were once more walking beneath branches.

'Don't get caught up in that nonsense, Shilly, or you'll be no help with this case. These trees are simply plants. Plants!'

She slapped her palm against a trunk. Far above us, the leaves shook and then there was flapping as unseen birds took to the air.

On Anna went, talking loudly of the ordinariness of oaks and ash and thorn trees, which I knew weren't ordinary at all.

We were deep inside the woods now and the path had grown narrower, less well-trodden. Anna kept on with purpose but I had my doubts.

'How will we find our way out again?' I said, and ripped my skirt free of a bramble's clutching fingers.

'Landmarks, Shilly. We'll soon grow acquainted with them and be as familiar with these woods as Mrs Haskell.'

That lowered my spirits even worse. I didn't want to know the place. I wanted to leave.

'Here's one such landmark now,' Anna said. 'The fallen oak.'

'Markers are no use if they shift about.'

Anna laughed. 'This oak hasn't moved since it hit the ground, Shilly. Look at the ferns that have grown over it. And the moss here.' She rootled in the green. 'I shouldn't wonder if this is a badger's sett beneath. A big one too.' She stood and clapped the earth from her hands. 'There's nothing here to be afraid of, though these strangers, whomever they are, whether they've taken the boy or not, they've done an excellent job of terrifying the inhabitants of Trethevy, both rich and poor.'

She took pity on my terror and squeezed my arm.

'Anna . . .'

She reached for my face and I closed my eyes, ready to feel her touch again, but it was not as I wanted for she was rootling in my hair as she had rootled beneath the fallen oak.

'How have you ended up such a mess when we've walked the same path?' she said, pulling twigs and leaves from my hair as if it was a nest she was unmaking.

'We walk in different ways,' I said.

'That I won't argue with.' She tossed the twiggy bits into the brambles and walked on. 'Mrs Haskell said to go left here, didn't she?'

The path was now so narrow we had to walk one behind the other, and the noise of the river grew louder with each step and kept us from talking, and that was fine by me for Anna wasn't listening anyway. We twisted and turned, and then something jutted from the trees. A wall. Tall but not wide, snaked with thorns and leaning over the path as if it strained against the thorns' clutches. This was the remains of the monks, then, and here the path forked. We bore left. A few steps further and we came to the river, just as Mrs Haskell had said we would.

By then it was too dark to see well but the noise told me the river was wide and fast-moving, and I was glad we didn't have to cross it to reach the summer house. Glad, too, that the women were on the other side.

The path became steep, then stepped, and the way much wetter, being so close to the river. That made our going slow. We were climbing and with every step the river became louder still, so I knew the waterfall must be close and the summer house beside it. But still I feared we'd never find the place, that the woods had closed over it as they had the monks' wall, its timbers softened into the wet earth. Sunk. Lost.

'There it is!' Anna said.

I looked up. It was a little white house with wooden slats, painted black, laid over the top. The white paint was bright in the gloom of the woods and of evening.

Anna gave me her hand and hauled me the last of the way, but then I saw there was still further to go, one more set of steps to climb, for the summer house had been built onto a crag of rock. Anna unlocked the door with the key Mrs Carne had given us and then I fair tumbled inside, tired and aching. But I found a scrap of strength from somewhere and shoved the door closed, locked it tight on Anna and me. The woods would be kept out if it was the last thing I did.

I couldn't keep out the water. The damp had crept up the walls, a foot high near the fireplace. I poked at the green fur with my boot.

'Hardly a surprise when one builds on a riverbank,' Anna said, dropping the blankets she'd carried. 'Still, I suppose the view must be worth it.' She went to the large window that faced the river. 'Not much to see but shadows now. Come the morning we might have a sight worth sketching.'

'Can you draw?' I asked.

'Not a line. And unless you've been hiding your artistic light under a bushel, I'm guessing neither can you, Shilly.'

'Never tried,' I said. 'Surely you must draw the patterns for the clothes you make?'

'That doesn't count.' She bent to look in the fireplace. 'Only cobwebs here.'

'Why don't the patterns count?'

'Because they're easy.'

'Only if you know how to do them. Like . . . like reading, and being able to write.' I gripped the back of a chair. The cloth was clammy. 'Will you teach me?'

After a pause, she said, 'I will.'

I was so pleased I almost forgot how to breathe.

'On one condition. You must keep from the drink.'

'I am, I haven't . . .'

'I know. But it's the sticking with it that's the hardest part. Having something to work for, to motivate you – that's what'll keep you from the bottle.' She was going to the door. 'If not a drop of alcohol passes your lips during our time in the woods then I'll teach you your letters. Now, I'll fetch something to burn before we succumb to the damp.'

'Don't go far!'

'If you could see your way to fashioning some kind of bed.'

44

And then she was gone, back out into the woods, leaving me to think about what she'd offered me as I looked round our new home.

There wasn't much to see. It was a single square room, filled with almost as many chairs and tables as the room we'd seen in Sir Vivian's house, but it would be ours until we'd done what was needed with the women across the river. What were they doing in that moment? Settling down for the night as we were? As I cleared the chairs and spread the blankets on the floor, were they pulling back their bedcovers? I went to the window. Across the water a woman might be looking back at me. The strangers in the woods. Which of us was which at that moment? I put my hand to the glass and thought of another hand likewise pressed against a window. Which of us . . . the witch?

The door banged open. Anna came in with an armful of branches, sending such thoughts away.

'I found enough for tonight,' she said, and dropped the branches by the fireplace. 'These were fallen. We'll need an axe for gathering more. What's wrong?'

'I'm afraid . . .'

'Not this business of the woods again. It'll all be better in daylight, I promise you. Something to eat would help. I shouldn't think Mrs Carne provided us with anything, did she?'

'No. But the squire did.'

I reached into the pocket of my dress and pulled out a napkinned parcel. Anna took it from me and frowned, but when she opened it, she grinned.

'Shilly, you rogue.'

She stuffed one of the fancy cakes in her mouth and when she had room to move her tongue again she told me I was wicked to have thieved, then thanked me heartily for doing so. I lit the fire and we ate our spoils before its dancing light. The cakes weren't so neat as when I'd slipped them from the plate. Some were smashed to pieces, and the cream in the middle had gone greasy from the warmth of being pressed against me. But we licked every last crumb from our fingers and praised the squire's cook.

'You were quick about it,' Anna said. 'I didn't notice a thing.'

When she was asleep I crawled to the bag I'd carried from Jamaica Inn that morning. She hadn't seen me take the bottle either.

SEVEN

I couldn't stay inside to do as I had need to, not after she'd said she'd teach me my letters if I kept from it. Not when my fingers itched to stroke her sleeping face. In the daytime, when she was striding about, wearing her false parts and hiding her yellow-haired self, there was a hardness to her. Her mouth was more often pursed than bearing the sideways smile I knew she had in her keeping. Her brow was furrowed, making her look older, fretful. But when she slept, all that left her. She couldn't hide the softness that was within her, and at the sight of it I feared even more to let her down.

I didn't want to go back into the woods, of course, for they were not to be trusted. But when we'd arrived at the summer house I'd seen a good place. It was a wooden shelf that ran beneath the window and looked over the water, thickly built and wide enough for chairs, but without a rail of any kind so I guessed this part of the summer house was still unfinished. It was a good place to be alone, but if I should roll off, smash drunk-heavy into the water and the rocks below, would Anna care?

That I didn't know the answer made me unstop the bottle and take my first swig. It was strong, unwatered stuff they sold at Jamaica Inn and I was unused to it. My eyes burnt and my head sloshed about. The feeling was like before, when Mrs Haskell had spoken inside my head and told me of the hatred in the woods, that I should see this if Anna couldn't. And hadn't I seen it already? Something had been shifting about. There was uneasiness in every leaf. To know this, to feel it, even when I didn't want to – what did that make me?

This worry made me take my second drink, and my third, and all the others that came after. Would that I was like Anna, able to walk the path and feel nothing more than wonder at a badger's sett. Would that I was different. Would that I was like I was before Charlotte Dymond had come into my life, for if the pair of women across the river were powerful, as she had been, I didn't want to be anywhere near them.

Or be anything like them.

A bell. A church bell. Calling us to worship. Calling me to stand. But I couldn't. My legs were twisted under me like matted roots, and like the roots I was beneath the ground and it was wet—

—save that of the bell that shines like a mirror, that catches the sun and rings and rings, though no hand touches it, and then the ringing becomes cries and the cries become laughing and there are two of them, their hair long and dark and thick as branches. Their backs are to me as they go about their work, their pushing and shoving and laughing and holding him down, the old man, in the pool, him gasping and crying out and—

—wrenching to get free, this old man, this not-flesh-and-blood man, this sainted man, this saint being drowned in his own holy water, his own holy well they're killing—

—ring louder now and I tell them to stop they must stop stop, please stop he's—

—them turning to look at me and I see that they are like me, women, looking at me their empty faces—

—there is no looking for their faces have no eyes their faces—

—ceases his thrashing but still the pool's water slops onto the slate and the drips—

—for it is raining

I could hear the drips. I feared I'd be soaked, soaked as the old man and that might be the start of it, the drowning and that pair with no eyes but seeing me anyways, coming for me.

That made me shift myself and I found my face against stone, a wall. I sat up, let the floor and the wall spin until they had spun themselves to stillness. The rain kept on, each drop a thump between my ears. But there was no rain, or none that I could feel. Only the sound, the drip drip drip. I pressed my ear against the wall of the summer house. The water was inside it, and I was on the shelf outside wretched with drink and seeing such terrible things again. For that was what brought such seeing. The drink.

The drips faded, stopped. I moved along the wall, listened in different places. Nothing.

I got a grip on my own fearful thrashes, drunk thrashes, and knew the old man to be Saint Nectan that Mrs Haskell had spoken of, and that I'd been shown his holy well. He'd been drowned, was lost. But the Haskell boy that was missing, he could still be saved.

And I could do the saving.

EIGHT

A dull thump. Another. It was a clitter, that noise, and coming from above. I kept my eyes closed and my face tucked into my chest, hoping that whatever torment now visiting me might soon be gone. But the noise only grew louder.

I managed to roll on to my front but it took longer for my legs to remember how they worked so that I could kneel and look up. The sun glared down on the river, so bright it made water stream from my eyes so bad that if anyone should see me I'd look like I was scritching. And maybe I was scritching. I felt wretched enough. It was the strength of the drink. Or my needing another. I wasn't sure if there was a difference between those feelings any more.

The magpies were jouncing around on the summer house roof. That was the cause of the clitter. And then I saw Anna at the other end of the shelf, looking out to the waterfall. Her pipe was clamped in her mouth and I caught the sweet prickle of its burning. She wore no wig, and had no paint on her face. She wasn't beautiful. She was all angles and scrawny, her nose too long, her lips too thin. But there was something about her true self, her – undisguised. Something I had no words for.

'I might be tempted to try my hand at drawing after all.' She pointed at the water with her pipe. 'Quite the picture.'

The spot where the river broke from its bed, tumbled, and so made the waterfall, was level with the summer house. The air was damp with spray from the water falling, crashing into the pool beneath. I thought the drop fifty feet, maybe more. From the pool the water raced on, rushing to be gone from the woods and out to the sea. I would rather have been at the bottom of the sea at that moment, beyond reach of daylight. Such were my thoughts as I tried to collect myself.

I got to my feet and there was a clunk. The empty bottle rolled and disappeared over the edge of the shelf. A pause, a breath, and then the smash. The magpies took to the air.

'I . . .' But I got no further for I had no words. She could see. She knew.

'Today,' she said, peering at the bowl of her pipe, as if the day might be caught within the sweet tobacco. 'We'll start the bargain from today. If from *this* point until we leave the woods you keep away from the drink, I'll teach you your lessons.'

'Anna, I—'

'That's reason to find the boy, find the guilty party and be gone all the more quickly, wouldn't you say, Shilly?'

There was something in her voice, something caught between sadness and hopefulness, that made me see, for the first time since I'd known her, that she wanted this for me. Wanted me to be better, to be free of the drink. But after last night, after drinking and seeing the blinded pair drown the saint, I knew the cost of giving it up. The cost for both of us, and I had to tell her that. It was only fair, the bargain we had struck to work together.

'What I can see, what you *know* I can see, Anna, it's the drink that shows me. I can't explain it, but I can't do without it. Not if you want my help with cases.'

She threw up her hands and was ready to tell me I was foolish, it was nonsense – all of this we'd done before. I kept on, though. It was the only way.

'Before Charlotte died she gave me a gift. Or a curse. I don't know yet which it is. It might be both. But understand me, Anna – without the drink, I can't do it. My part of the deal, our partnership – whatever you want to call it. You have to take me as I am.'

She charged at me and I said to myself, this is it now, Shilly. She'll have you over and smashed just like that bottle for you're too drunk-trembly to fight her as you did once before, in the grip of the moor's marsh.

But I wasn't taking my last breath, not yet awhile, for Anna stopped short of getting hold of me, though I could see in her tautness that she wanted to, by God she did.

'That's nothing but an excuse, Shilly, and some part of you, some part deep down not yet pickled by spirits knows that.' She was spitting like the cat Pigeon had spat and I couldn't look at her. 'The things you can do, can see – that's *your* doing, not the drink's. That's who you are.' She turned on her heel and marched away, calling back over her shoulder, 'When you're ready to accept that, I'll be here.'

Panic rose like bile in my throat. 'Where are you going?'

'To find these witches.'

I followed her inside and she didn't tell me no. We'd fought before and we'd fight again. I didn't need drink to know that Anna and me were as often fury together as we were care. It was the caring that brought the fury.

We put ourselves on, our hair and our cunning clothes, and I was Mrs Williams again. It was good to leave Shilly behind. She was a bad sort. I hoped she wouldn't follow me across the river.

We went back the way we'd come the night before, picking our way down slippery rocks and twisting past trees that sought to block the way with their roots or half-fallen limbs. I wondered that I'd made it up alive, given the gloom and the things I'd been carrying and my tiredness. But then I wondered if the way down was *not* the same, if it had remade itself while Anna slept and I saw blinded women drown a saint. I shivered and hurried after Anna.

The way levelled out again once we had passed the pool. I was glad to be away from the drop into the water for my head was still sloshing from the temptations of Jamaica Inn and I didn't trust myself. I was right to be so fearful of my own wanderings for the next thing I knew I'd crashed into Anna's back for she'd stopped walking and was looking about her somewhat fretful.

'It should be here, shouldn't it? We've not gone too far. And I would have seen it.'

'What?'

'The wall. The monks' wall.' She looked left then right then left again. 'I thought . . .'

'I told you. Markers are no use when they move.'

'It can't have moved, Shilly. It's a wall, for goodness' sake.'

And then the ferns rose up and spoke.

NINE

'Lost, are you?'

He was a big man, tall as well as broad brushing the broken ferns from his clothes. His face was all over whiskery, but his head was without a hair at all, the skin pinked from the sun.

Anna was without words for shock. I was much the same.

'Took fright, have you? Ah, my dears, I'm sorry for that. Path moved, see, and we had to find a new way. I go first when that happens for I'm biggest to crash through. Sit you down here now, on this bit of stone.'

He led Anna, oh so gently, to perch on a slab of moor stone that crowned the ferns and nettles.

Others appeared from the trees. Men and women. Seven of them. No, eight. They wore working clothes, most with slate dust about them, but they carried farm tools – rakes and scythes.

'We must go on, David,' one of the women said.

'Won't do no harm to rest a moment,' he answered.

'It might do all the harm in the world! It's been three days.'

She looked like she'd argue more but for being weary, as they all were. Pale and their eyes red-rimmed. The whiskered man, David, he put a hand on her shoulder but she turned away from him and scritched with her back to us.

'You're looking for the boy,' I said. 'Paul Haskell that's missing.'

'That we are,' David said. And then in a low voice, 'I fear it won't do no good now. It's been too long with neither sight nor sound.'

'I'm going on,' the scritching woman said loudly. She lifted her rake like to beat someone with. 'They're abroad again. If we can keep them in sight they might lead us to him.'

She pushed past him into the trees. All but David and another woman followed her. In a moment they were swallowed by the green, were gone. Their sound too. The only noises were the leaves *shh shhing*, and somewhere beyond them, the birds.

'Maria will drop dead before she gives up hope,' the woman said. She was well-fleshed and sweating in the close air of the woods. Down low, as we were, there wasn't the freshness the waterfall gave.

'Maria is the boy's mother?' Anna asked.

'She is. Beside herself, as we all are. Until that pair are dealt with we're none of us safe.' She spat, and a clump of ferns bore the spittle.

'Don't upset yourself, Sarah. It don't do no good.'

'The women, you mean, across the river?' Anna said. She got to her feet and was herself again.

'They're not *women*,' Sarah said. 'Not people at all.'

'Then what are they?'

Sarah dug her scythe into the ground with a splitting sound. 'They're creatures of the Devil. I've heard them, how they speak to him when they think they're alone. Heard their Devil tongue. It was him that helped them take the child, and he'll help take another unless we put a stop to them.'

'Saint Nectan will keep us from harm,' David said.

'He's not done a good job so far!' Sarah said. She wiped her face and neck with a handkerchief. 'And how can he when that pair has turned on him?'

56

'What do the women have to do with the saint?' I said, and thought of what I'd seen whilst insensible. Their blind looking.

'They're his helpers. Or they were.' She spat again. 'Sisters who served him. They've come back to plague us, taken up bodies, but without the saint they've gone to the bad. We shall never be safe,' she muttered darkly.

'Now, Sarah, didn't the saint ring his bell to warn us just before the boy was lost, as he used to warn the boats when the storms came, to keep them from the rocks?' David said. 'Doesn't that show he still guards us in the woods, much as he can?'

But Sarah only shook her head. 'Maria was right. We must keep going while the sisters are abroad.' She hefted her scythe and was ready to be gone, but then a thought seemed to strike her. She took a step closer to Anna.

'What's your business in these parts?'

'A sketching holiday. I mean to make a study of the waterfall for a larger work.' Anna shifted her black bag across her hip, by way of proof, I thought.

'Where are they living, these sisters?' I said. 'I shouldn't like to run into them.'

Sarah pointed at the river with her scythe and I saw there were flat stones rising from the water. Beyond, only more trees.

'This is where they cross. Their cottage isn't far along the path the other side. If you should see them, you get straight away. You've come at a bad time.'

'So I've heard,' Anna said scornfully, and I thought it foolish of her to mock the fears of people who knew their own place well. But that was Anna's way. She thought she had all the answers and that people like me, whether in the woods or on the moor, we were nothing but fools. Would I ever help her see different?

'The sisters don't confine themselves to their cottage, then?' Anna said.

'If only they would,' David said. He scratched at his whiskers with

57

his knuckles, making a raspy sound. 'No, they like to walk here, in the woods. They're out every day.'

'To take another child!' Sarah said. 'I'll be in my own grave before I see that happen. No saint will save us in Trethevy.'

She pushed past Anna and was gone into the green.

'You mustn't mind Sarah,' David said. 'With the boy lost . . . Well, if you should see anything while you're painting, any sign of him—'

'We'll go straight to the Haskells,' I said.

David nodded. 'I'd best be getting after them. If the path should change again . . .' He looked back the way he'd come, when he'd crashed through the ferns, then looked at each of us in turn. 'Keep away from them sisters, if you value your lives.'

'Oh we will, Mr . . . ?'

'Tonkin, David Tonkin.' He shook hands with us, which was a strange way to say goodbye. His grip was firm and his hands faintly stained. Blue they were, as if he was bruised but the bruises were fading.

'You live here, in the woods?' I said.

'I'm further upstream. Have the mill there. Last of them on the river still working.'

'A corn mill?' Anna asked.

'Yarn and blankets. Dyeing, too. Not that I been doing much of it since the boy went missing.' He shook his head. 'Poor wretch. I must go—'

'We were looking for the monks' wall,' I said.

'You're not far. Keep on that way.' He pointed back the way we'd come. 'Then bear left. You should see the wall not long after. That's if it hasn't moved again.'

Before Anna could tell him this wasn't likely, as she had been so quick to tell me, David Tonkin was gone, and once more the woods swallowed any sign of him and his whiskers.

'You see!' I said. 'The woods *are* shifting about.'

'I don't see any such thing, Shilly. We're still new to the place, that's all.' She started after David.

'Where are you going?'

'If these women are out walking then why shouldn't two others do likewise? The sooner we find them, the sooner we can find out if they really do know anything about Paul Haskell's disappearance.'

And she set off after David Tonkin who had set off after Sarah who had set off after Maria Haskell and the others. We would all be lost in the woods together.

The path we took was not one we had trod before, for the trees changed almost at once, becoming shorter and wider, which made me think of the squire, whose trees they were, after all. The ferns grew less thickly and in their place were low branches that reached for the mud beneath them, and for the river that they closed upon. Everything was narrowed, and inside my head was narrowed too without a sup to save me.

'What do you know of talking to the Devil, Shilly?'

'I don't know nothing about it!'

'I thought not. And do you know why? Because there's no such thing.'

'But that woman Sarah heard the women talking to him.' A whippish branch flew at me, caught the soft flesh just beneath my eye.

'She might have heard them talking. That doesn't mean they were conversing with the Devil.'

'That Sarah's not as honest as she makes herself out to be, that I *do* know.'

'Meaning?' Anna stopped to scrape her boots against a slate edge that poked from the ground, to rid them of the rind of mud that caked them. The mud made her feet look bigger than they were, like those of a man. I thought of Mr Williams.

'Well,' I said. 'Sarah told us she heard the women talking when they thought no one was there to listen. So she was spying, wasn't she?'

'I suppose she was,' Anna said. 'You were keen to ask her about this Saint Necktie.'

'Saint *Nectan*. There's no need to be scornful.'

'Did you discover Christianity at the bottom of that bottle, Shilly?'

'I discovered something,' I muttered.

'Something you'd care to share?'

She'd asked so I told her. I didn't see that I should have to fear those two blinded sisters alone, and if we were going to seek them out then Anna should know what was coming. That was only fair.

She told me it was nonsense, of course, even though it was because I *could* see such strangeness that she'd asked me to leave the moor and work with her, but she didn't like such talk. Neither did I, to be truthful. But it was what I'd seen.

I picked my way through moor stone and roots and all manner of unevenness. 'Them creatures I saw were of the kind that would speak to the Devil. They had the Devil in them to drown the saint.'

'And what of *these* creatures, Shilly?' She had stopped walking.

I looked where she was looking, and there they were, the pair. Not twenty paces from us but walking away, slipping through the trees. A flash of long brown hair, hanging loose, unpinned. A hand on a thin trunk, then gone. A wink of grey cloth. Their backs to us so I couldn't see if their eyes were as they should be.

Anna went after them and that meant there were three ahead of me, three women in the woods, walking amongst the green. I followed and made four. If David Tonkin and the others came across us now, with their scythes and their rakes, would they know which of us to strike?

TEN

There was no sign of David Tonkin and the others, even though they'd gone this way before us. Sent on another path by the shifty woods. But the trees wanted *us* to see these women newly come to the woods. See but get no closer, I realised, for no matter how fast we went after them, they drew further away, even though they seemed to go no quicker than we did.

'Hello there!' Anna called. 'Might we speak with you?'

I didn't think her voice would carry in the woods but it must have done for one of the women stopped. The ferns grew tall there, as high as my waist, and it looked as if she had no lower body. I held my breath for her to show her face, the smooth skin where her eyes should be.

Slowly, she half turned, her head cocked to one side as if listening to us as we crashed through the ferns to try and reach her.

But then the other, the one slightly ahead, she called to her. I couldn't hear the words but I heard the sharpness of the tone, and the woman who had stopped began to walk again. Neither had shown their faces.

'Are they cutting their way through?' Anna said, wiping the sweat beading at the edges of her false hair.

We were running now, or as close to running as we could manage in the thickety woods that made us twist and turn and climb over sudden logs and rocks. And still the women were ahead of us, still their backs to us as they slipped in and out of the trees.

'They're not slashing at anything, are they?' I said, doing my best to study them as we stumbled on. 'Look at them – they're just strolling.'

'Calm as you like,' Anna said. She leant on a mossy rock to catch her breath. 'Let's give it up, Shilly. We're not going to catch them.'

'And do you know why that is?' I said. 'Because the way is shifting!'

'Perhaps Tonkin and the others will have more luck. They'll know the woods better, know what special path these women have found. That they *must* have found.' She waved in their direction, but they were gone.

'What about the boy? Tonkin said he's been gone three days. Much longer and if we find the boy at all it'll only be a corpse.'

'I agree that time is of the essence, Shilly. But there are other ways to spend it than chasing women who don't want to be caught.'

'Back to the cottages, then – talk to the boy's family?'

'A much better plan.'

I hoped we might get ourselves a morsel to eat, too, for we'd had nothing since the stolen cake the night before. My head still felt as if the waterfall had worked its way inside my skull but the roar was quieter now and I was ready to partake of something other than that which came from a bottle.

We went back the way we'd come, me in front this time, for I was hungry and keen to be around people like Mrs Haskell again. Ordinary people. Anna kept glancing back. I feared the women had bewitched her and she would be lost to me, endlessly chasing them. I told her so and she smiled.

'You won't lose me to phantoms, Shilly. More like breaking my neck on a tree root.'

'I'm glad you've more humour than when I first met you and you were a glum man,' I said, 'but that's not funny.'

We came out of a thorny patch and there was the river again, wide and not too deep at this point. I thought we might be back at the place we had parted from David Tonkin, for a little way ahead were flat stones that gave a way to cross the water. If I was right then I was starting to know the place, as Anna had said I would, given time. But there could be many such places to cross, and this one, that now we stood before, might be another, leaving the sisters well served for ways to ford the river, for the taking of children.

'You'd better bathe that, Shilly.'

'Hm?'

'Your hand, look. You must have caught it on the thorns.'

She was right. There was a deep scratch across the back of one of my hands, and it was dirty. As if she'd given me the pain with her words, now I felt the sting. I gave her back the pain by telling her that her cheek was likewise scratched, cut right through the greasy paint she wore.

'We won't get out of here alive,' I muttered.

I knelt and lowered my hand into the water. The sting worsened then eased, mostly from the cold of the water that chilled my hand so I couldn't feel anything. It was like drinking. I wondered if I should plunge myself into cold rather than go for the bottle again. And then I wondered if I *had* been drinking that morning, for I heard a little voice ask, *are you there? are you there?*

'Looks like Peter Haskell is going to get another telling off,' Anna said, nodding upstream.

The boy was on the other side, up to his knees in water and digging in it, if anyone *could* be said to dig the shifting slip of water.

Anna and I made our way along the bank until we drew level with the crossing stones. Anna called to the boy but he gave no sign he'd heard her.

'Is everyone in these woods deaf?' she said, and gathered her skirt to keep the bottom from getting wet.

She called to the boy again as she crossed to him. Though she was much closer to him now, not five feet away, he remained digging the water and asking his question of the river – *are you there? are you there?* I began to cross. The water slipped cold between the worn seams of my boots.

Anna reached the boy and laid a hand on his shoulder. He gave a cry of fright and spun round, striking her hip with his spade. Then it was Anna's turn to cry, in pain. He was sorry at once and near to scritching so I had to get everything in hand.

'You're not meant to be near the water, are you?' I said, and grabbed the spade.

'You won't tell Grandmother, will you?'

'Only if you tell us what you're looking for,' I said.

Peter splashed his way to the bank, that belonging to Trunkett, the squire's neighbour, and sat down. He was pale with cold, and sat shivering, his head lowered onto his chest. I thought him to be about eight years old but I knew little of children besides them being good at lying. His hair was sandy and in need of a cut for it fell across his eyes. All the better to be tricksy, I thought.

Anna sat on the bank beside him but I stood, not minding my feet getting colder and wetter as I perched on the last crossing stone. Standing meant I was firm with the child.

'Well?' I said.

'I was looking for the grave,' he said quietly.

'Paul's?' I said, unsure whether to feel pity for the boy or be suspicious of him.

He shook his head and Anna gave a sigh of relief.

'The saint's grave,' he said. 'Saint Nectan.'

'And you think he's buried here, in the river?'

He frowned at me, as if I'd spoken something foolish. 'Of course he is. This is where they put him. I just don't know which part.'

'Who buried the saint?' I asked him.

'The sisters,' he said. 'Everyone knows that.'

'I think you'll have to explain it to Shilly and me,' Anna said. 'Saint Nectan is a stranger to us.'

'Well, I'm sorry for you, then.' Peter shuffled his backside backwards and eyed Anna and me to be certain we were listening. Then he began.

ELEVEN

'The furrin pair came first when the saint was dying. They knew to come because they're holy. Like he was.'

'And when was this?' Anna said.

The boy shrugged.

'A month ago? A year?'

He crowed with laughter at her.

'More like hundreds of years,' I said. 'It was forever ago, wasn't it, Peter?'

'Around then. That's the time of the saints. Before everything we have now, but not before ships because he came here by ship. That's why he thinks of sailors. Because his ship was wrecked but he survived.'

'Because he's holy,' I said, and the boy nodded.

'I see,' Anna said, and gave a great sigh. 'So in the days of forever ago, St Nectan came to these woods and after a little more of forever had passed, he was close to death.'

'In his chapel,' Peter said. 'That's where he was dying. It's the squire's little house now. The one he keeps empty by the falls.'

'The summer house is built on Saint Nectan's chapel?' I said.

Peter nodded and Anna gave a snort of laughter.

'That sounds like the work of poets to me,' she said.

I paid her no heed, thinking of what I had seen the night before, by not seeing. By drinking.

'These women that came for the saint, did they have eyes?' I asked.

'Shilly!'

But Peter didn't think it was a foolish question, or a fearful one.

'I don't know about their eyes. Grandmother might. She knows all the old stories. But they must have had some seeing for they put the saint in an oak casket and put that in the river bed. That'd be hard to do with no eyes at all.'

'Very true,' Anna said, looking at me.

'So the women put Saint Nectan to rest,' I said, ignoring, for a moment, the thought of them having drowned him first. 'You digging him up is hardly a kindness.'

'I have to!' Peter shouted. 'He said he'd come back when he was needed.' And then, more quietly, 'I need him. He'll find my brother.'

He was scritching again. I gave him back his spade to try and cheer him.

'Do you know who the women are?' Anna asked. 'The ones in the woods now, living in the cottage this side of the river.'

He wiped his eyes with his dirty sleeve. 'I told you. They're the same ones from before, the sisters that buried him. They've come back.'

'Why?' I said. 'What do they want?'

He shrugged. 'They won't say. I couldn't tell neither, though I went there most days, with Paul.'

'To the cottage? Why?'

'They needed things bringing, from Boscastle. And me and Paul did their snaring and skinning. They paid a ha'penny a rabbit. They ain't got no food now, and I'm glad of it.'

'Did you and Paul always go to the cottage together?' Anna said.

Peter nodded. 'But then I was ill and Mother said I was to stay in bed. Paul wasn't meant to go to the sisters' cottage without me, but we'd set a new snare and he didn't want it to go to waste, not when that pair would pay for fresh rabbits.' Peter pushed himself off the bank and into the water again. 'Mother was raging when she found he'd gone alone. Then when he didn't come home . . .' He dug his spade into the small stones of the river bed and turfed them into the water with a scattering splash, his actions quicker than before. Desperate.

'Poor soul,' Anna murmured. Then with deliberate loudness she said, 'Well, Shilly, we must be on our way. If only we had a guide to take us to the cottages where we met Mrs Haskell yesterday. All I have is this ha'penny—'

Peter stopped his work and we set off.

The boy didn't say much, though Anna tried to learn his secrets, as she had worked to learn mine when we had met on the moor. She was good at that. It was her talent.

The cottages came in sight and I was pleased to see the dusty quarry workers sitting outside amongst the piss bottles, for it meant we'd arrived at dinner time and there might be something spare, if Anna had more ha'pennies about her.

But she didn't need to spend them for Mrs Haskell saw us coming down the path with Peter and seemed to think we'd brought him to her, rather than the other way around. After she'd told him off again for going in the river, she bade us sit on the stone bench by her front door and pressed warm pasties into our hands. I noticed again that the Haskells' cottage was without the clutter of things that the others had, the things to keep witches away. Instead of piss bottles and hag stones, the Haskells had flowers in pots either side of the door, red and sweet-smelling.

I didn't ask why they didn't do the same as their neighbours, for I was eating and that was the better job then. No use knowing the questions to ask if you'd nothing inside you to keep standing. There was no meat in the pasties, for there was no money for it. I could see that, looking about me. Squire Vivian wasn't generous with his wages. But the pasties were filling and it was a kindness of Mrs Haskell to ask us to eat with her, and to feel the sun on my face. If it wasn't for the fact we were only there because a child was missing, I might have said it was pleasant.

Mrs Haskell wore the huge black shawl, same as the day before. It was made of wool and wrapped around her tightly, snug at the neck so that no skin showed below her chin. I said to her I wondered that she kept it on, such was the sun's fierceness.

'I can't be taking it off, my bird. Not with my flesh the way it is.'

'Have you sores?' I said, and Anna ceased chewing her mouthful of pasty.

'Scars,' Mrs Haskell said. 'From the fire. One of the mills went up, you see, years ago now. There's not many still living will remember it. I was stuck inside when the roof came down and the flames caught my dress. Took half my flesh with it when they pulled it off me.'

Anna marvelled that the flames hadn't touched Mrs Haskell's face, and the woman agreed.

'It was the saint, my sweet. He looks after us.'

'But not enough to stop the fire from happening in the first place,' Anna said quietly.

If Mrs Haskell heard this, she gave no sign, and asked if we'd like a drink. I wondered if they brewed much in those parts and was thinking how to ask that when a man came round the side of the cottage.

Mrs Haskell told us this was her son, James. He was lanky, and had the same sandy hair as Peter, though his was tidier than the boy's. Slate dust lay at his temples and on one side of his chin where he'd failed to wash it off. Anna told him we'd met his wife in the woods earlier, looking for Paul.

'I'm sorry to hear what's happened,' she said, and the care in her voice made me believe she meant it, that she wasn't only thinking of the reward. I liked her best when she showed this side of herself. It wasn't often.

James Haskell could only nod, his gaze on the ground.

'Maria's out there still,' Mrs Haskell said, patting her son's hand. 'And the others. We'll find him yet.'

James grasped her hand and squeezed it, and he seemed to draw comfort enough from this to work his tongue.

'You're staying in the summer house, Mother tells me,' he said.

'We are,' Anna said. 'It gives a fine view of the falls.'

'Damp, though,' I said.

'Thought it would be.' James leant against the door frame. 'Foolish place to build. You'd think the squire would have known that. But then he's never up there.'

'I'd imagine the cottage where the women are staying, the strangers, is less rustic?' Anna said.

'It's bigger, I know that. Needs to be, all the trinkets they've got with them.'

'You've been there?'

'When Paul didn't come back. I'd not gone before. Had no need to. Oh, now then!'

Peter appeared from behind, squeezing himself between his father and the doorpost. James wrapped his long arms round his son's shoulders and held him close.

'What have I got here then, eh? What have I got?'

The boy made out he was keen to be away but he wasn't. He was the cheeriest I'd seen him. James Haskell, too, had brightened.

There were shouts from down the path – girls' voices, squabbling. Cursing.

'Here's the peace gone,' Mrs Haskell muttered.

They appeared at once – three of them, each with the Haskell sandy hair but none of their father's leanness, or his quiet. Peter curled into himself, still held tight in his father's arms.

Mrs Haskell took the girls in hand, shouting that they should stop their racket, and truth be told they were as loud as the magpies who jounced and made their clitter on the summer house roof. They were introduced as Esther, Tamsin and Jenna. I forgot at once which was which but the youngest was ten and the eldest thirteen and the fight was over a comb and someone being pinched. The youngest showed her grandmother a red mark on the fleshy part of her upper arm, and blamed the middle sister, for which she was rewarded with another pinch, and a kick for good measure. I liked the spirit of the pinching sister. I thought that one was Tamsin.

Her grandmother smacked the back of the girl's legs and said, 'Go and see if Richard Bray has any fish. Your mother deserves a decent supper after searching all this time.'

'Richard Bray is a smelly old trout himself,' the youngest girl said. 'He leaves the guts all over the table.'

'You get going, my girl, and what's more you'll take your brother with you. Go on now, Peter.' Mrs Haskell gave the boy a shove into the flurry of his sisters and they swept him away with more shouts and curses.

James Haskell clasped his elbows, as if to hold fast the feeling of Peter there with him.

'I can see why the boys are close,' Anna said, when quiet had returned.

'Pair of nestle-birds, they are, keeping each other company. It does him good to be with the girls now, while Paul . . .' Mrs Haskell shook her head. 'It stops Peter digging.' Then she turned a sharp eye on me. 'That's where you found him, isn't it? In the water.'

'I'm afraid so,' Anna said.

'He said he was looking for the grave of Saint Nectan,' I said.

'He doesn't know what else to do,' Mrs Haskell said.

James went back inside the house without a word.

She watched him go, then said, 'We none of us do. The girls might look as if they're free of cares but they're weighed down by the worry of the rest of us. And Maria running herself ragged out there all hours, even in the dark when she's more likely to go over the waterfall than she is to find Paul. Oh my dears, my dears! That pair across the river, gliding about like they're innocent as the day they were born, when they've taken him! I know they've taken him!'

Then James Haskell was back with us again, setting a cup of tea in his poor mother's hand.

'Calm yourself, Mother. This won't help anyone.'

I thought Anna and I should be away, leave the Haskells to their grief. I stood but Anna pulled me back to sitting again and I saw that she was right, for if we could help, then maybe the grief could be ended.

When Mrs Haskell's sobs had eased, Anna spoke, and did so gently, with careful prodding.

'How do you know the women took Paul?'

'That's where he was last seen,' James said, looking up the path, as if his words could call the boy into view. 'At their cottage.'

'When was this?' Anna asked.

'Tuesday morning.'

'It was you that saw him there?'

'No, it was Simon. Simon Proctor. Said Paul was going up to the door.'

'And did this Mr Proctor see the women admit Paul to the cottage?'

'He didn't need to!' Mrs Haskell shouted, upsetting her tea all over her shawl. I worried she'd burnt herself but if she had then she was too angry to feel it, and perhaps old burns couldn't be burnt again. 'Paul was going to their door on Tuesday and now here we are on Friday and no sign of him. Where else could he have gone?'

'Anywhere,' I said, and then wished I hadn't for Mrs Haskell hung her head.

'Shilly's right,' Anna said. 'I'm sorry if that's cruel but it's true.'

'You talk to Simon Proctor. Paul was as good as seen going into the cottage.'

'It's not only that.' James Haskell picked some of the dead heads from the pot of flowers nearest him. 'I found his rabbit knife not far from the door, still wet with blood.' With the last word his voice cracked.

Mrs Haskell produced a huge handkerchief from inside her shawl and blew her nose loudly. 'And the other sign, James. Fetch that to show them.'

He nodded and went inside the house, returning almost straight away with an old tea tin. Something rattled inside it.

'May I?' Anna said. She took the tin and tipped it. A small black lump fell into her palm. A lump of coal.

'I found it near the knife,' James said.

Anna peered at it. 'Drawing charcoal.'

Mrs Haskell snatched it and dropped it back in the tin, snapping the lid closed. 'One of them draws, like you do. The boys told me of her pictures.'

'There's been much talk of the coal,' James said. 'Here in Trethevy, and in Boscastle.'

'We heard of it too,' I said. 'In Jamaica Inn.'

'They're talking about Paul as far away as that?' James said.

'It's a good story,' Anna said, 'and good stories have legs that cross a county in an instant.'

Mrs Haskell rattled the tea tin. '*This*! People are saying *this* is what those women turned Paul into. That he's been cursed.'

'You don't believe that, do you?' I said.

'Of course not!' Mrs Haskell said. 'Paul went to their cottage as flesh and blood, and as flesh and blood he'll be returned to us.'

She got up and pushed past James into the house. The sound of crashing crockery followed.

'Do you believe the women talk to the Devil?' I asked him.

'I don't know about any of that, but the older of them shouts loud enough.'

'Have you been able to search their cottage?' Anna asked.

'Maria and I did, the day Paul didn't come home. No one else will go near the place.'

'And you found no sign of the boy inside?'

He shook his head. 'The women say they had nothing to do with it, but they're strangers here, aren't they? Won't state their purpose.

What are they wanting, coming here, if not to do us harm?'

There was a pause then, hot with discomfort, for weren't Anna and I the same – strangers? And lying about our purpose, too. That didn't make us likely to thieve children, though. The same could well be true for the pair across the river. We shared more than a few likenesses.

James Haskell cleared his throat. 'How long you staying in the summer house?' he asked.

'It depends to some extent on our access to provisions,' Anna said. 'We would be glad of food and drink being brought. For payment, of course.'

She and James Haskell talked of bread and rabbits and pennies, and I left them to it, wandering onto the path that ran between the cottages. The Haskell girls were a little ahead, fighting with other children and poor Peter looking on, looking lost. To not know what had happened to someone you loved – I had felt that pain. And how it worsened, once my girl had been found, and I had learnt what had been done to her.

A fishy stink was on the air, and I followed it to a cottage with greasy windows and cats prowling the doorstep. This must be the home of Richard Bray, I thought, the trout Mrs Haskell had sent the girls to, to seek their mother's supper. It wasn't fish that made me go closer. There were more bottles outside Bray's cottage than any other and I reasoned they couldn't all hold piss and pins.

When I peered in the doorway I knew that I was right, for Bray himself stank of brewing. He was fat and old and shiny with fish oil and sweat. His smock bore the stains of fish gutting. Bray was singing some bold song about a woman with a liking for sailors, swaying and stumbling in what might have been a jig, the cats dodging his boots and the spillings of his beer as they fought for the fish scraps. I was going to ask him for a sup. But then I thought of poor Peter Haskell digging the river, of his mother fighting her way through the woods, and I asked instead where I would find Simon Proctor. Him that last saw Paul.

'Simon? He's along at the manor house,' Bray said, sending his fire irons clattering to the floor. 'In the stables. Been losing again, has he? Ah that boy. Vice it is.' He let free a belch and took another swig.

'Losing what?' I said, but Bray was singing to his cats about the faithlessness of men who put to sea so I left him to his trilling. The air outside his cottage was the sweetest I had known.

Anna was looking for me, and as I left Bray's cottage his roar rang out and the cats dashed past me onto the path and away, their tales fluffed fat in alarm. A magpie shot overhead.

'I didn't touch a drop,' I said, seeing Anna's mouth opening and knowing only too well what she'd likely think. I told her where we'd find Simon Proctor.

'It wouldn't be a bad thing if the squire were to see us making enquiries,' Anna said as we left the cottages behind and were back beneath the trees' gloom. 'He'll see then we're working for the reward.'

Always she was thinking of money.

TWELVE

We followed a wide drive of gravel that led to the back of the house and then through an arch cut into a thick hedge of yew. There was a cobbled yard beyond, and four stable boxes in a row. A set of steps clung to the wall at one end of these, leading to a door in the roof. Only the horses watched us climb to the door, watched me open it. Behind it was a snug room built into the eaves, with a bed and a small table next to it that bore a jug and basin, both of which were chipped. Working clothes were thrown across a chair and lay on the floor.

'Proctor's room?' Anna said.

'I'd think so.'

Everything smelt of horse, and I had no doubt the person who slept in such a place would smell that way too. No matter how much they scrubbed their skin, the traces of their working life would never leave them. There would be no escape from it.

Anna was moving the clothes from the chair to the bed.

'What are you looking for?' I asked her.

'I'm not sure yet. Something to tell us who Simon Proctor is.'

'How about these?' I knelt and picked up the playing cards beneath the bed.

Anna found another pack under the pillow.

'Bray asked me if Proctor had been losing again,' I said.

'It certainly looks like he enjoys a game. See how grubby these cards are.'

A sound from below – a door opened. Murmuring. I knew it to be someone speaking to the horses for I knew the kind of soft talk people used when alone with beasts.

We crept back down the stairs to the yard. The murmuring was coming from the closest box.

He had his back to us. I put my hands on the half door, made the bolt clang, and he whipped round with a start. His lean face was struck with terror, I thought. But when he saw who we were, he let out a breath.

'We startled you, Simon,' Anna said. 'You look as if you're expecting someone. You *are* Simon Proctor?'

'Yes,' he said, his gaze flicking between us, as if we might still turn out to be those he feared. As well we might. 'If you're here about the reward, then you'll need to call at the house.'

He reached over the door and undid the bolt, sliding nimbly from the box in one quick movement that put me in mind of a fox. He went into a small room filled with saddles and ropes and the smell of oiled leather. We followed him, and he looked troubled by this.

I stood in the doorway to show we weren't going anywhere. 'The Haskells told us you were the last person to see the boy that's missing. Young Paul.'

Simon fiddled with a saddle flap, making out he was oiling it but I'd done plenty of that in my time and could see it was only to keep his hands busy and save him having to look at us. His cloth was filthy for a start.

'I don't know about that,' he said.

'You weren't near the cottage on the morning Paul went missing?' Anna said. 'The one across the river, where the strangers are living.'

'Well I . . .'

'Yes?'

'I was there, but I didn't stop.'

'So you didn't see Paul?' I said.

Proctor's hand on the saddle flap stilled.

'Or you did see him,' Anna said. 'Going up to the door.'

'I . . . I did see him. But I didn't stop.'

'Tuesday, wasn't it? Around ten in the morning.'

'It might have been. I've no watch so . . .'

'What were you doing over that side of the river, anyway?' I said.

'I don't see that's any concern of yours.'

He began sorting some pails, which made a terrible clanging. If he thought that should stop our questions, he was wrong. I just spoke louder.

'Did the squire know you'd left your work to cross the river that morning?'

The colour leaving his face was answer enough.

Anna changed her questioning then, grew soft with him. Like a friend. 'The boy is still missing, Simon. You could help us find him if you'd tell us a little more. You saw Paul Haskell near the cottage on Tuesday morning, didn't you?'

'Yes,' he said quietly.

'How close were you?'

'Twenty paces, maybe. Not at the door. I never said he was at the door. Mrs Haskell, she was so upset. When people started saying the boy was missing, I went and told her I'd seen him there, but she didn't hear me right, or maybe I gabbled a bit. I don't know. Everyone was scritching and talking about the coal and the knife.'

I wondered if he might start scritching himself, he was getting so flustered.

'So where *was* Paul when you last saw him?' I said.

'By the old gatepost. He was kneeling there, taking a rabbit from a snare. I don't think he even knew I passed him.'

'And you saw no one else? No sign of the women?'

'No, they were . . .' He fussed with the pails again.

'They were what?' Anna said.

'I didn't see anyone,' Simon said. 'Just Paul Haskell and his rabbit. Now, I . . . I must get on.' And he nipped past me, out into the yard, looking over his shoulder as he went. He was no fox now. He was Paul's rabbit running.

We made our way back through the yew hedge and so to the house, for that was the way back to the woods, but Anna said we should go round the other side of the house this time, on a narrow path that ran close to the house itself. For people this was, not for carts and carriages like the gravelly drive, and I guessed she was still hoping to be seen earning her fee.

'Proctor was keen to tell us he didn't stop at the women's cottage, wasn't he?' she said. And I heard the tapping noise I knew to mean she was thinking. It was her false teeth that sat in her jaw as if they were her own. Her tongue fidgeted with them. She never knew she was doing it, but I liked the sound. It was part of the finding out of things.

'Twice he told us he didn't stop at the cottage,' I said.

'Now, why wouldn't he want people to know he'd been near there, I wonder?'

Climbing plants trailed the walls, heavy with white and pink blossoms. I brushed them with my fingertips as we passed, and the soft petals fell on me like warm snow, but then my fingers caught the brick beneath.

'This part of the house is newer,' I said, more to myself than to Anna walking ahead of me.

'Hm?'

'This is brick. The front part is made of moor stone. These plants would never get a foothold in that.'

Anna came back to where I stood and looked where I was looking. 'So? Many people make additions to their houses.'

'And Sir Vivian has the quarrying to pay for it,' I said. 'It's like another house stuck on the end of the old one, and with its own garden too, look.' I nodded at the little square of green bound by low walls that sat in the crook where the old house joined the new. A chair was set in the shade of the overhanging plants, next to the door. 'A fine spot for doing nothing when you've others labouring for you.'

'We need to get on with our own labours,' Anna said, moving away.

I put my hand on her arm. 'Look.'

Lady Phoebe was at an upstairs window of the brick part. Her hand against the glass. But as soon as she saw us looking she was gone in a rush of her many white layers.

'This must be the east wing,' Anna said, 'where the squire said no one else was to go, in case she was disturbed.'

'Do you think he lets her out?' I said.

'I hope so. Making her a prisoner won't help her health, even if she is a delicate thing. And besides, I don't want to add rescuing a damsel in distress to this quest, Shilly. We haven't got time for that.'

The woods were one reason we were short of time. It took us hours to find our way back to the summer house, even though we had walked the same journey the night before, when we had arrived. Now as we chased our own tails Anna claimed she had purposefully chosen the long way round. But I knew it was the woods' creeping and shifting that kept us from where we did want to be.

When at last we came upon the monks' wall Anna gave a cry of joy, making it plain to me she'd been anxious, even if she kept saying there wasn't anything strange about the woods.

'I'll make a map,' she said. 'That'll help us get about more quickly.'

I laughed. As if those woods would be stilled by setting them on a piece of paper! Mrs Haskell had said that hate had stirred them, and I wondered – was it these strangers coming, these sisters? Had they brought hate with them, unpacked it from a travelling case and stowed it in their cottage from where it had spread to the trees, to their roots and so to the earth, the water? Peter said they'd come first to bury the saint in the river. I'd seen them drown him in his holy well. But that was what stories were like. They changed. Some parts stayed the same – the saint, the pair of women, the water. But others were different. The difference between natural dying and life being taken.

At least the last part of our journey was staying fixed. We climbed the slippery rocks that ran next to the waterfall, as we expected to. The black and white of the summer house came in sight above, the saint's chapel, the place where he had died. Of old age or from drowning? I had no drink with me, and that lack was a bad business. But I took comfort from the fact that, without it, I might keep myself from such a sight again.

As we drew closer to the summer house there came a terrible noise – a squabbling squawking ruin of a sound. We hurried the last of the way and then beheld magpies fighting on the summer house steps. I ran at them, flapping my arms and squawking, as if I was a bird too. They took to the air, but only after I'd colped them round their heads. It was then I saw the cloths and the basket scattered across the steps, and within these the pasties and bread, some apples. The birds had only managed to unfold one of the cloths so most of the food was still unpecked.

'Those birds are braver than most are wont to be,' I said. 'And bigger, too, than magpies should be.'

'If they often enjoy Mrs Haskell's pasties then it's no wonder,' Anna said as we collected up our feast. 'James Haskell is as good as his word. He can't leave food out though, not with these birds.'

She eyed the magpies who had settled in a tree nearby, a lone tree in the clearing where the summer house had been built. The tree wasn't tall but it was finely shaped – slender branches that made me think of arms reaching out, not in anger, not to strike, but to hold me in kindness. The tree made me think of my mother. I shook such a sad thought away.

'The Haskells will be glad of you paying them for food,' I said to Anna. 'They won't be earning any more from the pair across the river.'

'True.'

I picked up a stone jar of tea that had rolled on its side. The stopper had held, thank goodness. 'Those women will be hungry now, I should think.'

'I don't doubt it, Shilly.'

'We should take them something. We can use the food to make them answer our questions.'

Anna ceased her stooping and looked at me. 'You'd use their hunger as a means of interrogating them, Shilly? The gangs of the East End would have nothing on you.'

I shrugged. If you didn't have food, you had nothing. You'd die. Anna had never faced being without it. I had.

We went inside and I locked the door against the woods and the trees. And blinded women too, if they were abroad that night.

When I was close to falling asleep I heard water dripping inside the walls again. Such was the damp of the summer house, I didn't think it'd be long before it softened and slumped into the pool beneath the falls and then washed out to sea.

Would that we were gone before then, and Paul Haskell safe, back with his family.

THIRTEEN

I was woken by a man's voice, then Anna's, then a great thump of something heavy and the sound of the door being closed. I opened my eyes and there was her travelling case, taking up most of the small summer house.

Anna laid her hand on the battered leather, as if it was some special friend she had missed. All her other selves were stowed inside it. And mine too, if I should choose to put them on.

I unfolded myself from the blankets, shielding my eyes from the bright sun streaming in the window.

'Good, you're awake. Well, Shilly.' She clapped her hands. 'It's high time we crossed the river.'

We set off to the cottage where the pair of women lived, taking a basket of food to force their secrets from them. Anna was dressed in something orange and shiny, the colour close to rust. She had kept the wig of dark knotted hair she'd worn since leaving Jamaica Inn, and looked fine enough. But not as fine as Mrs Williams who went with her. Of course, the mud did nothing for such finery and I soon gave up trying to keep the bottom of my dress from getting dirty. I was glad I'd kept my own boots, rather than give Mrs Williams shoes from the case.

We came to the monks' wall, which had kept itself where it should be, and the crossing stones in the water beside it. I looked out for Peter Haskell but he wasn't there. Was he digging for Saint Nectan's grave in another part of the river today? I hoped his grandmother had found a way to keep him from that grim task.

We reached the other side and were now on Mr Trunkett's land. Though the mud and the ferns and all the rest of it were the same as on the bank we'd just come from, that which belonged to the squire, the going was harder here. My boots felt heavier, each step took greater will. I couldn't catch my breath so well.

Something made me look back across the water. A movement there. Some bird?

There was a woman on the opposite bank.

Her back was to me. She was wearing my old working dress, the one Anna had told me she'd got rid of. The woman's hair was my hair. The paleness of her arms, my own. I was looking at myself across the river, my sister self. I called to this sister on the other side, and after a moment she turned, and then I saw her eyes were gone.

I heard screaming, and then came the hot slap of Anna's hand across my cheek. She was right to hit me. It made my sister vanish.

'Again!' I shouted, wanting to keep her gone, and when Anna didn't do as I asked I grabbed her hand and held it hard against my cheek to show her that I meant it. And so she slapped me.

Then there was only Mrs Williams and Anna Drake facing each other, one of them shaking, one of them confused, upset. And then they were stumbling from the water, into the trees. Holding hands.

A drink, I thought. My god, a drink.

Once the river was out of sight Anna sat me down on a large flat stone. She didn't ask me what was wrong, but like as not she knew.

When I could speak again I said we should talk of the boy, of Paul, for that was what would keep me in the woods and keep me with her. Keep me from myself.

We set to walking again, and talked of what we'd learnt yesterday from Mrs Haskell and her son. Reviewing the evidence, Anna called it, and I was grateful for the words to fix on.

'There's the bloodied knife,' she said. 'Paul could have been killed on the spot and we're looking for a body rather than a living boy.'

'Or the blood's from rabbiting. Peter said they'd set that snare, that Paul was certain they'd catch something.'

'And Paul did the skinning then and there, hence the blood?'

'Why not?' I said. 'He was going to sell the meat to the women. Makes sense he'd ready it for them while he was so close. Why go home to do it, only to have to bring it back again?'

We were following a path, not as well trodden as the one on the squire's side of the river but a path all the same. I kept my gaze on my feet, putting one in front of the other, and was glad again of my own boots. They made me believe I was looking at my own feet. Not those of some other woman.

'There's the drawing charcoal, too,' Anna said.

'Found with the knife, James Haskell said, didn't he? That looks bad for the women.'

'It would certainly seem to incriminate them, given that everyone in the woods knows they're here to draw.'

'But they think that of us, too,' I said, 'and that's a lie.'

'Well, let's see what truths we find at the cottage, shall we?'

As we went on our way I realised something, that the weighed-down feeling that had beset me since coming to the woods was eased here. It wasn't that there were fewer trees, or that there was more light between them on this side of the river. Those parts were the same. The place *looked* the same. But the air was different. The hatred Mrs Haskell had spoken of, that I had felt so badly, it wasn't with me now.

The path bent to the left, away from the river, and after we had climbed a slight slope the space around us opened and the trees weren't so tight together. A moor stone pillar, four feet high, stood a little way off. I left the path and went over to it, the ground around it ferny, and in the ferns, blind nettles.

'Presumably this is the gatepost Simon Proctor mentioned,' Anna said, coming up behind me. 'This is where he saw Paul Haskell.' She ran a hand over the moss that clung to the pillar's top. 'Whatever gate was once attached is long gone.'

A little way beyond the pillar was a bank of earth and stones beset by the roots of trees growing from the bank's top. The stones were wedged this way and that, some all but forced out by the roots and so teetering. I thought of Anna's false teeth.

I made out the dark eyes of holes between the stones, and knelt to better see them and judge for creatures living there. In doing so I put my hand into the ferns. Something stabbed me.

As I cursed my hurt palm, Anna rootled amongst the ferns and after a moment held up a short length of wood about the thickness of my wrist. At one end was a loop of wire and it was the sharpness of this that caught my hand.

'The boys' snare,' I said. 'See the way the wood's cut to a stake at one end, for driving into the ground? It must have fallen over.'

'Or Paul had pulled it out ready to set somewhere else.'

'Then why is it still here?' I said as Anna helped me to my feet. 'Paul would want to set it again or take it home with him, surely? He was earning money from it.'

'Simon Proctor said he passed Paul without the boy even knowing he was there.'

'So someone else could have crept up on Paul once Simon had gone. That would be a reason for the snare being left.'

'That theory works if you believe Proctor had nothing to do with Paul going missing,' Anna said.

I wrapped the wire loop around the wood so that there was no more sharpness sticking out, and then tucked the snare into one of the many pockets in Mrs Williams's dress. Peter should have the snare back, at least.

'Simon Proctor's reluctance to admit what he was doing here doesn't cast him in the best light,' Anna said.

'He could be in league with them, the women.'

We went back to the path, walking deeper into the trees, and hadn't gone far when we heard shouts. A woman's voice. I couldn't make out the words. A few steps more and we found the cottage.

Black smoke drifted from the squat chimney and gave the air the smell of burning. The shouting was loud and though we were close now, close enough to look through the narrow windows either side the door, I still couldn't understand the words.

I grabbed Anna's hand. 'They *are* speaking to the Devil!'

I tried to drag her back the way we'd come and so away, out of these fiendish woods, but she wouldn't move, just cocked her head and listened. I was afeared she'd be turned into a lump of coal if we stayed there much longer.

'Anna, please!'

She laughed. She laughed!

'Ah, Shilly. If that's them talking to the Devil then the Devil is fluent in German.'

FOURTEEN

Anna knocked on the door. All at once the shouting stopped. In its place were hurrying feet, mutters, the sound of furniture being pushed about. A moment of silence, and then the door was opening. I held my breath, held myself steady for what might come for us – the blinded sisters who had drowned the saint.

And then my breath came back to me, for the woman before us could see as well as Anna or me. Her eyes were where they did belong to be.

She had opened the door with her face set haughty – her pointy nose raised, her lips pressed together, not quite smiling. But on seeing us her manner changed. Her shoulders slumped and her mouth fell open into ugliness. We were not who she hoped for. And who was that, I wondered?

'Yes?' she snapped. 'What is it that you want?'

These words I could understand, but her way of saying them was strange, as if her throat was closing. She glared, put out by us and our unexpectedness.

'Forgive the intrusion,' Anna said. 'We're staying across the river and thought to make your acquaintance. I am Miss Drake, and this is Mrs Williams.'

I bobbed my head and smiled, all polite, which Shilly would never do, but other women might. I must have done it wrong, though, for this woman on the doorstep recoiled as if I'd spat on her boots. And I felt like spitting, truth be told, for there was no friendliness from her as she looked me up and down.

'You have come to . . . *call* on us?' she said, as if this idea was the most foolish thing she'd ever heard, and at that moment I shared her feeling. This woman was never going to answer our questions.

Whispers behind her. The woman made to stop whoever it was coming to the door, saying something sharply in what I guessed must be the German talking of theirs. But she wasn't quick enough. A younger woman appeared beside her, sixteen years of age or so. She thrust out her hand to me and was all smiles, eager.

'I am Miss Wolffs.'

'Shilly,' I said, forgetting Mrs Williams.

She caught sight of the basket Anna carried and her eyes widened, for Anna had made sure the cloth was pulled back to show the food. She turned to the older woman and some silent conversation was had between them. Both looked in a bad way. Their faces were sallow, pinched, and there were shadows round their eyes that didn't come from tiredness. They came from hunger. So did the bitterness on their breath. I knew such signs. Had lived them, not so long ago.

'My apologies, we've called at an inconvenient time,' Anna said.

We turned to go, but of course they stopped us, as we had known they would, and the younger one, the one called Miss Wolffs, all but dragged us into the cottage, her eyes never leaving the basket. I caught sight of something as we crossed the threshold – a heap of little brown shells dumped by the door. For witching?

It was gloomy inside, and more so once the older woman shut the door. She stayed close by it as if ready to turn us out. I wouldn't have minded that, for the cottage was airless as well as gloomy. The fire smoked badly and made me cough.

'I am Miss Franks,' the older woman said, like this was a grand thing to tell us.

Not sisters, then, as the people of Trethevy called them, but then they were thinking of another pair, an older pair. These two shared no likeness in looks. Miss Franks was slight, with narrowed shoulders and a narrow waist. Her face was likewise narrow. Her hair was brown, and caught up behind her head, not like when we had seen them the day before. But it was badly done, falling more to one side than the other and with strands escaping. More like gorse, which grew any old way it wanted to. There was slate's greyness in her hair in places. She wasn't old, though. Perhaps thirty.

Miss Wolffs was squarely built, with a wide face. Her hair was brown too but darker, richer in colour, and just as badly pinned. She wore the grey dress I had seen the day before. There was a pattern on it, some flowery thing. The cloth was very fine, but the dress had foolishly wide sleeves. They would be forever catching in milk or on door handles. Miss Wolffs must have likely found that for one of her sleeves was stained dark with something or other.

What were they to each other, these women in the woods? If not sisters then they must be friends, and I wondered if they were *very* close friends, as Anna and I might be again, one day. But if these women were friends then the friendship was sore at that moment. The older one, the Miss Franks, was saying something German at Miss Wolffs, something angry, for Miss Wolffs clutched her skirts and flapped her hands, which only sent the smoke coursing around the room even worse.

'We cannot make it go up. Up up!' she said, waving at the chimney breast.

I raised my arm across my face and peered into the hearth. There were thick logs in the hearth. Smoke poured between them but there was no sign of a flame.

'You haven't laid it right,' I said. 'Have you no one to help you?' Meaning someone like me, of course. A servant.

Miss Wolffs shook her head. 'Gertrud and I, we—'

'It is made badly,' Miss Franks – Gertrud – said. 'The chimney.'

She had folded her arms across her chest and was glaring at Miss Wolffs. I guessed the fire was the cause of the shouting we'd heard as we came upon the cottage.

'You've paper here, look,' I said. 'Let me get that between the wood and it'll help the fire take.' I grabbed some of the sheets lying on a chair and was about to scrunch them when Miss Wolffs grabbed them back again.

'That is my drawings!' she said, and I saw that the pages did bear something, some lines and colour, but I had no chance to look closely for she was smoothing out the sheets. One of her hands was all ashake. And only the one.

'You do not need them all,' Miss Franks said. 'We must have the fire. Here.' She thrust a handful of pages at me. 'Do it. Make the flames to come.'

'But I have not so many papers left,' Miss Wolffs said, before another glare from Miss Franks silenced her. Her shaking hand grew worse and she tucked it behind her.

I didn't want to burn the drawings but I didn't think I had a choice now, with this Miss Franks standing over me. I scrunched the paper and knelt by the fire, coughing and spluttering as I poked the scrunches between the logs. When I stood up I was rewarded for my efforts by Miss Franks looking me up and down again, for I had muddled her with my fine dress and my willingness to kneel on the floor. I was not as good at disguise as Anna.

Anna herself had taken up the drawings that had survived the burning. 'These are some fine sketches. Can I ask where they were made?'

Miss Wolffs smiled shyly. 'That one, it is Boscastle. It has the harbour with the fish boats. The sea there, it is very beautiful. We stayed for some weeks before—'

'You will sit down, yes?' Miss Franks said loudly, and shoved a chair at Anna. 'Miss Wolffs – the tea.'

Miss Wolffs looked afeared at this, her shaking hand shaking worse as she picked up a dented cooking pan and peered at it.

There was only one other chair. Miss Franks pointed at it so I sat. Miss Franks herself perched on the edge of a large wooden box upended on the floor. She arranged her dress so the folds hung neatly. It was as fine a dress as Miss Wolffs wore, though plainer, and very grubby about the collar and the cuffs. She was an odd sight and no mistake, sitting haughty and dirty on a box.

Miss Wolffs was shilly-shallying about the tea, all jittery, looking to Miss Franks for help.

'I get water,' Miss Wolffs said, 'and then I get . . . I get . . .' She turned to the fire as if the answer to making tea lay somewhere in the smoke.

I felt sorry for this poor girl and thought it best to help her or we'd die of thirst.

'Here now,' I said, 'here's your kettle, look, with water in still. Enough for us all. I'll set it on the trivet to boil and you show me where the cups are, and the tea.'

The smile she gave me spoke her relief, such great relief that I felt ashamed for all I'd done was set the kettle boiling. I followed her into a small scullery where the smoke wasn't so thick but there were flies in its place. They buzzed about the unwashed plates and cutlery piled up. The plates and such looked very fine beneath the crusted food – china, I thought. But much good that was doing this strange pair, stuck in a poor cottage in the woods.

Miss Wolffs began hauling cups out of the piles of dishes with such carelessness I worried she'd scat the whole lot on the floor and then Miss Franks would be shouting again and we'd have no luck with our questions. I told Miss Wolffs to let me get the cups if she'd find the tea. While her back was turned, I grabbed a cloth that was nearly clean and gave the cups a wipe.

'Is here,' Miss Wolffs said, handing me a fancy tin that had drawings on it, of girls, I thought. Girls, dancing, drawn in gold. The tin was light, and when I opened it there was barely a spoonful of tea at the bottom.

'Have you no more?' I said.

Miss Wolffs shook her head.

'We'd best not have any, then.' I gave her back the tin. 'We won't take your last leaves.'

She gripped my arm with her shaking hand and the tremor ran through me. 'She will be angry.'

'But . . .'

'Please!'

'All right, then. No need to fret over weak tea, is there? We'll soon have a pot made.'

She smiled. 'Your name, you say it *Shill-lee*?'

I nodded.

'I am Mathilda, but Gertrud – Miss Franks – she makes us be proper so you must call me Miss Wolffs if she hears. Is good, though, to know true names for friends.'

'Yes,' I said, but I couldn't meet her bright, sweet eye for there was a lie between us. The lie of Shilly.

I followed her back into the main room. Anna was talking.

'I believe we saw you out walking yesterday, Miss Franks.'

Miss Franks sat silent and rigid on her box.

'I had hoped to make your acquaintance,' Anna said, 'but we weren't able to catch up with you.'

After a long pause Miss Franks said, 'We were engaged.' She didn't look at Anna. Her gaze was fixed on the basket of food we had brought.

'Of course.'

I knelt by the fire to see to the tea, and Miss Franks made no effort to stop me doing so. The floor was flagged with slate, and cold, despite the warmth of the day outside. A dead mouse was curled in the corner. The fire was at last drawing better, which meant the smoke had eased and I was able to see the many things the room held, besides the dead mouse.

James Haskell had talked of there being trinkets here, and I had to call these things the same, for none of them looked purposeful to me. Dishes too small to put anything in, shaped like ducks and cows, and babies, too. Little boxes of polished wood and metal, and maybe even the same stuff Anna's false teeth were fashioned from. A fine clock, all gleaming small cog parts and a shiny, white face – stopped. And small china people – that was what there was most of. Men and women, boys and girls, dressed up in hats and ribbons and lace, fine-coated and pink-cheeked, holding flowers and birds and fruit. The room was crammed with such bits and pieces, and all of them covered in the smoke's dirt.

These weren't witching tools, were they?

They looked very ordinary, not the kind to foretell a lover or rid a girl of pox. Not the kind to ill-wish either. But the shells at the door – did they have a secret use? These women might have cursed everyone in Trethevy for all I knew. But then I asked myself, if they were witches, wouldn't they save themselves from starving?

'The woods are wonderfully picturesque,' Anna was saying. 'And the waterfall – such an inspiring place for the artistically minded. You take walks often, Miss Franks?'

'Every day,' Miss Franks said, still looking at the basket.

'It is what we do here,' the girl Mathilda added. 'We walk.'

'And that is why you have come to the woods, to walk and to draw?'

Mathilda hesitated, her gaze flicking to Miss Franks who got up and went to a table wedged beneath the small window. There were so many things on it there was barely any tabletop to see. She picked up an enormous metal teapot, all tall and pointy like a church spire. This she thrust at me.

Taking her place on her box again, she said, 'Like you say, Miss Drake. We come for walking and to draw.'

'You have come a long way,' Anna said. 'From Germany – yes?'

'The woods, they are very famous now. In the travel guides, the poems.'

'Still, you must have sights to rival these in your own country. Why come to this isolated corner?'

'Travel – they say it broadens the mind, do they not? Woods here in Cornwall hold more for us than woods at home.'

'Such as?'

'Ferns. The hart's tongue, it grows here. For Miss Wolffs to draw this is a great thing.'

'You must be quite the botanical enthusiast, Miss Wolffs.'

Mathilda let out a shrill sound, a gulp of laughter that was all nerves, before catching hold of herself again.

'You must be wanting to draw every fern here, to have all these belongings with you,' I said. 'You going to stay a long time?'

'I . . . I do not know,' Mathilda said. 'It will depend—'

'We stay as long as it takes,' Miss Franks said quickly.

'To draw the ferns?' Anna said.

'To draw the ferns,' Miss Franks said.

And then a tight silence fell and I was glad to make the tea so I had something to do. As I tipped the few leaves into the grand teapot I was aware of Mathilda leaning forward in her chair, her hands clasped to hide the shaking one, watching me. Delighted. Relieved. The kettle began to whistle and I looked for a rag to lift it.

Anna cleared her throat. 'I gather you've been well looked after by the people here. They've brought you food and such.'

Miss Franks began to tap her foot against the floor.

'Is stopped now,' Mathilda said. 'They stop it. They say . . . bad things.'

'Lies!' Miss Franks hissed, jerking her head up. 'All of it lies! The things they say, they are mad! Paul Haskell, he come here often, yes, with his brother. They bring food and I pay them. Then his parents come and say we are wicked, that we take the boy. That we are . . .' She threw up her hands and made a noise of great annoyance, something like a grunt.

'Witches,' I said.

The word took all sound from the room. Even the fire's crackle dropped away.

FIFTEEN

'We do not hurt Paul,' Mathilda whispered. 'They are sweet boys, the Haskells. I want him to be found.'

Her hand was shaking badly now. Miss Franks took hold of it to still it, with no kindness in the touch.

'It is a sad business,' Anna said, 'and I understand that Paul was last seen very close to here. His brother believes he was going to bring you a rabbit from his new snare. Did you see him that morning?'

'We were walking.' Miss Franks straightened on her box seat.

'Near here?' I said.

'Across the river,' Miss Franks said.

'You went to the waterfall?' Anna asked.

'The manor house,' Mathilda said.

Miss Franks stiffened slightly.

'And what time did you reach the manor house?' Anna said.

'At twelve o'clock,' Mathilda said. 'I hear the clock chime when the maid, she come running. She chase the cat. It have a bird in its mouth.'

'A bird's *leg*,' Miss Franks said. 'A game bird. Expensive.'

Mathilda grinned. 'The maid shout and cry, and the cat, he just run faster!'

This sounded very much like Pigeon.

'And when you arrived back here, did you see any sign of Paul Haskell?' Anna said.

'No sign,' Miss Franks said. 'No rabbit, no bread. We think, Peter and Paul forget to come. Then the parents come. They say we *steal* Paul, when it is us who have been stolen from.'

'Things have been taken from here?' I said.

'Special things,' Miss Franks said. 'Valuable things.'

Mathilda nodded eagerly.

'Such as?' Anna said.

'Silverware – spoons and knives. A frame for a picture. They even take our shoes! So many things – gone. We lock the door and still they get in. Like snakes!'

'When did these thefts occur?' Anna said.

Miss Franks shrugged. 'They go little by little. We do not see until we look. The thieves – they are clever. Take piece at a time. They wait, and when we go out, they come and take, and then they accuse us!'

'And they listen,' Mathilda said.

'Yes!' Miss Franks hissed. 'They are spies. All of them. At the windows. They think we do not know they are there but we know. Always we know.'

'So why do you stay here?' I said.

'We cannot leave Trethevy,' Miss Franks said.

'Not even for a morning?' I said. 'To go to Boscastle and get yourself what you need?'

'Not for a morning. Not for a month. We must stay.'

'Surely the ferns aren't worth all this?' Anna asked. 'What is it that truly keeps you here?'

'That is not a question a stranger can ask.'

'Well, I hope we won't be strangers for long.' Anna picked up the basket.

Miss Franks and Mathilda leant forwards. Their hunger was so bad I felt it had a sound, that the dirty cottage moaned with it.

'Given the situation you find yourselves in,' Anna said, lifting out a pasty, 'I thought you might appreciate—'

Mathilda snatched the pasty.

'What *have* you been finding to eat?' I said.

'How is it you say?' Mathilda said through her chomping, her cheeks fat with pastry. 'The snails.'

The shells by the door. Ordinary things. No malice there, just hunger.

Miss Franks reached to take from Mathilda what remained of the pasty but Mathilda wasn't having any of that and wriggled away. Then Miss Franks muttered something in their language that made Mathilda hang her head. She let the pasty go. Miss Franks returned it to the basket. I marvelled at her strength in doing so, for she was hungry as Mathilda, I was sure of it.

'You will forgive Miss Wolffs,' Miss Franks said. 'She forgets manners. We will not eat without our guests. I will get the plates.'

She stood but Anna bade her sit again.

'Please, that's not necessary. We will leave you to your meal.'

And now relief was clear on Miss Franks' face at not having to share, but she tucked the relief back inside herself and found her haughtiness again.

'As you wish, Miss Drake,' she said, as if she didn't care either way if we stayed and shared the food. 'You may call on us again, if it would please you.'

It would please *her* very much, I thought, if we came with baskets of food each time. I hoped Mrs Haskell wouldn't learn who was sharing the things we bought from her. She wouldn't like that much, and I'd enjoyed the welcome of Trethevy. If we could only find Paul, we might be forgiven for feeding witches.

We stood to go. Miss Franks stayed seated, gripping the basket of food. Mathilda followed us to the door and said goodbye, her hand shaking all the while. She'd all but closed the door when she put her face to the gap and whispered, 'You come again. We must eat. I will starve if she—'

103

A hurry of footsteps and then the door slammed shut.

'They'll be ripping those pasties apart,' Anna said.

'We should have a look about, shouldn't we? They'll pay us no heed while they're eating.'

Anna followed me round the cottage, through the tangle of greenery trying to choke the place.

'Mathilda could just stay here all day for ferns to draw,' I said.

Anna snorted. 'I don't believe they'd endure this much hardship for a few plants. They're used to having help – that's clear enough from the pantomime about making tea.'

'And the poor pinning of their hair. They haven't much practice at that.'

'I don't expect they've done much for themselves in life, until now,' Anna said. 'They've clearly been well off in the past, but what has caused their change of fortune?'

The back of the cottage had one small window. I peered in and saw a bed, no other furniture, but the room was crammed with fiddly things just as the front one had been. No wonder it had taken this pair a little time to notice their belongings had been stolen.

'If we come again,' I said, 'if we bring more food, they might tell us what has befallen them. Mathilda – that's Miss Wolffs – she's wanting to talk. Needs to, I should think.'

'That Miss Franks . . .' Anna said. 'We'd have more luck questioning Peter Haskell's spade.'

'She was happy to talk about thieving.'

'Wasn't she?' Anna got hold of the window frame. The sash slid up easy enough. 'Locking the door seems a futile measure. But I wonder . . .'

I heard her false teeth tapping, her thinking noise. But I was thinking too and I was ahead of her.

'You don't believe them, about the thieving.'

Anna lowered the window back into place. 'It could be a way to cast themselves as victims rather than villains, to elicit sympathy instead of fear.'

'To un-witch themselves,' I said.

'In a manner of speaking.'

I made my way round the other side of the cottage, so that we should make a circle of it. There weren't so many ferns and brambles so the way was easier.

'There isn't much menace to them, or otherworldliness,' Anna said, coming up behind me.

'You mean you don't believe them to be witches?'

'Do you?' she asked.

I turned to face her.

'Are you asking because you want my answer, Anna, my real answer, or are you mocking me again? And I ask *you* that because I can't always be sure, even though you told me we would work as equals.'

'Well, you can't deny they're flesh and blood, Shilly. And that they have eyes. I certainly don't believe them to be reincarnations of the sisters said to have buried St Nectan in the river.'

'Or drowned him.'

'Whichever. Legends aside, do you believe that Miss Wolffs and Miss Franks are engaged in . . . supernatural practices?'

'I don't know,' I said. 'They've set up home here with a great many possessions but no money, no food, and they won't say why they've come. And Paul is still missing. That's a fact.'

'Indeed it is.'

We began walking back to the river, to our part of the woods.

'So,' Anna said, 'the women arrive in Trethevy for a mysterious purpose and then Paul disappears. I cannot believe the two things are unrelated.'

'Then they're bound somehow,' I said. 'But what's the binding?'

'It must be whatever has brought the women to the woods.' Anna was all at once sprightly – a plan was coming. 'To find Paul Haskell we need to learn more about them, and quickly if we're to find the boy alive. Mathilda said they stayed in Boscastle before they came here. We'll go there ourselves, ask—'

'To Boscastle? Oh, I can't. I *can't*, Anna!'

'Because of Charlotte?'

It was all I could do to nod, sent dumb just thinking of the place my girl was born, had lived before she came into my arms.

Anna took me by the elbow and set me walking again. 'It won't be easy, Shilly, I know that. Don't think me cruel in suggesting it. I could go without you.'

'And leave me on my own? In this wretched place? I don't think so, Anna Drake!'

Part of me wondered if she'd come back, if leaving me to go to Boscastle wasn't the first step in leaving me forever. Charlotte had wanted to leave me. I feared Anna going too.

'I'm coming with you.'

'That's settled, then,' she said. 'We'll speak to those who knew Miss Franks and Mathilda in that place, see if we can't learn their purpose in coming here.'

'Yes,' I said, but trembly still.

She held me closer. 'There's something you can be certain of when we go to Boscastle, Shilly, and that might be of help to you.'

'I'd be glad to hear it.'

'The one person in the world I can guarantee *won't* be there is Charlotte Dymond.'

There was truth in that, of a kind, for my girl was in the ground in Davidstow churchyard. Her flesh and bones were, at any rate. The other part of her, terrible and raging, that was on the moor still, but Boscastle wasn't the moor. It was the sea. And didn't I have someone else now, someone better, holding me up, holding me close?

But then she, too, was slipping from me, for Anna's foot had caught something in the ferns and she stumbled, then righted herself and picked it up, this tripping thing. A piece of china, I thought, until Anna told me it was called por-s'lain. I didn't know about *that* but I could see it was a little person, like the many others the women had in their cottage.

This person had been broken at the waist and it was the lower half Anna had kicked. A woman, for the bottom of her dress was clear to see. It was pale pink and shaped like a bell. Or a man wearing a dress. Such things were possible, I thought, because Anna dressed as a man, had been Mr Williams when I first met her, so why not the other way around? Gathered at the woman's feet were several birds. They burst from the por-s'lain, as if trying to fly away.

Anna turned the broken woman this way and that, peering at her. 'A fine piece. There's a maker's mark on the bottom.'

'Let me see.' I thought it was letters maybe, but to my eye they were tangled as washing wrung by the wind.

'The top half – can you see her?'

We kicked aside the leaves and parted the ferns, but there was no trace of the broken woman's other parts.

'Miss Franks was telling the truth, then,' I said, 'about having things taken.'

Anna stowed the piece of woman in her black bag. 'And this unlucky lady could have been dropped by the thief as they left the cottage.'

'Which means there's a good chance the thief was going to cross the river,' I said, 'go back to the squire's side.'

'And Paul Haskell saw something he shouldn't.'

We went back the way we had come and soon there was the river before us, and the stepping stones to cross. No sister waited for me on the opposite bank. Only the trees and the gloom, and the hatred Mrs Haskell had warned us of, the hatred that stalked the trees. I could almost see it. Smoke, but clear. Smoke, without smell. We would breathe it in. And then what would become of us?

SIXTEEN

We crossed the river watched by a hundred pairs of eyes.

The birds filled the branches and their chatter filled my head so that all I could think were bird thoughts, bird noise. When Anna spoke all I heard was bird, until she shouted.

'What has made so many gather?'

I had no answer. No answer but fear, for it wasn't natural to see so many birds in one place. I wondered if it was a sign of something, something bad. But there being so many kinds of birds muddled that notion, for there were magpies and blackbirds and small brown ones, and some other littler ones with blue bits on. Signs were one thing only, weren't they? I didn't know what to do with all these different parts, save for sticking my fingers in my ears and running, hoping soon to be shot of them.

But that wasn't to be, for when we came to the fallen oak there were more of them, and closer now, perched on the log in a line of beady watching. I ran at them and flapped, I cawed to be rid of them. It worked – they took to the air. But when we were only a little way past the oak there came a flap flap behind us.

'Would you look at that?' Anna said.

I didn't want to but I did, I turned. The birds had returned to their line on the log.

'People must feed them,' Anna said.

'I doubt many in Trethevy have food to spare for wild birds,' I said.

We pressed on to the cottages with stops and starts and turnarounds when the path bent a way other than we wanted it to, or brought us to lumpy rocks we hadn't seen before. At least the birds didn't follow us, and we found no more ahead. As their cawing and crying died away my breath became easier, my heart less racing. Anna was only curious, and mildly so at that. Still she didn't feel the woods' strangeness as I did. Still we were apart on that.

The first of the cottages came in sight, and then, a little way down, a knot of people crowded at the door of one.

'News of Paul Haskell?' I said to Anna.

'Good news, let's hope.'

We hurried over. I spied David Tonkin, him of the mill, him of the whiskers, and asked what the to-do was.

'They're at it again,' he said.

'The women across the river? What have they done?'

'They've taken Sarah's mirror, the one she keeps above the fire. Her father's, it was.'

'How do you know they took it?' Anna said.

A man nearby swung round – Richard Bray, the stinking, drinking fishman. 'This is how we know!'

He thrust his hand at Anna. In his palm lay a black lump. Coal.

'It was left in place of the mirror,' David Tonkin said. 'They're laughing at us.'

'But why would they take a mirror?' I said.

'They have a liking for fine things,' Richard Bray said, whisking the coal away and giving it to the woman Sarah, who I recognised from our meeting in the woods, where we had first met David Tonkin too. 'Like magpies, they are,' Bray said. 'Nasty wenches! And it's a fine mirror, isn't it, Sarah?'

Sarah nodded sadly. 'My father bought it down Falmouth. Come off a wreck, it had. Lovely frame, all curly metal. I'd only gone out to see the chickens. They witched it away.'

David Tonkin shook his head. 'A bad business.'

'But we were just at—'

Anna pulled me away by my elbow.

'But it's important, what I was saying.' I wriggled out of her grip. To be held by her was a fine feeling, but only when she wasn't telling me off. 'We were just with Miss Franks and Mathilda, which means they can't have taken Sarah's mirror.'

'I agree, but given local opinion of the pair, it doesn't seem wise to admit our recent visit. Now, turn your thinking round, Shilly. What matters is what was left behind, not what was taken.'

'You mean the coal? Because that was found where Paul was last seen too.'

'Which means?' Anna said.

'That the thief who took the mirror is the same person who took Paul. If we can find who that is, we can find the boy.'

'I'd say so, but that way of thinking weakens the case against Miss Wolffs and Miss Franks, given we know they didn't steal the mirror as it's only just been taken.'

'The squire will be teasy about that,' I said. 'He wants rid of them. He mightn't pay us if he doesn't get what he wants. I knew we shouldn't have said yes to him. That was all your doing, Anna.'

'So we should have refused to help find a missing child? You're more heartless than I thought.'

'Me!'

'If one of the squire's tenants is to blame for Paul's disappearance, then I'm sure that information will be just as welcome to the squire. Surely that's all that matters in the end, to discover the truth?'

A magpie swooped low overhead and I ducked. 'By any means?'

She was about to speak then caught herself. 'If you're referring to what you claim are the revelatory effects of alcohol, then I disagree.'

'I thought you might.'

'Then why bother asking?'

She was cross. Her voice was sharp with it. Sharp as the sounds of slate-splitting that reached us on the air. We were near the quarry and so the manor house beyond it and then the road – to Boscastle, to learn more of Miss Franks and Mathilda's doings there.

'Because you won't listen to me,' I said.

'You ought to be grateful I won't. I'm saving you from yourself, Shilly.'

Two more magpies flew over us, swooping through the trees and out of sight. A pair. A coupling. I felt like hurling a slate at them, them who were together.

On a little more and the light grew stronger ahead, making my steps stronger to reach it and be free of the woods, if only for a time.

'How are we to get to Boscastle, then?' I said.

'We'll ask at the manor house, and while we're there, it might be worth asking another question too. I'd like to know if Miss Wolffs and Miss Franks were walking here on the morning Paul went missing. They might not have taken Paul Haskell, but they're clearly hiding something.'

We broke from the trees and followed the path to the house. I guessed it to be noon by then for the sun was high overhead. Now we were free of the tightness of the woods I could feel a bit of breeze, meaning it was less hot than the day before, but still my scalp itched warmly beneath the false hair of Mrs Williams, and I was glad I'd left her fur hat back at the summer house.

Mrs Carne the sour-faced housekeeper let us in, as teasy as when we first arrived. She showed us into the room we'd waited in before, and we waited again while she fetched the squire. I didn't mind all the paintings of woods this time, nor all the wooden things in the room, for I was getting the measure of the place now. I mightn't like it, but I had seen its tricks, at least. Mrs Haskell had explained things to me.

The squire arrived with his usual bellows and bluster, shouting at us, 'You have the answer? You've come to claim the reward?'

'We're making good progress, Sir Vivian,' Anna said.

He thumped himself into a chair and fixed her with his one good grey eye, an eager smile on his fat, flushed face. 'You have it, then? Proof of the women's guilt?'

Anna licked her lips. 'We're pursuing some important avenues.'

'That's why we're here,' I said. 'To ask you about it.'

He sat back and his smile was not so fulsome. 'How may I be of assistance?'

'The two women claim they were not at home on the morning Paul Haskell was seen near their cottage,' Anna said.

'You have spoken to them?'

'Of course. To establish if they played a part in Paul's disappearance—'

'There's no "if" about it, Miss Drake. They are guilty.'

'So you have said, Sir Vivian.'

'The fiends are lying about not being at home when the boy disappeared.'

'It would be useful to confirm that,' Anna said. 'They say they were walking here, near the house.'

'Here!' he bellowed. 'What nonsense! They came nowhere near the house that day.'

'I see, and—'

'The fiends *do* come here, you understand, to threaten Lady Phoebe. We are plagued by them.'

'But they didn't come on Tuesday?' I said.

'Correct, Mrs Williams. They did not come *here* because they were taking the boy. It is all quite clear.' He spoke as if we were soft in the head.

'How is Lady Phoebe?' Anna said.

He studied his huge hands, the fat fingers clutching one another. 'She cannot rest. Frets so, and will do until those women are gone from here.'

He looked up, his good eye roving between us, the lazy one so fixed, so still. I found myself wondering if the child would be likewise afflicted.

'It has been worse since you came,' he said. 'I was mistaken in introducing you to her. Hourly she asks what you have discovered, if the boy is found. My attempts to reassure her fail for I can find no way to ease her questions.'

'That's to be expected, isn't it?' I said. 'She fears for him, like everyone in the woods.'

'Of course, of course. But my wife is such a fragile soul, and she has wanted her own child for a long time. Knowing that you are here, investigating, she fears your activities will upset things. Force the fiends' hand.'

'I can assure you, Sir Vivian, that we are working with tact,' Anna said.

'*Haste*, Miss Drake! That is what should concern you most. I need the women gone.'

'These things cannot be rushed, but know that we are doing our best.'

'Our best to find Paul Haskell,' I added quietly.

He stood and so we were to go, I guessed. We were all but out the front door when the squire said something that took all the colour from Anna's face.

'I offered the reward to hasten the removal of the women across the river. If the task should not be completed in good time, I will have no choice but to seek help elsewhere.'

'You have others offering their services?' Anna said, trying not to sound like she minded but I knew all too well that she did. She had already counted out the thirty pounds in her head. Had already spent it on our future.

'Not yet,' the squire said. 'But the next person who calls at this door will be considered. Good day to you both.'

And so we were out on our ears.

Before Anna had a chance to worry at these words, I was off.

'Where are you going, Shilly?'

'To see about a cat.'

SEVENTEEN

The kitchen window was ajar, to make use of the breeze, I thought, for it was hot in there with the big stove lit and pans all bubbling and steaming.

The girl who'd brought the tea when we first came to the manor house, Lucy, she was in the kitchen working pastry. Her little hands were red and coarsened, and she had flour everywhere, all over the floor and on her sleeves, which she hadn't rolled up to save from the mess. Her fair hair had half-escaped her cap, as puffy as a dandelion's head apart from near her face where the puff was gone and it was lank and stuck to her slick skin. By her side was a pie dish with the filling full inside it, smelling rich and good and reminding me of my hunger. Chicken, I thought, and my mouth watered.

Anna caught up with me and I was about to open the door, go in and ask the girl my questions, when I thought it better to wait, to watch through the open window, for her doings were odd. She fussed at her sleeves, looking as if she *was* going to roll them up, but she didn't. Only rucked them with her floury hands, making a great mess that made no sense to me. A few times each arm she rucked. Scratched her arms.

Something slipped against my leg and I made a noise. Lucy looked up from her work and saw me, but saw something else too, something that made her pick up her rolling pin and shout, for Pigeon had leapt and forced the window's catch with his mighty stripedness, and was now on the inside window ledge.

'Don't you dare!' she shouted. 'Don't you bleddy dare!'

Pigeon stalked along the ledge towards her. He was no fearful scuttler or a slinker. He was all shoulders, prowl and swagger. I quite loved him, I realised, for his boldness. For him making clear his wants. But if I had been in Lucy's shoes I wouldn't have loved him for he would be a devil in the kitchen. He sprang for the table and was within a thick whisker of getting his paw into the untopped pie and flipping out a piece of chicken. But then Anna was rushing through the door. She helped Lucy push Pigeon to the floor and shooed him out – a pair of curses, four clattering heels.

The beast charged out of the kitchen, past me still outside. I feared for my ankles.

'The door!' Lucy shouted.

I slipped inside and made it fast behind me. Lucy was quick to shut the window with a thump.

'You had a near-miss there!' I said.

'He's why I can't have the door open.' She mopped the sweat above her lip with a floury wrist and gave herself a white moustache, as if she was an old man, though truly she was only a little younger than me – seventeen, I thought. 'Window open is risk enough,' she mumbled. 'But I'd be fainting without some air coming in.'

I thought she was likely right. The heat of the kitchen pressed against me like a damp sheet. I pulled out a chair to sit and Lucy remembered then that she had two strangers in her kitchen.

'You wanting Mrs Carne?' she said.

'That woman is the last thing we want,' I said.

Lucy grinned. 'You've met her, then.'

'We have had the pleasure,' Anna said.

She told Lucy that we were Miss Drake and Mrs Williams, for that was who we had brought to the kitchen, and said we'd been walking in the woods. She asked if we might have a drink for it was so hot outside. Lucy fetched us both a cup.

'He's a tinker, that cat,' I said, trying to hide the kindliness I felt for him.

'Isn't he just!' Lucy said. 'I have to have eyes in the back of my head.' She started working the pastry again and every so often tugged at her sleeves, but tugging hard. Tugging to scratch the skin beneath, I thought.

'Does he often make off with food?'

'He tries regular enough. One of these days that cat will find himself in a Pigeon pie.'

I caught sight of a few long, stripy hairs being worked into the pastry but I thought best not to say.

'What about on Tuesday, around lunchtime?' I said. 'Did he get away with anything then?'

Her hands stilled on the pastry and I saw that they were very badly reddened indeed, almost rash-like, braggaty with it. Much more so than ordinary work would make them.

'How do you know about that?' she said.

'We met some fellow walkers in the woods today,' Anna said. 'A pair of women. They were quite amused by Pigeon's antics, told us a story about him making off with a pig's foot.'

Lucy gave the pastry a vicious prod. 'That bleddy animal . . . I got in so much trouble. Mrs Carne said she'd dock my wages the cost.'

'So it did happen?' Anna said.

'Oh yes. Pigeon ate like a lord. But it was a leg of pheasant, not a pig foot. Pig foot wouldn't have been so bad,' she said sadly. 'I seen them furriners when Pigeon took off. They didn't try and catch him, and I was glad of that, even though it meant the leg was lost.'

'Why didn't you want them to catch Pigeon?' I said.

'Well, he'd have only scratched them, wouldn't he, and then I'd have been for it. They'd have turned me into coal, like they did Paul Haskell. That's what women like that do, isn't it?' Lucy picked up the rolling pin like she'd brain someone with it.

'Do they walk this way often,' I said, 'the furrin pair?'

'I only seen them a few times,' Lucy said, 'being stuck in here, but Simon – he's with the horses – he says he seen the furriners here most days.'

'And what do they do when they come this way?' Anna asked. 'Go down to the road?'

'They don't go nowhere. Just come out the trees and then they wait, looking at the house.'

'Do they come up to the door?' I said.

'Not so close as that, and that's the worst of it. They don't do nothing when they come. Just stand and *look* at the door. Even if the weather's dirty, they stand there. 'Tis a fearful sight. I'd rather they rang the bell.'

'And this worries the squire?' Anna said.

Lucy nodded. 'That's why Lady Phoebe's moved into the east wing, to be away from the furriners when they come. She's to be by herself for she's needing quiet. None of us servants are to go down there.'

A bell rang somewhere deep within the house and Lucy was all of a flurry. 'That's for dinner and the pie not in yet. She'll have me strung up from the chimney.'

'Mrs Carne?' I said.

'Lady Phoebe.'

'We'll leave you to get on,' Anna said. 'Thank you for the drink.'

I was opening the door, watching for a striped trap waiting to spring, when I remembered we didn't know how we were to get to Boscastle, and I made myself ask the way, though fearfulness was creeping up on me, going to that place.

''Tis easy enough,' Lucy said. She laid the pastry across the top of the pie and cut away the hanging-over bits quick as you like. 'The road goes straight there. Only a little more than two miles. It's a good road, too.

And on a day like this, be quite lovely, I should think, to be going down to the sea.' She sighed and scratched her arm, but when she caught me watching she stopped, quicker than she'd cut the pastry. 'When you reach the road you must go right,' she said. 'That's the way to Boscastle. Don't pass the old mill. That way is to Bossiney.'

We thanked her and left her to the kitchen and the worry of the dinner being ready. I'd done enough of that in my few short years. It was good to be free of cooking and cleaning for other people, even though I'd changed them for sometimes darker things. Uncertain things. Missing children and blinded women.

We passed Pigeon as we walked away from the house. He was sitting on the low wall that marked the little courtyard, facing the kitchen. His tail hung down behind him and he swished it to and fro, slow and steady as he planned his next attack. I scratched him behind one of his great big ears, and he leant into my touch. Lovely beast, Pigeon was.

'Did you forget that Miss Franks said it was a game bird's leg that Pigeon took?' I asked Anna.

'No, it was a test. If we'd given Lucy all the information we were seeking, we might have led her in her answer. Because she corrected me, the two accounts are more likely to each confirm the other.'

'But the squire and Lucy, they say different about Miss Franks and Mathilda being here on Tuesday. Of the two of them, is it the squire lying?'

'"Lying" is too strong a word,' Anna said. 'What's more likely is he simply didn't chance to see Mathilda and Miss Franks and so he believes they weren't here, because that tallies with what he thinks happened – that they were across the river taking Paul Haskell.'

Pigeon jumped from the wall and ambled back to the kitchen window.

'But if we believe Lucy,' I said, watching the beast try to force the window open with his thick paw, 'then Mathilda and Miss Franks were away from home on Tuesday.'

'It would seem so. To reach here by noon, they would have been

121

on their way by ten when Simon Proctor saw Paul near the cottage. Boscastle might still hold some answers, though. We need to know more about their past to make sense of what they're doing here now. I'm sure that's connected to Paul Haskell's disappearance.'

'So, if we learn more about the women, it'll help us find Paul?'

'I hope so. Time is running out for him.'

The road came in sight, where we'd left the coach when we arrived. That was two days previous, and though we had done a great deal of thinking and asking of questions, we were still without a name for who had taken Paul, and no trace of the boy himself.

On the far side of the road were more wretched trees but they were not so thickety there, and I knew that beyond them was the sea. To our left was the bridge we had crossed on our way to Trethevy, and near it the mill Lucy had talked of. I hadn't seen that from the coach for by the time we passed it the trees had appeared and made me fearful.

'Is that David Tonkin's mill?' I said. 'Where he does the dyeing of cloth?'

'He said that was upstream, didn't he? No, that must be where Mrs Haskell was burnt all those years ago.'

I squinted but couldn't see the state the mill was in. It still had something of a roof and at least two walls. There were brambles up the side but there were brambles up the side of everything in the woods. They were just as needed as stones in a wall, far as I could see.

'Come on, Shilly!' Anna called, setting off along the road at a fair pace. 'We don't have time for rummaging about in mills.'

'What about Lucy, then? Do we have time to think of her?'

'What about her?'

'Her scratching. Surely you saw it.'

'She wasn't comfortable in her own skin, I'll grant you. But I don't see what that has to do with anything.'

'I'm just saying my thinking out loud. You do it often enough, Anna. Why can't I?'

'Ah, but my thinking aloud is relevant to the matter at hand, not idle speculation.'

'Lucy's scratching might be important,' I said.

'I hardly think a scullery maid having lice is significant to finding Paul Haskell.'

'You can't know that, not yet. We don't know everything, do we? We don't know how one thing might have a bearing on another.'

'I think the only bearing Lucy's lice have on anything is whether we catch them. She probably got them from Pigeon. They spend enough time together.'

I gave up arguing. There was nothing to be gained. I was growing used to her stubbornness, though that didn't mean I liked it.

The road was twisty and turny but without hills, at least. The sun was warm and I didn't want to be climbing. The trees on our left thinned out then thinned away and the sea was all at once before me. I laughed in surprise that it should creep up on me like that, such a huge thing, so fine-looking. There all the time, and yet I was only now coming to know it.

EIGHTEEN

It was better for me to walk without talking, to try and forget where we were going. But the sea wouldn't let me forget. Wouldn't leave me alone. Its sounds reached me on the warm air, and I found that they were good. The sounds were of rolling, the water strange breathing and sighing, and the calls of birds cutting through. The sea's birds were not like those of the woods. The sea's birds were white, or maybe white-grey. They flew near enough for me to see their orange beaks and hear their squawks. I had seen them once or twice when I had lived on the moor. They were blown in by bad weather.

The only thing blowing in on that fine day was the smoke of Anna's pipe. It drifted around me in the warm air. Just as Anna herself was around me, there and yet *not* there. For she was still a stranger. The sun caught my ring, Mrs Williams's wedding ring that she had given me, made it wink. That decided me.

'Now that we are working together,' I said.

'No good ever comes of such statements from you, Shilly.'

'We should know more of each other. What of your family?' The question made her cough with surprise so I knew I was on to a good line of thinking.

'My family? I don't see that's important to the here and now.'

'It's important in knowing who you are. You know about my family – my mother dead before I went to work on the farm. My father signing me into farm service to save himself from feeding me. Him drinking.'

'*Him* drinking?'

'And my sister. Somewhere. She left years before my mother died. Now, your turn.'

She drew deeply on her pipe. 'I have no family.'

'You mean, none living?'

'I mean none at all – living or dead.'

I stopped walking. 'Why must you do this?'

'Shilly, I—'

'Why must you lie all the time? Am I not deserving of some truth from you? After all that we have seen together, the promise you made on the moor that we should be equals, that we should work *together*. That means we must know each other, Anna. You can't ask me to be in those wretched woods, seeing all the terrors—'

'Not the sisters without eyes again, Shilly.'

'Yes, the sisters!' I shouted. 'Yes, my hatred of the woods! That is who I am. Now, I would know, before I go one step further on this road with you, who *you* are.'

She was looking at the sea, as calm as I was angry. 'You know who I am,' she said quietly.

'I know that you are a seamstress, that you worked in that theatre place. I know that you recognise the German way of talking. I know that you know what por-s'lain looks like. That you are not from Cornwall, and that you might be from London, although whether that's true I can't say. I know you use the name Anna Drake.'

She drew on her pipe and blew the smoke out to sea. She scratched the end of her thin nose. I wanted to strike her.

'What more do you need to know?' she said.

126

'Everything!' I said.

'You ask for the world, Shilly, and it's not mine to give. But I can give you a little, if that'll help.' She swallowed. She took a deep breath. 'I am a foundling.'

And then she looked at me, at last, and I wished that I could take back my words and strike my foolish self with Lucy's rolling pin, for I hadn't meant to be so cruel.

She wasn't going to cry. She wasn't going to wail, as I had. She was simply hollowed out. Blank with it. As she herself was blank. I saw then, as I hadn't seen before, that she hadn't kept herself from me for spite, or for not liking me, or because there was something terrible at the heart of who she was.

She had kept herself from me because she didn't know *who* she was at all.

She cleared her throat and began walking again. 'Whoever left me on the butcher's doorstep didn't want to be found.'

'There was no name for you?' I said.

'None. If a note was left, in the shawl in which I was wrapped, say, it could have blown away, been lost somehow.'

It was as if she was speaking of someone else's life. Her voice was the one she used to review the evidence. And yet the evidence was her past. Herself.

'The only thing worth remarking on,' she said, 'apart from the fact my mother had given birth before her time, was a piece of felt tied to my wrist. It was cut in the shape of an animal. Can you guess what that might have been, Shilly, hm?'

'A duck,' I said.

'How very clever of you!' She said this with meanness, because she didn't believe me to be clever at all. 'I chose "Drake" myself,' she said, 'but that was later, when I was another girl.'

'And "Anna"?' I asked.

'The butcher's wife liked the symmetry.'

I frowned.

'It's the same forward and back,' Anna explained. 'The neatness of it has always pleased me so I've kept it. If you keep from the drink and keep our bargain, Shilly, I can show you how to write such a word.'

'The butcher and his wife – are they living still? Do you see them?'

She walked a little faster. 'That's a story for another day.'

We went the rest of the way without talking. I didn't know what to say, and even if I'd found some words, I doubted she'd want to hear them. It was best to keep to the matter at hand, as Anna was always telling me. If we strayed from it, into ourselves and what we meant to one another, we would lose our way.

There was a heavy rattle behind us, and I turned to see a wide cart coming on, and a second just behind it. We pressed ourselves against the hedge to let them pass.

'Boscastle looks to be a busy port,' she said, in an everyday Anna Drake sort of way. I was grateful for such calm talk, such quiet talk. To leave the painful things behind us on the road.

The carts were going towards the port, as we were, each piled with the storm cloud colours of slate. I wondered if they were from the squire's quarry. Then another cart was coming, up from the port, and I feared they wouldn't have room to pass, but just as I thought their sides should splinter against one another, the horses leaping in fright, the carts were passing, the horses trotting on. The cart that came towards us was covered in sacking, hiding its wares, but when the driver spurred his horses all was set to wobbling and something bounced from the cart bed into the road. I picked it up and my hand was all at once filthy, for I had hold of a lump of coal.

'I don't expect many houses burn coal in this part of the world,' Anna said.

'Some people must do,' I said, watching the heavily laden cart round the bend and disappear.

'But at great expense if the coal is brought by ship, even if it only comes from South Wales. Your tin and copper mines don't do much for warming a house or cooking a stew.'

'They do if you're the one selling the tin and the copper,' I said, and pocketed the coal. 'On the moor, people burn turf. Cut it themselves. It gives a bit of smoke but the smell is good.'

'We're a fair way from the moor now, though.'

'Plenty of wood,' I said, and thought about setting fire to the trees.

'And yet a piece of coal was left in Sarah's house only this morning.'

'It must have come from someone with money,' I said, 'and the only place like that in Trethevy is the manor house.'

'Did you notice if the fire was laid when we saw the squire earlier?'

'It wasn't. It's too warm to need it in the downstairs rooms.'

'What about in the kitchen?'

'Well, I didn't go poking in the stove, did I? There was no smell to speak of, but that could be because the flue is working right.'

'There may be coal fires upstairs,' Anna said. 'And if there are, there's bound to be a store of coal somewhere.'

'Which anyone in the house could take a lump from.'

We had come in sight of roofs and the road began to slope down. The white-grey birds with the orange beaks were closer now, making a terrible racket, and the air was thickening with the smell of Richard Bray's cottage but riven with something else – salt, as if someone was trying to salt Richard Bray, keep him from rot through the winter. It was the smell of the sea.

We had arrived in Boscastle.

NINETEEN

I told myself I mustn't be afraid. I told myself that firmly, meanly, even. I pinched the soft part of my arm, above the elbow, to make it true with a bruise. Anna was with me. Charlotte was dead. Boscastle was just a place we had reason to visit, and then to leave. A place I shouldn't mind so much.

A place of ropes. That was the first thing I noticed about Boscastle. More than the smell and the noise of all the loading and unloading, the men and women shouting, the children running, the birds diving for the fish brought ashore in little boats, the big boats with trees growing out of their middles a-creak a-creak. I saw all those things, heard and smelt them too, but it was the ropes that struck me. They were all over the place, as if some giant hand had tried to tie the port down, stop it moving. But the whole place strained against being bound – everyone fetching and carrying, calling and heaving. It was all of a jostle, the port of Boscastle.

A river cut through the jostling and tumbled to a wide patch of sand, and beyond the sand was the sea itself, held small between two cliffs. A wall jutted from each cliff, but neither wall went all the way across the water, and one was set further back than the other. I knew the walls from Mathilda's drawings. She had made a good likeness of the place, but as I looked at it now, with my own eyes, I found that I was pleased and fearful in equal measure, for people drowned, didn't they, in the sea?

'Which do you think the worse way to die,' I asked Anna, 'being drowned, or having your throat cut?'

'Drowning,' she said, without pausing to think. 'It's much slower than people imagine.'

She pointed across the river to the sign of an inn and at once I knew my own death. Insensible and falling, insensible and fighting. Sickness, and its loneliness. The drink gave so many ways to die.

'We'll ask in the inn about lodgings,' Anna said, 'see if we can find where Miss Wolffs and Miss Franks stayed when they were here.'

We crossed the river by a steep little bridge, and my steps quickened as we drew close to the inn even as I willed my body to keep from the drink. Not to be that person any more.

'I'll wait for you here,' I said, and caught hold of a wooden post all tied with ropes as if I was a boat to be kept from the tide.

Anna nodded and left me, and I wondered if saying we'd go to the inn had been a test on her part, for she'd have known how much I needed a drink, us coming to this place. The shake was on me so I turned from the inn and looked at the sea again. Thinking about drowning was better than thinking about drink.

But my eye was drawn from the water, drawn from death, by a young man on a stool near the river's edge. He was dressed in working clothes and wore a red handkerchief knotted at his throat. He was talking to an older man who stood before him, the older man all in blue, like the sea had dressed him. He wore a blue hat too – a cloth thing, with some lettering on the front in gold. His cheeks and chin were ginger whiskery. A sailor.

'My mate, he said he paid four pence,' the sailor said.

'That was only for one knot,' the other man said. He held up a piece of rope, the length of my arm. 'This has two. Costs double.'

'You can untie one, can't you?'

'Not once it's tied. We'd all get scat about, wouldn't we?'

'I'll have a different one, then.'

'It's this or none. Can't make a new one until this is sold.'

The sailor grumbled but took some coins from his pocket. He counted out the money, on purpose slow. The other waited, holding the rope strangely, out in front of him with one hand over each knot as if to hide them.

At last the sailor held out the coins. The other pocketed them swiftly somewhere inside his shirt and then handed over the rope. The sailor ran his fingers over the knots with caution, as if he feared them, and this drew me closer, for what could there be to fear in a knotted rope, in that place of ropes?

''Ow long do it take to work?' said the sailor.

'When you've untied it? That depends.'

'On what?'

'All sorts of things.'

'Sounds like a load of old codswallop to me.'

'If you'd rather risk going without it . . .' the other man said.

The sailor turned to look at the sea rolling beyond the two walls that made the harbour. His hand tightened on the rope and then with one last grumble he went stomping off.

I gave a start – the man on the stool was looking at me. His eyes were small and he was missing one of his front teeth.

'Why'd he buy that rope?' I said.

'You putting to sea?' he said.

'No. Is that what it's for?'

'Mostly.'

He straightened his back, settled himself, and took another short length from a pile of such ropes beneath his stool. He ran his hands up and down it, and I wondered that they weren't made sore by such doing.

'Don't have to be at sea to need a good head of wind,' he said without looking up.

'How can a rope bring the wind?'

'What *does* bring the wind?'

I didn't have an answer for that. If I'd been chapel then I'd have said God is the one brings the wind, and brings the sun and the rain and all of that business. But it'd been some time since I'd gone to chapel and then it was only because someone had said I had to.

The man was tying a knot in the rope. An ordinary knot, no fancy lashed-up thing. He was pulling it tight.

'Four pence,' he said, and handed it to me.

'I . . .'

I heard my name. Anna was on the bridge. I shook my head at her, waved and pointed, meaning that for once she should come to me. And she did, and that pleased me. But when I told her I wanted four pence for the rope, she wasn't at all pleased.

'Are you planning on restraining suspects?' she said.

'When I untie the knot, the wind will blow. I want it for the woods. It's so airless, so closing-in all the time. I'll untie the knot and then—'

'Is this some sort of joke?' A spot of red was growing in each of her thin, pale cheeks.

The man said nothing, just ran his hands up and down another length of rope.

'Doesn't matter if you don't like it,' I said. 'You owe me.'

'Oh do I?' she said.

'Days we been working together, Anna, and I've had no pay.'

'We haven't been paid yet!'

'Call it an advance on wages, then,' I said, and hung the rope around my neck for carrying.

'Shilly . . .'

'I'm not moving a step from this spot unless you buy me this rope.'

After much show of being cross and put out, she found her coin purse and paid the man. He didn't acknowledge her at all, but he spoke to me.

'Be careful. Using it inland, it will be very strong. At sea the space is greater.'

I thanked him, and Anna threw up her hands and rued the day she'd ever met me. But I didn't care. I had something to make the woods a better sort of place to be, and that was a mercy for I'd have to stay there a while longer to find Paul Haskell.

And now I was in Anna's debt for it.

TWENTY

'So?' I said as we made our way back to the bridge.

'So what?'

'What did you learn at the inn?'

'I'm glad you still care, Shilly, given your diversions into quackery.'

I waited for her storm to blow itself out. Anna was her own knotted rope sometimes.

'The landlord of the inn had no recollection of the women staying,' she said at last.

'They're not easy to forget.'

'True. But the landlord did tell me of two lodging houses to try, both of which are here, on this side of the river. This,' she said, shielding her eyes against the sun, 'is one of them.'

It was a foul-smelling place overlooking the water. Anna rootled out the owner from a dirty corner and described Miss Wolffs and Miss Franks to him, but he said they hadn't stayed. I wasn't surprised. I didn't think Miss Franks would put up with the stench, even without much money to her name. The second lodging house was higher up the cliff. It gave the view of the harbour but without the stink of the fish-gutting. The owner, a Mrs Teague, remembered the women well.

'The foreigners? They were here . . . oh now, let me think.' She was a dumpy soul, wearing a shiny dress of wide bright stripes that made her look more dumpy still, and which was a close match for the curtains of the parlour she asked us into. 'They stayed a month at least. I hope nothing's the matter?'

'I have a letter for them, a letter of great importance,' Anna said, ready, as always, with a lie. Perhaps that was a talent of foundlings taken in by butchers.

'A letter! Well, wouldn't you know. After they'd waited so long.'

'I'm afraid I don't quite follow,' Anna said.

'Well, they sent so many letters, you see,' Mrs Teague said. 'Always asking for paper and ink, and quite firm too, was Miss Franks. The younger one, Miss Wolffs, now, I liked her. As pleasant as Miss Franks was fierce.'

'These letters they were writing,' Anna said. 'You don't happen to know where they were sent?'

''Fraid I don't. Posted their letters themselves, though my Samuel offered to take them. Miss Franks was quite bad-tempered when no replies came, but that didn't stop her sending more. Quite furious with writing, she was. Used to sit there, at that little table in the window, day after day, and Miss Wolffs at the other end doing her drawing. Such lovely scenes she did, and with her hand so shaky! She gave me one of her sketches, you know, and my Samuel made a frame for it. I'll fetch it—'

'That's quite all right, Mrs Teague,' Anna said. 'I have just a few more questions you might be able to help us with. Did the women speak of what they were doing in Cornwall?'

'I did ask them, only in the course of things, you understand. I'm not one to pry.'

Oh, Mrs Teague, I thought to myself, I reckon you *are* one to pry. I should think you peer at keyholes, rootle through bags and steam open letters before you've even served breakfast.

'They said they were here for a drawing holiday,' Mrs Teague said. 'We've lots of artists staying, and writers. They've not got much to spend, more's the pity. That pair were the same. Took the cheapest room and paid weekly.'

'They didn't book the whole month of their stay upfront?' Anna said.

'Week by week Miss Franks wanted it. Each Friday I said to my Samuel, they'll be off tomorrow, you wait, and then Miss Franks would ask to take another week.'

'Did they talk about where they'd come from?' I said.

Mrs Teague shook her head. 'They said very little, really, just Miss Franks asking if any letters had come and Miss Wolffs busy drawing. They talked to each other, of course, but no one here could understand what they were saying, them being foreign. Nothing in the guestbook, either.'

'And when they did leave,' Anna asked, 'did they give you a forwarding address in case any letters should come for them?'

'Well, that's the strange thing. They didn't, and I said to my Samuel how surprised I was, because they'd been wanting replies so badly. I offered to forward anything that came but Miss Franks wasn't interested, when for weeks all she'd spoken of were her blessed letters. It must have had something to do with him coming.'

'Him?' I said.

'Their visitor. They only had the one. He was already with them in here when I got back from fetching the bread. Samuel had let him in, and then Miss Franks had the cheek to shut the door! Even though one of our rules is no private use of the parlour. I couldn't believe it, and my Samuel, he's not one for being stern, so I came in.'

'So you saw him, this visitor?' Anna said.

'Only a glimpse. Miss Franks was up on her feet raging, shouting at me to get out of my own parlour. Well! I wasn't going to stay there and be so insulted.'

'The visitor, Mrs Teague, what did he look like?'

'He was in working clothes, that I do remember. Big chap, and he had an eyepatch.'

'An eyepatch?' I said. 'Are you sure?'

'Of course I am! You don't see them every day, do you?'

'No, you don't. Which eye—'

'Did you hear any of the conversation?' Anna said.

'Are you suggesting I would eavesdrop on my guests?' Mrs Teague huffed and puffed and made out she was truly hurt by such accusing.

We waited until she'd finished being affronted, and then she admitted that she had lingered by the door.

'The door of *my* parlour that Miss Franks had *shut*! I was waiting to give her a piece of my mind, as I had every right to do.'

'And did you hear anything?' I said.

'Only that they weren't getting on. It sounded like an argument.'

'Which language were they speaking?' Anna asked. 'English or German?'

'That I can't tell you. The door . . . Well, it's too thick.' Even for a nosey crow like Mrs Teague with her ear pressed against it. 'Miss Franks was apologetic once he'd gone, well, as apologetic as that woman is ever likely to be. Miss Wolffs was quite upset. I didn't see her drawing again, and they left the next day, owing me for some unpaid suppers, I might add.'

'When we find them we'll let them know,' Anna said. 'I'm sure they'll send you what's due.'

I almost laughed, thinking of Mathilda and Miss Franks eating snails in the woods.

We took our leave of Mrs Teague, who had been more helpful than she could have known.

'Why didn't the squire tell us he had met the women before they came to the woods?' I said as we made our way back down to the harbour.

My words made Anna stop and her mouth fall open.

140

'That's who you think their visitor was? The squire?'

'Don't you?' I said. 'Mrs Teague said he was a big man, that he'd covered one eye. The patch was to hide his lazy one.'

'"Big" could mean anything, and as for the eyepatch, many people have blindness. You keep telling me about these women without eyes stalking the woods.' She started walking again. 'It's not enough, Shilly. That man could have been anyone.'

'It's the reward, isn't it? You won't admit we can't trust the squire because it could mean we won't get paid and that's all you care about.'

'I'm not the mercenary you think I am, Shilly. But on an unrelated point, you must see that we can't keep taking unpaid work or we'll be the ones surviving on snails.'

'Never mind snails. What about the squire? We have to ask him why he met them here. We'll go straight to the manor house.'

I hurried past her but she grabbed my arm.

'No! *If* the squire does know more about Miss Wolffs and Miss Franks than he has so far stated – and I say that only to humour you, Shilly – then we must use caution. Fortunately, I know someone who can help us find out one way or the other. Someone you know quite well, Shilly.'

'Who?'

'Mr Williams.'

TWENTY-ONE

I wasn't pleased to hear of Mr Williams again. He was the first of all Anna's people I had met, and I had found him to be stern – forever saying I was slow or late or something worse, saying I was drunk, even when I wasn't. Once Anna had shown herself to be the yellow-haired woman hiding beneath Mr Williams's disguise, I hadn't minded him so much. His faults were those of Anna's and those I had learnt to forgive, but the mention of his name made me remember a time when I hadn't liked her, and I didn't wish for that again.

Anna seemed pleased to be speaking of Mr Williams again, and chattered of him all the way back to Trethevy, as if Mr Williams was a welcome visitor soon to call. When Mr Williams had first taken himself apart before me, Anna told me she carried on in such a manner because she had to. Passing as a man let her find out things a woman wouldn't be able to, for solving crimes. And I had believed her then, because I didn't think anyone *would* do such a thing unless they had to.

But seeing Anna quicken her step now as she talked of Mr Williams's arrival, seeing the flush in her cheeks, I knew better. Anna *liked* to dress in men's clothes. It caused her excitement. The same excitement I felt when she passed as her true self – the yellow-haired woman with the scrawny hips. Her claiming she had to pass as a man was only an excuse to hide what she wanted most.

'It will be odd to have Mr *and* Mrs Williams together,' she said now. 'In the past I've only been able to have one roam at a time.'

'We'll be a proper married couple then.'

'Yes,' she said faintly.

Her blushes made me bold. 'We should do as all married couples do,' I said.

'Bicker? We're doing a fine job of that already, Shilly.'

We had come to the manor house. Our path back to the woods took us in sight of the little walled garden with the chair, where we had seen Lady Phoebe at the window. As we were passing now I caught sight of someone seated in a corner made shady by some branchy plant that swarmed the walls. Just their feet, their little slippered feet, and the paleness of their skirts. The rest of her was shrouded by the plant's overhanging, but I could see enough to know who it was. Lady Phoebe.

I pointed her out to Anna.

'At least she can escape the house, then,' Anna said.

'But she's not gone far. The squire can fetch her back easily enough.'

'Quick, Shilly. Before she sees us.'

But we were too late.

'It's Miss Drake, isn't it?' the soft voice called, barely reaching us in the still, baked air. She was getting to her feet.

'Please – don't let us disturb you,' Anna said. 'We were only passing.'

But we were stopping now, with Lady Phoebe wanting to speak to us.

She stepped from the shade of the trailing plant and I saw she had a book with her. She marked her place with a blue ribbon, made sure the ribbon was laid flat, then closed the book and pulled the ribbon taut, with a quick jerk, the way some women lace others into their stays. Then she set the book carefully on the little chair and eyed it, as if there was some part of it she wasn't sure about, then she straightened it, making the book's corners line up with those of the chair.

Anna and I watched all this from the other side of the low wall. I'd seen such tricks before. Those who did the paying liked to make us wait, those of us being paid. It made us remember we were beholden to them. But then I chided myself for such thoughts, for wasn't she soft-hearted, and so soft-headed too?

Even with her expecting the child, there wasn't much of her. Just a scrag of a thing. The baby will be little as the mother, I thought, if it lives long enough inside her to be born breathing. She was so pale, I wondered there was enough blood in her body to give life to them both.

'You haven't found poor Paul yet?' she said now, crossing to join us. She shielded her eyes against the sun, which set her face in shadow.

'I'm afraid not,' Anna said. 'But as I told your husband this morning, we're doing—'

'You came this morning? Vivian didn't tell me.' She clutched the wall. The earth left a brown mark on her cream dress. 'What did you need to see him about? You've found something?'

'He don't want you fretting,' I said.

'Fretting? A child has been taken. Is there a greater crime in this world?'

I had plenty of answers to *that*, because being taken left the chance of being returned. There was no body yet. If your throat was cut it was a different thing altogether. But Anna was speaking before I could put Lady Phoebe right.

'Please, don't upset yourself,' Anna said. 'We came to confirm a detail with your husband, that was all.'

'About the sisters? Their part in this horror?'

145

'About the quarry,' Anna said. 'Mrs Williams and I have been considering the tunnels.'

'Oh.' She let go of the wall and there was a great sag about her, as if she were a pair of bellows and talk of tunnels had taken the air from her.

'So you see, there was no reason for the squire to inform you of our visit.'

'Yes . . .' Still she held her hand before her face to keep the sun from her eyes. Still she was hidden. 'But if you should find other things, you will inform me, too, I hope?'

'I don't know about that,' I said, and glanced at Anna who was looking uncertain about what to say. 'It's the squire paying us, and he's wanting to save you the worry.'

'That is Vivian's way. To offer the reward, to bring people to the woods without telling me of his plans.'

'It's a kindness,' I said. 'I've known men who care more for their dogs than their wives.'

'Shilly!' Anna hissed.

'It would be a greater kindness still to tell me what you find out,' Lady Phoebe said. 'If we could come to an—'

Someone coughed behind her. Mrs Carne was in the doorway to the house.

'Doctor's here, ma'am.'

Lady Phoebe clutched her belly. 'I'll just be a moment.'

'Sir Vivian's with him,' the housekeeper said, and there was something in her voice, just a touch of a push, that meant the men weren't wanting to wait.

'We won't detain you any longer,' Anna said.

She nodded and turned away, with great sadness, I thought. Then she was lost inside the house, her book left so neatly on the chair, forgotten. Mrs Carne shut the door with force.

'It *would* be a kindness to tell Lady Phoebe,' I said. 'As it is, she's left to fear the worst.'

We began walking again, taking up the path we'd followed before coming across Lady Phoebe.

'The greater kindness was my lying to her,' Anna said, 'telling her we'd come to ask the squire about the quarry rather than the movements of Miss Wolffs and Miss Franks.'

'But we don't yet know if that pair have done anything wrong, apart from staring at the house. That is strange doings, I'll grant you.'

'I don't think we can risk the truth with Lady Phoebe. Belief can be a powerful thing, Shilly, especially for an already anxious mind. You keep telling me these woods are bewitched, and no amount of reassurance from me is convincing you otherwise.'

And there they were, before us again, those wretched trees. There was no escaping them.

Anna slipped into the gloom without a backward glance, left me. I had my knotted rope around my neck and clutched at it now, thinking of untying it to blow our way clear of the tightness of the place and crowding birds and the like. But as I followed Anna into the woods I stilled my hand. The place was going to get worse before it got better. I should wait until things got very bad indeed before I unknotted my rope.

That things *had* worsened since we'd gone to Boscastle I soon knew, for the path had narrowed to almost no path. Before, it had let me and Anna walk side by side almost as far as the quarry, but now it was hardly wide enough for us to pass at all. The brambles snaked their way across it. Lumps of moor stone had rolled in and taken root. There was a cry above me, then the sound of washing being shaken out. The birds were back.

They shuffled on the branches, barely room for them to perch and stare at me with their eyes that gleamed even though there was so little light. Most of them magpies. They began to jump up and down so that the trees shook like they were having fits. I feared the creatures would fly at me if I moved so I tried to stand as still as I could. There was no sign of Anna.

It was then I saw something else moving. The trunk of a tree twisting, turning, as if – as if *undoing* itself. A shadow opening, reaching.

A shadow that spoke.

TWENTY-TWO

'You got the basket all right, my bird?'

She had been sitting on a fallen tree, her black shawl making her a part of the woods until she chose to reveal herself. To let me see.

'My sweet?' she said. 'Not ill, are you?'

'No, I . . . You frightened me, Mrs Haskell.'

'Not me you should be frightened of, my sweet. Not me.'

She moved a little, resettled herself, and I saw her scarred hands. All the rest of her scarred too, she'd said, from the fire, aside from her face which was marked only with age. Her face tilted now to look at me, her eyes bright as the magpies'. I had the feeling that everything around me at that moment was leaning in, trying to get close to me. Close enough to hear my heart stuttering.

'The food, now,' she said. 'Did you get it?'

'Yes, thank you. Though the magpies, they got to it first.'

She chuckled and shook her head. 'Ah, yes, with the ash tree there, by the summer house. I should have thought to remind the girls.'

'The squire should chop the tree down,' I said. 'He can't be liking the birds crowding so close to the summer house. They make a terrible clitter on the roof.'

'That would be a mistake. The magpie tree is sacred, my bird. Saint Nectan planted it himself.'

I was glad, then, that Anna had gone on without me. She'd have called such a tale fanciful and stopped the telling. She had no heart for the ways of the people in my country.

'Someone has done it once before,' Mrs Haskell said. 'Cut down the magpie tree and suffered the consequences.'

'What happened?'

'His legs went.'

'They disappeared!' I said.

She laughed. 'No, my sweet. I mean they stopped working. He was crippled. His arms too – no strength in them. He knew, this man, that it was his own fault, and he bade his daughter plant a new ash tree on the same spot. The tree grew and the birds returned, and the man's weakness was taken from him.'

'So all was well?'

'For a little while. The tree grew tall and there were many strong branches. Another man—'

'It's always men in these stories, Mrs Haskell.'

'And what does that tell you?'

'That men cut things down,' I said, 'destroy things. It's daughters do the planting.'

'You're wiser than your years, Shilly. But some daughters cut down trees, too. Some set fire to whole forests. Don't forget that.'

How could I forget? I'd been thinking it. To burn the place, to be rid of the closeness. The hatred. And she knew.

'But the second man,' I said. 'What did he do to the tree?'

'He cut a branch to make a wooden nail.'

'And he was afflicted?'

'Of course. He lost an eye.'

'Did the nail go through it?' I felt my stomach heave as the words escaped, but I couldn't keep from asking, nasty beast that I was.

Mrs Haskell shrugged. 'The story doesn't say. But I'd imagine so. He deserved nothing less.'

A cripple and a blind man. The woods weren't kind to bodies. And to mine – what might they do to *my* flesh and *my* bones? To Anna's, too?

I asked Mrs Haskell if Anna had passed that way.

'She did, my sweet. Passed right by me but she didn't see me.'

'Anna doesn't know how to look,' I said.

'Not like you, my bird. Your eyes are wide open.' Mrs Haskell patted my arm. 'On you go, then, fly away home. You don't want to be too long out here, things being the way they are.' She sat down on the fallen tree again and pulled her black shawl more tightly around her – so tight she might crush her throat, I feared.

'But what about you?' I said. 'Will you be all right out here, on your own?'

Her back was to me. She seemed to sink into the tree beneath her, to find the place she slipped into shadow.

'Me? I'll be right enough, my sweet. And I shan't be on my own, don't you worry. He is here.'

'Who . . . who is with you?'

'Why, the saint, of course. He's with us in the woods.' Her voice was growing fainter, even as she sat a few feet from me. I reached out to touch her, to prove to myself that she *was* there.

The birds took to the air.

I ran.

I found Anna at the cottages. She was talking with a young woman I didn't recognise – a pretty thing with red hair and the bones of her cheeks sharp enough to draw blood, but her face was grey with slate's dust, which I knew Anna wouldn't like. Anna was all for washing. But I hastened over all the same. Anna was mine. No one else's.

I needn't have worried. The talk was thieving, not kissing. Two more things had vanished since that morning – a brooch belonging to this young woman, and a christening spoon of Richard Bray's.

'Both silver!' the young woman said. 'And precious too. Poor Richard's in a bad way because of it. Weeping, he is!'

'Where did you keep your brooch?' Anna said.

'In a box beneath the bed, but I'd had it out this morning, hadn't I? To show the baby. She was fretting. And the shininess of the brooch, she likes that. Takes her mind off whatever it is that's giving her pain. I left it on the bed to fetch something from the other room, and when I came back – this!'

She held out a small lump of coal.

'And your bed,' Anna said, 'it was near the window?'

The woman nodded.

'And the window was open?'

'Course it was! 'Tis hot, isn't it?'

'Did you see anyone nearby before the brooch was taken?' Anna said.

'Well, people were passing, like always, but none of them strangers. I didn't see the sisters from across the river. But the Devil helps them cast spells, don't he? So they can hide. That's how they took Paul.'

A man was hurrying towards her, carrying a bawling child, which he thrust at the young woman as if ridding himself of a violent animal.

'Oh my dear, my dear!' she said, taking the baby. 'They'll come for you next and how shall we stop them turning you into a lump of coal?'

Anna and I left them to their worry and made our way past the cottages in the direction of the summer house.

'The thefts are increasing,' Anna said.

'And all costly things. But Miss Franks and Mathilda are too well known to pass by here unnoticed, surely?'

'If they haven't enlisted the Devil to turn them invisible.'

'That's not funny, Anna.'

She waved away my telling-off. 'It's true, though. The thief must be someone known here, someone no one thinks will steal.'

I glanced about me as we passed the last few cottages, and met stares in return. Folded arms. Children herded indoors and doors banged shut, bolted. The Haskell girls, making their way home, skirted us, their squabbles forgotten. We were strangers in that place.

It was late by then – too late to cross the river and see Miss Franks and Mathilda to ask them about what we'd learnt in Boscastle, too late to ask the squire the same. Climbing the steps to the summer house door I caught sight of something stowed beneath the wooden slats. A basket, the cloth cover tucked in tight to keep out the birds. But the care wasn't needed today, for in the magpie tree there was only one bird. If the tree was Saint Nectan's, did that make the bird the saint's own too? The magpie watched me take the basket and make my way inside, and I was sure it watched me long after I'd locked the door.

We were tired after our day asking questions and didn't have words left for each other as we ate the food brought us – bread and hard cheese, some salted fish that dried my mouth so badly I wanted to stick my head under the waterfall.

When we had finished eating, Anna took from her black bag the broken piece of por-s'lain we had found outside Miss Franks and Mathilda's cottage – the bottom half of the woman in the pink dress, birds gathered at her feet. Anna put it on the window ledge, and next to it I put the lump of coal I'd taken from the road to Boscastle, and Paul Haskell's rabbit snare.

'Three clues,' Anna said. 'And two of them missing something.'

'The snare has no rabbit. The woman has no body. And the coal?'

'Is itself standing in for missing things – a mirror, a spoon, a brooch. And a boy.'

'Do you think Paul Haskell is dead?' I said.

'I don't know. I . . . I fear it.'

'If I were to have a drink—'

She blew out the candle.

153

TWENTY-THREE

I woke and the first thing I saw was black fidgeting at the window. Fidgeting flickering. Five or six of them, birds' tails, hanging from the roof. A creak, then the summer house sighed with the relief of them going – the magpies, swooping across the river. To the women on the other side.

We were to follow the birds. It was barely light but that was light enough for there wasn't time to waste while Paul was still missing. I felt better for my knotted rope. Anna didn't notice I'd brought it until we were on the last of the crossing stones and I stumbled, the rope slipping free of where I'd tucked it in the waist of my dress.

'Four pence for a knot,' she said. 'That rope-seller is no better than whoever is thieving in these woods.'

'You won't be saying that when I blow away all the ill feeling in this place. You'll be thanking me then.'

'Oh, will I? And when do you intend to unleash the fury of the weather, Shilly?'

'I'll know.' I tucked the rope back inside my dress. The roughness of it grazed my skin.

'Well,' Anna said, 'I look forward to seeing what my four pence has bought.'

'*My* four pence.' I sloshed through the shallows and stepped up onto the bank. 'Come on, Anna. We don't have time for your shilly-shallying.'

There was no smoke from the chimney today, and no devilish shouting either. Anna went to knock on the door but I didn't think we should give Miss Franks a chance to say we couldn't come in, so I shoved the door with my hip, calling out we were coming as I did so.

We found them much as when we'd come before – seated by the hearth and surrounded by unwashed plates. Mathilda jumped to her feet and got hold of my elbow.

'It is Shilly! Shilly, come again!'

I found that I was pleased to see her, this smiling girl with her wide cheeks and her badly pinned hair, her hand ashake. I had the sense she would hold nothing back in life. Her every hope and fear and love would be spoken and meant truly.

My feet brushed something. Paper. It was everywhere – scattered across the table as well as on the floor. And amid the paper, jars. Filled with murky water, little sticks in them.

Miss Franks' face made me think of the quarry workings – hard lines, worn deep.

'You . . . you just come *in*?' There was disbelief in her voice, but below that, rage. 'You take liberty—'

'We took the liberty of bringing you something to eat,' Anna said, handing her the basket we had brought.

Miss Franks' fingers twitched on the handle. 'That is . . .'

'Is kind, Gertrud,' Mathilda said. 'That is what you must say to our guests, yes? You are kind, Shilly, Anna. Thank you.'

There followed awkwardness as we waited to be asked to stay, even though we were going to anyway. There was a cost to the basket of food. I hadn't kept back bread the night before for nothing. Miss Franks fought to keep her anger in check, while Mathilda fretted beside her, afraid of her companion but happy to see us at the same time. I decided to make things easier for everyone. I sat down.

'Have you been out drawing the ferns?' I said, picking up a bit of paper from the floor. 'Oh, but this one is the sea. And this one, too.' I gathered up those scattered around me, and Anna did the same.

'Why, they're all of the sea,' Anna said. She smiled at Mathilda. 'I don't believe the famous hart's tongue fern holds any interest to you at all. I think you are a natural landscape artist rather than a botanist.'

Mathilda gasped with pleasure. 'You think so? I like to draw the sea, and to paint it. The colours, the movement. This one, Shilly, it is after the big waves and the wind. You see – I want to make it peaceful but still the storm that come before. Still there.'

Miss Franks set the basket on the table, so roughly some of the trinkets teetered then fell. She didn't pick them up. I thought of the broken por-s'lain woman we had left at the summer house.

'Is too dark, I think,' Mathilda said.

'This one is Boscastle, isn't it?' Anna said.

'Yes. A good place for me.' Mathilda gently touched the bridge in the picture with the tip of her little finger. 'A good place.'

'We were there yesterday,' I said.

'Ah! You are lucky, Shilly. You saw the fish boats come in?'

'I didn't,' I said. 'We'll have to go again. You could come with us.'

'I would like that,' Mathilda said, with great seriousness.

'We could stay there,' Anna said. 'We found a lodging house yesterday. I believe you know it, Miss Franks.' Anna turned to look at the older woman brooding by the table. 'The landlady is Mrs Teague.'

'I do not know it,' Miss Franks said.

'Really? Because Mrs Teague remembers you both well. She remembers your visitor, too. Quite a distinctive look to him, with the patch over his eye.'

Miss Franks' own eyes widened and she started forwards.

'You *do* know Squire Orton, then?' I said. 'Is he the reason you've come here?'

And then Miss Franks screamed.

'Spies! Everywhere in this place, people spy! In Boscastle, that woman at the keyhole, wanting to post my letters so she could read them. Her husband always asking why do we come where we do not belong. Every day he says that to me.'

'Gertrud,' Mathilda said, going to her side and plucking at her sleeve. 'Please, be calm now.'

But it did no good. Miss Franks was beyond being calm. And it was all our fault.

'We leave Boscastle and find only worse things in these woods. The people watch at the windows and put their filthy hands on my possessions. They are here, all the time. Watching. Listening. And now *you*.' She spat out that last word and jabbed a finger at Anna and me in turn. '*You* come like it is *your* house, you do not ask, and then you say that you ask questions of us in Boscastle. You are no better than the rest.'

'Miss Franks, Gertrud, I'm sorry to have upset—'

'Out!'

'But—'

She hauled Anna to her feet and dragged her to the door. Mathilda was scritching, talking in German but I could guess the sense of her words. She was begging. It did no good, though. Miss Franks wrenched open the door and threw Anna out – properly threw her, like she was Pigeon being banished from the manor house kitchen. I didn't wait to be so thrown myself and scuttled outside.

Miss Franks seethed and spluttered in the doorway.

'I will not be hounded!' she shouted. 'No more! I wait and I wait. That is enough.'

She ducked inside and I was going to run away but then she was back, throwing something at us. The basket of food and everything in it tumbling into the ferns.

'You will not come here again!'

And she slammed the door shut.

Anna uttered a curse. 'You should have knocked, Shilly, made more effort to act polite caller than spy.'

'But we are spying, aren't we? Anyway, it was saying the squire's name that was the problem, not me barging in.'

I helped her to her feet and we gathered the scattered food before the birds should come. Anna was all for leaving then, going back to our side of the river, but I told her to wait, and crept to the back of the cottage, taking with me a knocked-about half loaf. The window was easy to open, just as before, and I dropped the bread onto the bed below it. Miss Franks might be teasy but that didn't mean she deserved to starve, nor smiling Mathilda.

When I joined Anna on the path she was making her thinking noise, tapping at her false teeth with her tongue.

'You're right that mentioning the squire touched a nerve,' she said.

'Which proves he *was* their visitor in Boscastle.'

'I don't know about that, Shilly. But if they won't tell us if they know *him*—'

'We'll ask the squire if he knows *them*,' I finished for her. For that was what had to be done, no matter the risk to the reward.

'Mr Williams will ask,' Anna said, 'and he will go alone. He needs to appear entirely unconnected with our investigation. Shilly, you can—'

'I'll join the searchers. The luck we're having finding Paul Haskell, it might be the most useful thing I *can* do.'

'If you think that's for the best,' she said coldly.

'Will Mr Williams be the newspaperman he was when I first met him?' I said.

'Of course. That's who he is. He can't be just anyone.'

'But won't he need a new name?' I said, 'to stop the squire thinking him my husband?'

'An excellent point, *Mrs* Williams.'

We went on a few paces and then I asked a question I had been wanting to for some time. 'Is he the only man in your travelling case?'

That surprised her, and she couldn't meet my eye. 'There might be others, Shilly. Would you like to . . . to meet one of them?'

'I might,' I said.

She didn't say anything for a moment, and then she said, as if we had been speaking of a clue, 'Well, that is something we shall have to see about.'

And so the talk of us becoming men was put aside. But I wouldn't give it up. Anna's travelling case held many chances to become someone else. She'd already given me one just by helping me leave the moor. I was keen to try others.

We had been walking back towards the river but Anna stopped now beside a wide stump made lumpy with moss and said it was as good a place as any to bring out Mr Williams. I saw then that she had him in her black bag. He'd been with us the whole time.

'Remember,' she said, 'if you should see Mr Williams, who will be wandering the woods with his new name, you don't know him. His status as an outsider must be preserved if we're to have the most use of him.'

'I know, I know. I'm not soft in the head, Anna.' And I left her. She was already reminding me too much of the wretched Mr Williams and she hadn't even put on his thick spectacles yet, or taken up his limp!

The path was up to its usual tricks as I made my way to the cottages but I was ready for it now and didn't grow so afraid as when we had first arrived, for that was how to become lost in the woods – giving in to them. It was what they wanted, the huddling trees. Perhaps that was what had happened to Paul and I should even now come across him wandering about, dressed in clothes made of ferns, eating snails like Miss Franks and Mathilda. That was a better thought than him drowned in the river or buried by the quarry workings.

A magpie landed on a lump of moor stone a little way ahead. I passed it, and it flew ahead of me again. It did this watching and catching up all the way to the cottages and I was quite breathless when I reached them for trying to outrun the bird.

A few people were about, and I caught sight of the red-haired woman who had lost her brooch the day before. She was outside her cottage, surrounded by piss bottles. The baby was squalling in her lap, a miserable thing, curled fists and sweaty with rage. As I drew closer I saw the likely cause of the child's misery – her arms were sore-looking, covered in red pinpricks. I took a few steps back for I didn't want the pox. I wouldn't be much use to Paul Haskell if I had to take to my bed, or if I should die.

I asked the child's mother if there was any news of Paul.

'No, God help us. Nothing.' She clutched the baby to her. 'Why you asking, anyway?'

'I was looking to help. Join the searchers.'

'Well, they're at the quarry. Going to search the spoil heaps. Squire finally let them stop work to do it.'

I went on my way, towards the quarry, to see if I could be of some use. But then I passed a place that held more usefulness, better usefulness in finding Paul.

Richard Bray was snoring loud enough to raise his roof and neither heard nor saw me creep inside. From the smell coming off him, when he woke his head would be so sore he'd never miss the bottle. Without Anna there to chide me, to forbid, I could do what I had need of – for myself and for the missing boy.

I knew where to take my prize. I'd thought of it the day before, on our way to Boscastle when I first saw the ruined mill by the bridge. That's why I'd stopped to look at it. Anna didn't guess. She never did. Mrs Haskell was right. Anna didn't know how to look, and Mr Williams's thick spectacles would make her blindness worse, rather than let her see.

My hands on the bottle shook and I feared I'd drop it. Just a sip on the way, I told myself. Just a little one, to keep my feet moving, my breath coming. I'd be more like myself in no time, and the trees wouldn't have me.

If I could just get to the mill. Get to the mill and then I could have it. I couldn't let them see, let them know, those good people. Those Haskells. Anna. I told myself to run. Past the quarry and the search for Paul, because my help was something different. Something better, even, yes? Yes. Run, Shilly, run. There was the light beyond the trees, there was the path opening out, there was the manor house and Anna inside it, Mr Williams inside it, and I was running, no – flying. Flying past the house and there was the road and there was the old mill, burnt beyond use to all but me. Fly away home. Fly away, away to the bottle at my lips, the good taste, the best taste, oh that it would never end, that I should die at that moment and not have to go another day without a drink and Anna shaking her head, hating me for what I was. Look at her shaking her head, her eyes red-rimmed, red-veined. Her nose red too. Her hair lank. Her skin sallow. The bottle to her thin, pale lips. Her lying lips. Her saying, Shilly, what have you done?

And then I saw that Anna's mouth was my mouth, Anna's words, my words. My own hateful face staring back at me.

I had found the stolen mirror.

TWENTY-FOUR

Because I couldn't bear to see myself, I looked away, and took in where I was. The mill I had run to, run to like a desperate animal. A bird, I had thought. Flying. No. A rabid dog, more like. Something that should be shot.

I was lying in a pit of blind nettles and broken slate, the bottle beside me, not empty yet. I put the stopper back. I managed that, and told myself that was a start, at least. I got to my feet and saw my palms were scratched. How had I done that?

All four walls were still standing, and most of the roof, though a corner had fallen in and left the shattered slates beneath my feet. They scraped and ground their rough edges together as I stepped this way and then that, picking through the brambles and fallen beams that took up most of the floor. A millstone was propped against one wall, and there were stone troughs nearby. Sarah's stolen mirror had been tucked behind one of these, but had slipped from its hiding place, pushed into view by one of the scurrying things I could hear but not see. Rats, I thought, but forced myself to peer behind the trough. Sure enough, there were other treasures.

I pulled out shining knives and forks and spoons, and amongst them one I thought likely to be Richard Bray's christening spoon for it was smaller and thicker than the others, and looked too good to eat with. The other cutlery I guessed belonged to Miss Franks and Mathilda. A bit more reaching and fiddling behind the trough, trying not to think about the rats and trying not to feel the pain when the moor stone of the trough grazed me. My hand closed on something small and sharp. A silver leaf with a pin worked into it. The red-haired woman's brooch. More fiddling and I had a frame for a picture. The woman inside it looked very much like Miss Franks. Then a pair of shoes fine enough for Mrs Williams to wear, all lacy bits and silver thread.

I felt very pleased with myself for finding so many fine things, like a magpie must feel when she looks at the trinkets she has gathered. I gathered them up and thought how pleased Anna would be when I showed her. But then I put the things down again, for I knew what Anna would say. You have the stolen goods, Shilly, but you don't have the thief. Better to leave the things and wait to see who comes for them.

And so I stowed them all behind the trough again, as I had found them, all but the framed picture. That was small enough to carry and I could see a use for it. Miss Franks had turned us out. Food wasn't bait enough for us to get back inside the cottage, but a treasure might be. I remembered how sad she'd been when she told us what had been taken, and the woman in the picture looked so much like her that I thought she must be a relation.

I decided such cunning deserved another sip. Only a sip, mind, and then I would have had enough to go back into the world and try again to be good and worthy of being taught my letters. But I took the bottle with me. For Paul, I told myself, and was on my way to the summer house before I could think that mightn't be the truth of the matter.

'Anna, you won't believe—'

A man was by the window, his back to me. He spun round as I burst in to the summer house, his hand fumbling to free itself from inside his fly. From rubbing at himself. He was speechless, open-mouthed. But we needed no introductions. His neat but thick moustache, his spectacles. The disappointment on his face at seeing me, along with the flush of shame. I knew him all too well.

Mr Williams had returned.

'If you've a need,' I said, starting towards him, 'I can—'

'I was just . . . changing my clothes.'

I didn't look away while he was taken off and packed back into the travelling case, Anna revealed beneath him. I enjoyed her blushes, her failure to meet my eye. I had been right to think she took pleasure in men's clothes, and I would find a time to make use of it. For now, though, there were other things to speak of.

'Did you see the squire?' I asked her.

'He wasn't at home to callers, according to the *delightful* Mrs Carne.' Anna sat down to put her stockings on. 'All I learnt was that Mrs Carne was forced to do the washing because Lucy has taken to her bed.'

'Why?'

'Why did Mrs Carne tell me? Because she has the same capacity for sympathy as this chair.'

'No,' I said. 'Why has Lucy taken to her bed.'

'Ill, apparently. Mrs Carne told me, at great length, I might add, about the overwork she faces as a result.'

'I wonder . . . The baby belonging to the woman that lost her brooch, the one with red hair. The baby has marks—'

'Mr Williams's visit wasn't completely in vain,' Anna said, not heeding me. 'He met someone as he was leaving the house. Someone else looking for the squire.'

'Who?'

'The quarry captain. I forget his name, but he was pleased to tell Mr Williams of the fineness of Trethevy's slate. Not so fine as that of Delabole, which I gather is the best in these parts, but Trethevy has the advantage for they are closer to the coast for shipping.'

I went to the window and looked out at the waterfall for its tumbling was more interesting than Anna's slate rambles.

'Mr Williams was delighted to hear all about the quarry, of course,' Anna said, 'given that he is writing a piece for his newspaper about Cornwall's mineral extraction.'

'Is he indeed?' I said, jealous of Mr Williams being able to turn to whatever strangers chose to tell him. And admiring of Anna too, of course.

'The captain shared all *sorts* of insights,' she said. 'About inclines and drainage, how they winch up the larger blocks using that wheel on a tripod – that's a "poppet head", he told me.'

'How interesting.'

'The most interesting thing is how they get it out of the ground in the first place. They blast it, Shilly. With explosive powders.'

'Hm.'

'And do you know what they do before they set the charge?'

'I'm certain you're going to tell me.'

'They ring a bell.'

I looked at her then. 'What?'

'It's an alarm, to warn anyone nearby that a blast is imminent. It's not a dead saint that has been ringing a bell of warning. It's the quarry captain.'

'But the people here, they live so close to the quarry, they work in it. They'll know the blasting bell, won't they? Why would they mistake that for another? There must be two of them being rung, two *different* bells. The saint is here, Anna, looking after his people.'

'No, he isn't. It's the quarry captain who's doing the looking after, stopping people being blown to pieces. And the reason the inhabitants of these woods have mistaken the sound of their own blasting bell is because they're afraid. Afraid of two foreign spinsters so poor they're eating snails.'

I leant against the wall, not minding its damp fur for once. Could it be true what Anna said? She was still speaking. She had all the answers, and yet, and yet . . .

'So,' she said, 'now that we've solved that mystery, what's that you've got?'

'What?'

'In your hand there.'

She took the frame I'd forgotten I was holding. The bottle was safe in the ferns beneath the magpie tree. Anna looked at the drawn woman in the frame.

'Does she remind you of anyone?' I said.

Anna tilted the picture to make use of the light. 'The resemblance is quite striking. The same shaped face, and the mouth. The dress is old-fashioned – the lace at the collar.'

'Miss Franks' mother?' I said.

'A close relation, certainly. Where did you find this, Shilly?'

'The ruined mill, on the road. I was looking for Paul there.'

She frowned at me. 'I would have thought the mill had been searched already. Are you lying to me?'

I told her of the other things I'd found, and that I'd left them there so that we could find the thief.

'And if we catch the thief, we find Paul,' Anna said. 'The boy must have seen something he wasn't meant to, that day near Miss Franks and Mathilda's cottage. The thief needed to silence him. That's our motive. We just have to hope the boy is still alive.'

'Even if he isn't, the knowing is worth something.'

We were quiet then, thinking of Paul, before Anna upset all my good detective work by asking a hard question.

'So how do you suppose we catch the thief, Shilly? We can't keep watch on the mill all hours of the day. We can't put all our eggs in that basket.'

'I . . .'

She gave a tight smile of satisfaction, which did away with the last of her embarrassment at having been caught enjoying herself. She was in charge once more.

'Don't fear, Shilly. I have an idea. We'll need to go upstream for once, rather than down.'

'Upstream, why? What's there?'

'Not what, but who. David Tonkin.'

She told me of the plan as we walked. We would ask David Tonkin for the dye he used to colour cloth, and then we would paint it on the stolen things.

'Only the undersides,' Anna said. 'We don't want the thief to see anything is amiss before he or she has picked them up.'

'And then the dye will mark the thief – a sign of their guilt.'

'Exactly.'

I had to own that it was very cunning, but I only owned that to myself. Anna was prideful enough as it was.

'What shall we say to David Tonkin if he asks why we want the dye?' I said.

'We'll tell him . . . Well, what *shall* we tell him, Shilly? Time you decided a lie. I know you've a talent for it. Don't think I can't smell spirits on you.'

I quickened my pace and put all my thinking into what to say to David Tonkin.

By the time we arrived, having fought our way along the riverbank, through brambles and ferns and falling over the fallen trees and lumps of moor stone hidden there, I had my lie ready.

David Tonkin was hard at work, lifting and dropping a big club into a big tub, grinding at the dark water thickened with cloth. He greeted us like old friends, and told the lad helping him that we were 'the two art ladies'. This was helpful for my lie, for I told him we needed dye for our painting.

'Well now, I've never been asked for that before, and there's plenty other painters come to the woods. Modern painting you're doing, is it?' he said, his whiskers twitching, as if such a thing were fearful.

'I . . .'

'Quite right, Mr Tonkin,' Anna said, and saved me. 'We're experimenting with some new techniques. A wash, for which I think a dark dye might be just the thing. The river here, it moves so beautifully in the shadows cast by the trees.'

That put him at ease. 'Oh yes, she's quite a sight, isn't she? That's why so many come, and I always say to them, to you artists, I say, do you know the name of such a fine river as this here in Trethevy?'

He beamed at us with great expectation, and I took this to mean we were to ask for this answer, so ask him I did.

'What is the river's name, Mr Tonkin?'

''Tis the *Duwy*, my dear, which in the language of these parts means—'

'Dark River,' I said.

'How poetic,' Anna murmured.

'Isn't it?' he said. 'The poets come too. Scores of them.' Then his expression darkened, dark as the river he'd been speaking of. 'And they'll have something for their poems now, won't they? The tragedy of the lost boy.'

We were all three silent a moment then, only the river loud outside the mill, but then the young lad coughed in the poor air and the spell was broken.

'Now then,' David Tonkin said, 'let me get a little pot for you. I'd like to see the painting when you've finished, Miss Drake. See how a wash of dye looks.'

'Of course. I'd be delighted. Would you have a cloth I could take too?'

Still the better liar of the two of us.

We left one mill and went straight to another – the ruined one on the road. Anna was too fearful of the rats to be much use. After much

169

shrieking and cursing that would let all the thieves in Cornwall know we were there, she climbed into one of the empty stone troughs. From the safety of that spot she told me how I should place the dye, and then how I should do it better, so things were much the same as usual. Her talking, me doing, and both of us grumbling at the other.

'Make sure you put some dye on each of the shoes.'

'Do I have to? Waste of a fine pair, if you ask me. Miss Franks would likely think so too.'

'Well, she isn't going to know, is she? And it's a small sacrifice if we catch the thief and it leads us to Paul Haskell.'

Her words made me put a great wash of dye on the bottom of each shoe, caring less now about how the fine lace wilted in the dark splashes.

At last I was done with it, and a messy job it was, too. I straightened up and looked for a place to hide the pot of dye and the cloth.

'Shilly, doesn't something about this mill strike you as odd?'

'I know you don't like the rats, Anna. You've told me enough times. Just let me put these things behind this beam and we'll be off.'

'It's not the rats. Look around you. What do you see?'

I did as she said. 'I see an old mill with the roof coming down and brambles keeping it upright.'

'That's what I see too.'

'So?' I said, my patience all but gone.

'So what *don't* you see?'

'That's one of them foolish questions you only ask to make *me* look foolish. Well, I won't be a fool, Anna Drake. I hope the rats get you.'

I made my way towards the doorway with its half-hanging door more rot than wood. Wood. I put my hand out. Damp wood.

I spun round. 'There's nothing here been burnt. The place has just fallen down.'

Anna nodded, still standing in the trough, looking as if she floated above the ferns and brambles. 'And yet Mrs Haskell said there was a fire here. That she'd been burnt in it.'

'Why would she lie about that?' I said.

'Why indeed?'

I gave Anna my hand to help her climb out of the trough.

'Nearly everyone in Trethevy has a secret to hi—'

A bell rang.

TWENTY-FIVE

'Shilly, wait!'

I ran across the road and scrambled down the side of the bridge. The trees stood so close together it was as if I faced a wall. But I knew I had to find a way through, to get back inside the gloom.

'Shilly!'

'It's the saint, he's warning us.'

I pushed my way between two tight trunks and then was forced to step high through the brambles, like some leggy wading bird. The bell rang and rang. A low peal. A sad peal. It was the song the trees would sing if they only had mouths.

Anna had caught up with me but dithered at the treeline. 'I told you – it's the quarry's bell.'

'Something bad is going to happen,' I said, and tumbled free of the brambles and into the woods.

'A *blast* is going to happen.'

She grabbed my arm but I got myself free. There was a rough path ahead. An animal track, at least. I looked about me. This wasn't a part of the woods we'd been in before. I tried to get my bearings.

'The quarry must be that way, mustn't it, away from the river? Where's the ringing coming from?'

'Shilly, please. We can't go near the quarry. It's not safe.'

'Believe what you like, Anna, but the bell rang when Paul Haskell disappeared. Some other bad thing might be happening right now. We can't just ignore it.'

'But—'

I set off in the direction I thought the quarry, for that would lead to the cottages, and crashed through all manner of green and scratching thing. Anna followed me and I followed the bell. It grew louder but my blood pounded in my ears and my body was tolling, tolling, and the light was fading. Too fast for dusk. The woods' anger took the light. The branches seethed.

At last I found the path to the cottages and I made for it, if only for the sight of something known in that unknown place. At once I was in a river, but not the Dark River that ran through the woods of Trethevy. This was a river of people, surging with panic.

The quarry workers were streaming back, grey and frightened, calling names. Men and women grabbed children, shoved them indoors. All about me the children scritching. The birds screamed above. And still the bell rang, and my feet slowed, stopped, for the noise was inside me, as if my heart had been plucked clean out and a clapper left. I was so very afraid.

'Jenna! Where is he? Where's Peter?'

Maria Haskell had her eldest daughter by the arm and was shaking her.

'I don't know!'

'What do you mean, you don't know? I told you not to let him out of your sight.'

'I tried! He went off while I wasn't looking.' The girl was scritching and clutching at her collar, her voice rising to a wail. 'He kept saying he wanted to dig the water.'

Maria looked up and down the path, her hands pressed against her mouth but I could hear her moans still as I went to her.

'It's Peter,' she told me, 'he's out there somewhere. They'll take him. Oh, dear Lord, whatever will we do?'

The poor woman fell to the ground. Jenna covered her face with her skirt and howled. Faces appeared at the windows of the neighbouring cottages, but no one opened their door. There was no noise but the bell and the scritching, as if the world had folded in on itself and there was nothing left but the ground we stood on and the grief and fear that swelled from it.

I couldn't stay there a heartbeat longer. If I did I'd lay down in the dirt myself and never get up. I wrenched Jenna's skirts from her face.

'Where did you last see him?'

'The summer house.'

I ran, Anna behind me, calling I should take care. Past the cottages and left at the fallen oak and I knew it was the right way for the bell was louder now, calling me on.

Ahead, the river came in sight, and then the path rounded on the monks' wall. I skittered to a stop. There was no sign of Peter Haskell there, on his way back, or anyone else, for that matter. I spat the froth of running and pressed on, climbing now, towards the summer house. Towards the ringing. And then Anna cried out behind me. I turned to see her crumple away, vanishing into a clump of thorns.

I went to her side, tried to help her stand but the effort only made her cry more.

'What's wrong?' I said.

'I tripped. This wretched root!'

Her left foot was caught in the snarl of it. I reached down, her leaning on my shoulder.

'There,' I said, yanking her free. 'Now, come on!'

But she couldn't stand, could only cling to me. I had no choice but to let her sink into the ferns.

'I'll come back for you.'

'Don't go, Shilly. Please!' Her face was leached of colour. She tried to grab me.

'I have to. The saint—'

'Don't leave me!' she said.

A burst of wings above us but no birds to be seen. Between each peal of the bell the air tightened. I could feel it, as I had felt it before in that place. And now Anna could too. The trees put forth malice like other, more ordinary plants would put forth buds.

'You can't leave me here alone,' Anna whispered.

'You have your knife?' I said.

She nodded.

'Then use it if you have to.'

'Will it . . . will it work on . . .'

'If you try then you'll know, won't you?' I said. 'Drive it home. Don't hold back.' I pulled free of her grasping hands and carried on, into the bell's noise.

I climbed to the summer house, my legs heavy as fallen beams, my heart heavier still with dread, but still I climbed. The bell called me on, louder than ever, even as I drew close to the waterfall, which should have drowned it out. If it had been an ordinary bell, that was. I didn't look back at Anna below, tried not to think what might be waiting for me above. Made myself concentrate on each foothold, each step taken.

At last I neared the top of the climb, the roof of the summer house coming into view, and beyond it, the top of the magpie tree. The birds were at home, the branches heavy with their black and white tumbling, for the birds were all a-scurry in the bell's noise, making a clitter to beat it, so that as I came level with the summer house I walked into a great terror of sound. The saint was ringing his bell for all he was worth. So loud it made me want to shut my eyes, as if that would ease it, but the saint wanted me to see. He stopped my eyes from closing. My lids were fluttering like I was having fits and before me was the black and white of the birds in the saint's tree.

The black and white of the summer house's wood, and beneath it, Peter Haskell.

Peter Haskell being dragged by a black cloak.

TWENTY-SIX

The boy looked to be screaming as he fought but there was no sound save the bell and the birds. I shouted but my words didn't leave me, only thrummed through my body. I was struck dumb.

Peter saw me. He slackened his fight and called, silent as I was, and then the figure saw me too. They were next to the summer house, at least thirty paces from me. If the cloaked figure should drag the boy into the changeling trees on the other side of the clearing I might never find him. The boy would be lost as his brother had been lost. I couldn't let that happen. I unbuttoned my skirt and reached beneath it. My fingers closed on the coarseness of the rope. I set about the knot the man at Boscastle had tied, my fingers fumbling, useless.

The figure was dragging the boy again, Peter weakening in the fight, I could see it, but the knot was loose. I nearly had it.

As the knot came free the rope jerked in my hand, as if someone was pulling it. I threw it to the ground where it writhed like a grass snake. I stepped away, and found myself on the edge of the drop I'd just climbed, but better that than to be near such strangeness. As I stared at it, the writhing rope blackened, then crumbled, became ash. I braced myself for what must surely come now.

But nothing happened. Nothing.

The cloaked figure struck at Peter's face and he went limp.

And then I felt it.

A great breath rose from the ground, scattering the ash of the rope to nothing. The wind lifted my skirt, made my sleeves flap and for a heartbeat the power of it hung over me, sent my hair swirling across my face and my body near blown over.

The figure stopped. Head cocked, as if listening. Then it turned, slowly, to look at me. I caught a glimpse of a face beneath the hood and my breath stilled.

The creature had no eyes.

A snap and the wind shot across the clearing, whisking through the saint's tree as it passed. It sent the magpies into the air in a tumble – upside down and furious. The gust struck the cloaked figure and it went down, Peter too.

The bell stopped. The wind dropped. As sudden as candles snuffed, both were gone.

In the silence I forgot that I could speak, that there was noise other than bells and breezes. It was Peter that reminded me. He was running towards me, gabbling and scritching, his shirt torn and a red mark across his cheek. I reached out for him.

But he didn't want me. He wanted to be away, ran past me, all but hurled himself over the ledge and down the path that would take him home.

'Peter – wait!'

But he wouldn't, or couldn't. Some devil fired his limbs to run.

I turned back to the clearing. The cloaked figure had gone. A single magpie had returned to the tree, but it had no care for me. It was eying the spot where the figure had been, next to the summer house. I heard voices below. Many voices. Crying out. But for once in that place of sadness and fear, the crying was that of relief.

I peered over the ledge. Anna had managed to stand somehow, awkward and with pain clear on her face, but she held tight to Peter Haskell as if she feared he'd take off again. They were next to the riverbank. The waterfall roared above them, but louder than the water were the calls of Maria and James Haskell running to their boy. Anna let him go to them, and I scuttled down the slippery steps to her.

As she sagged in my arms I told her what had happened, of the figure with no eyes, how the rope had leapt and burnt, how it had brought the wind, just as the man in Boscastle had said it would. Her doubt was clear on her face, but there was no time for rowing for Peter was loudly gabbling to his parents.

'That one,' he said, and pointed at me, 'the one always muttering, she saved me. It would have had me else, I know it.'

'Why did you run away from Jenna?' his mother asked between kissing his sandy hair and pressing him to her.

'I needed to find the saint and Jenna wouldn't let—'

'Never mind that now,' James said. 'You're safe, that's the main thing. And we have you to thank, Mrs Williams.'

It took me longer than it should have to remember that was who I was in the woods. That was my name.

'Did you recognise it, Peter?' Anna said quickly, limping over to the Haskells. She took me with her for she was leaning on my arm.

'It had something wrong with its face.'

'A mask of some kind?' Anna said, stealing a glance at me.

'I don't know . . . It could see me but I couldn't see its eyes.'

'Nothing of this world would look like that,' James said. 'This proves the furrin women took Paul.'

'I'm not sure it does,' I said.

'It don't matter,' a voice said. A crackly voice. One I knew.

Anna flinched into my side. She'd seen something in the trees, and then I saw it too. A trunk stirring, turning. Mrs Haskell was there.

'You've left the girls!' Maria shouted. 'It got away – it could be taking them even as you stand here!'

The old woman shook her head, shook away the telling-off. 'One wasn't enough for them. They'll take them all. All my birds.'

'You go on home, Mother,' James said. 'We'll bring Peter. Go on home to the girls.'

Mrs Haskell turned back into the trees, but not because her son told her to. She was a woman who wouldn't be told. Far overhead, a magpie crossed, flying towards the cottages. I wondered if it was the one from the saint's tree, giving up its watch.

Anna was still searching for answers where easy answers didn't lie.

'Did the figure speak to you?' she asked Peter.

'No,' he said. 'It just grabbed me and then kept yanking my arm.' He rubbed his shoulder, as if only just remembering the pain he no doubt felt.

'Was there anything else you noticed? Anything about its clothes, its hands? The way it smelt, even?' Anna sounded desperate, and her ferreting for scraps only upset the boy. He pressed his face into his mother's hip.

'Did you at least see where it came from?' Anna said.

James Haskell gently set the boy to look at Anna who in that moment had no warmth or care about her. She could only speak in questions.

I knelt by Peter, and without my holding her Anna sagged on her bad foot, but I let her sag. There were others who needed kindness.

'You must tell us what you can,' I said to the boy, 'and then we can find Paul. This creature, it might be the one that took him.'

A trembly sound from his mother, but I carried on.

'Now, what did you do after the girls left the food?'

'I walked slower and slower, so they wouldn't notice they were leaving me behind. I let them get far ahead and then I climbed back up to the summer house.'

'Why?'

'To get on the boards that look over the waterfall. Grandmother says the summer house was the saint's chapel so he might be buried close. A waterfall's a good place for a holy burial. It's like blessings on your head all the time.'

182

'You weren't going to climb down there?' his mother said. 'Under the waterfall? Peter – what have I told you!'

'I'm not soft, Mother. I knew I needed a rope.'

'Lord preserve us,' James muttered. 'If the sisters hadn't taken you, you might have been your own end.'

'I thought there could be something in the summer house that I could use,' Peter went on, 'so I was trying the door. I heard water, like it was raining inside, but then the bell rang. I turned round and it was there.' His voice trailed into a whimper. 'My . . . my spade fell over the edge.'

He looked to the river as if he might see the lost spade floating there, offered up as a gift. But I knew the river to be a force so careless it ran on, ran on, drowning and saving as it saw fit. I saw the boy there, face down. Bobbing past on the current, bobbing as if he was laughing. Mouthfuls of water. Throatfuls. Bellyfuls. Until he was more water than he was anything else. Known only by his sandy hair and a knife in his pocket for skinning rabbits. Was that his brother's fate?

'We'll get you another spade,' James Haskell said.

'No we won't!' Maria said. 'No more digging. You can't be trusted in the woods, and your sisters are no help. Neither is your grandmother.'

'It's not their fault I—'

'You'll come to the quarry with me and your father, where we can keep an eye on you. You'll be safer in the cutting shed than you are out here.'

'But the saint!'

'I don't think you need worry about him,' I said. 'Saint Nectan's doing just what he should from his grave. He rang the bell today, didn't he? That's how I found you.'

I caught a scornful look from Anna.

'Yes . . .' Peter said, 'but the saint needs to come for them, for the sisters. Otherwise we'll never find Paul, will we?'

No one spoke then. The boy looked at each of us, and none of us could meet his eye.

'Come on, my sweet,' his father said, pushing the boy gently in the direction of home, away from the river.

Maria took my hand in both of hers and pressed it, as a chapel preacher might. Her face bore all that she had felt today – the exhaustion of fear, the softening of relief. But still there, the grief she'd borne for days now. One son found, one still missing. She had no words for me and I had none for her.

She followed James and Peter. The light was fading and they were soon lost to us.

'So my four pence were well spent,' Anna said at last.

'That knotted rope is the only reason Peter's going to sleep in his bed tonight.'

'Not a loose stone that tripped them, this cloaked figure? Not a stray root? I've fallen foul of one myself today.' And as if I needed proof, she limped towards a lump of moor stone and leant against it. 'It's not too much of a leap to believe the same was the reason the figure failed.'

'The rope turned to ash, Anna! With no burning, no light of any kind. You still doubt me. Doubt the things I've shown you to be true.'

'You haven't shown *me* anything today, Shilly.' She rubbed her ankle. 'Other than that you were prepared to leave me, injured.'

'Well, you showed me something, Anna Drake.'

'Did I indeed? And what was that – an example of effective questioning? Because that's what we're here to do, after all. Or have you forgotten that with all this talk of witching?'

'Oh, I've seen that often enough, how you hound people to get what you want. No, what you showed me was that you *do* feel the strangeness of this place, however much you tell me there's no such thing. You feel the hatred in the woods. You were afraid when I left you. Admit it!'

'I was afraid you were going for drink, and that you'd be the one going over the waterfall. That I'll admit to.'

'So you do care for me, then.'

She turned away, and after a moment she said, 'I didn't want to

184

spend the night out here if I couldn't climb up to the summer house without help. That was all.'

'Oh Anna, when will you stop lying to yourself?'

'When you do the same,' she said.

Her back was to me. The sharp lines of it clear even with the light going. I went to her, ready to hold her, but my steps stopped.

The bell rang.

Anna whirled round, frantic as a cat startled from sleep. She looked up, towards the summer house. 'What now?'

'It's not coming from there.'

'Then where is it?'

'Across the river.'

'Miss Franks and Mathilda,' she said.

We were slow getting to the crossing stones, with Anna's hurt foot. I thought about leaving her again but I couldn't bring myself to do it twice in the same day. Not if that figure without eyes waited for us at the cottage. I had no more knotted ropes.

Anna did her best to run but hobbling was all she could manage, and that pained her. I grabbed a sapling's branch fallen near the path and made her lean on it. The bell's din grew louder as we neared the cottage of Mathilda and Miss Franks, and my heart pounded worse and worse with every ring, every step.

We'd reached the old gatepost, where Paul was last seen, when the bell stopped. The silence was worse than the noise.

'Does that mean the threat's gone?' Anna said.

'Or we're too late. Look.'

The door to the cottage was open.

TWENTY-SEVEN

I peered round the door. The room was all but lost in the gloom of dusk for the only light was the fire and that had burnt down.

'Hello?' Anna said, still on the doorstep. 'Miss Franks?'

If something should be crouching in a corner, waiting—

Anna pushed the door wide open, letting in the last of the day's light. I made out two figures seated by the fire. Their backs to us. Skirted and shawled. Neither stirred. There was no sound.

Anna leant her walking stick against the wall and took out her knife, so I took up her stick to use as a club. I picked my way towards the chairs, all but blind in the near-dark, stepping on the unwashed dishes and sheaves of paper that were scattered about just as before.

As we drew closer, I saw an arm hanging over the side of a chair. Closer still we crept, and I saw the pattern of the dress. It was Miss Franks. Her hand was reaching for a handkerchief on the floor beneath it. But the hand was still.

A noise made me turn – a scratch scratch coming from the other chair.

'Mathilda?' I whispered. 'It's Shilly. Are you all right?'

Something was moving in her lap. Her hand, jerking back and

forth. She didn't look up at my speaking, gave no sign she even knew we were there.

Anna touched Miss Franks' shoulder and muttered words I didn't catch. Then there was a metal clunk – Anna had dropped her knife.

'A light – quick, Shilly!'

'What's wrong?'

'I think . . . I can't see a wretched thing.'

There was the sound of her bumping into the table, trinkets falling and chinking into one another. Anna's curses.

'Mathilda,' I said, 'do you have spills, for the candles?'

She didn't answer, so I grabbed from the floor one of the bits of paper lying there and made a spill myself. I plunged it into the fire's embers and after a moment the twist of paper caught.

'Anna – here.'

She snatched the spill and held it close to Miss Franks' face. I lit a second.

I stumbled back, nearly falling in the embers.

Miss Franks was glaring at me. Only one side of her face was clear and the clearest thing about it was the eye fixed on me. It was huge. Unnaturally so. It bulged in her face. Dark and glassy.

'Miss Franks . . .'

Anna lit the candle ends she found amongst the table's muddle and set them close by. In their light Miss Franks' cheeks looked very red. I made myself go closer. The redness was blood, and raw flesh. Her skin had been torn. Raked. Deep slashes made her forehead, nose and cheeks a ploughed field of themselves. Her other eye, the one not glaring at me, was burst and lay like a bad egg in the broken shell of the socket. Her lips were torn. Amongst the blood was the white of dried spittle.

I choked back bile. 'Dear God. What . . . Mathilda!' I spun round and held my light close to the girl to see if she was harmed. Her hand jerking so strange was her doing some drawing. In the near dark?

188

With a dead woman beside her? There were marks across her knuckles. Scratches. They were bleeding.

'She's hurt too!' I said. 'Anna – Mathilda's been cut.'

'But she's alive, at least. Hold this.' Anna gave me her candle. She pulled away Miss Franks' shawl and undid her collar, then peered at her neck.

'What happened to her?'

'I'm not a coroner,' Anna said.

'But you can guess?'

'There are no marks of strangulation, but that eye protruding, the strain in her cheeks. I'd say she's been smothered.' Anna touched Miss Franks' throat. 'Still warm. Whatever happened, it happened very recently. And yet the girl sits here as if nothing is untoward.'

It was true. Mathilda had remained in her chair, moving the charcoal over the paper but without looking at what she was doing. Her gaze was fixed on the fire's remains.

Anna bent down and when she straightened she held her little knife again. 'Mathilda,' Anna said firmly, as if speaking to a child, 'can you tell us what happened?'

No reply. Still the charcoal moved across the paper.

'Did you quarrel?' Anna said.

Scratch scratch across the paper.

Anna and I were like doorposts flanking the girl. The black lines she'd drawn were ragged and wiry, without neatness. But within the tangle was something firm that Mathilda kept drawing over and over. A shape. Curved at the bottom, like the underside of a bowl, the sides reaching into peaks, and between these peaks other lines were scratched to join them. The quarter-moon, set on its back.

I put my hand gently on Mathilda's, the one that held the charcoal, trying not to press the cuts in her flesh.

Anna raised her knife and it hovered now not far from Mathilda's face. 'Be careful, Shilly.'

Still Mathilda gave no reaction. Her hand moved beneath mine, as if I was drawing. I felt the tautness of it.

'She won't harm us,' I said. 'She's afraid.'

The flush that usually warmed the girl's cheeks was gone, replaced by a grey pallor. Sweat gleamed at her temples, above her lip, though the room was cold. Her lips moved. I leant closer but could glean no sound from her mouthing. Without meaning to I caught a glimpse of her companion's strained and bloody face beyond, her arm hanging down to the floor.

'Mathilda must have seen what happened,' I said. 'The shock has sent her mute.'

'Or it's guilt that keeps her silent.'

Anna grabbed Mathilda by her fleshy forearm and hauled her to her feet. The paper in the girl's lap slid to the floor but she still drew the shape in the air before her, as if the paper was there to press on. Her gaze remained fixed on the fire.

'Did you kill Gertrud?' Anna said, and shook her.

Mathilda moved soft and wobbly, as if her bones had left her. Anna let her go and she remained as she was, standing, looking into the fire, her lips twitching silent words. I put a hand on each of her shoulders and gently pushed her back into her chair.

'You'll get no sense out of her tonight,' I said. 'We need brandy, for the shock.'

'Don't go looking, Shilly. That's the last thing we need.'

'So what *do* we need?'

'A coroner, to establish cause of death, and then the magistrates will—'

Mathilda screamed.

I thought my heart had stopped, that I'd be a second corpse on Anna's hands.

'No, no, no,' Mathilda said, looking at us at last. 'No more spying.'

'It's not spying. It's the law.' Anna stood squarely in front of her. 'We must let the magistrates know there's been a death. An inquest will follow.'

'No!' Mathilda said, her voice hoarse. 'No strangers. Gertrud, she will not like it.'

'Gertrud won't know anything about that,' I said gently. 'She's gone. You don't have to worry about her now.'

'No strangers. The shame of it – it follow her. She could not bear it. No shame, no shame, Mathilda.'

'Perhaps,' Anna said, moving closer to Miss Franks' body, 'you wish to hide your own part in this, Mathilda. Save yourself from the gallows.'

'No one must know,' Mathilda murmured. 'No one must know.'

Anna's candle sent shadows across the dead woman's face, making her look like some giant fish left for gutting on Richard Bray's table.

'You wish to hide your crime?' Anna said. 'To hide how you killed her?'

Mathilda shook her head, which set free a small sob. 'The crime? Is two. Both hidden. In her now, too. Is hidden.'

'But the dead can speak,' Anna said. 'What secrets will Miss Franks spill once we've sent for the coroner?'

'She say no more. Her throat. It stopped. Stop stop, yes? Like a bottle.'

'Stoppered?' I said. 'What do you mean?'

'Look. See.'

Anna hesitated. She'd been so cocksure, goading Mathilda, but now she looked uncertain. In the end her curiosity decided her.

'Take my candle, Shilly.' She glanced once more at Mathilda as if checking for tricks, then peered into Miss Franks' mouth. 'The tongue is swollen, as I would expect. Some blood. Her teeth gnashing at the end. There's nothing—wait. What on earth . . .'

'What is it?' I said, leaning closer. Hot wax slipped from the candle to the floor, just missing Anna's fingers as they opened Miss Franks' spitted lips.

'There's something down there,' Anna said, 'in her throat.'

She widened Miss Franks' mouth and reached into it, pushing her fingers down the dead woman's throat. I gagged.

Without looking up from her task, Anna said, 'Don't turn your back on her.'

But Mathilda had no interest in what we were about. She was drawing again, even though she held no paper. She was drawing on her skirt.

'I have it!' Anna said, and she began to pull.

Her fingers came clear with a horrid sucking sound, as if Miss Franks was herself letting them go. A thin pointed thing, white-ish, was leaving Miss Franks' mouth. Mathilda began to sob.

Anna kept pulling, had to lift her arm high for the thing was long. The pointed end gave way to something black, something thick.

'My God,' Anna murmured.

A foot long. Two. Three. And still it came, this thing that had been driven down Miss Franks' throat, that had stopped her breath.

At last the end of it came clear. Anna held it away from her, as if not wanting to risk touching it more than she had to. She laid it on the table, amid the broken trinkets. Sodden and stinking of bile, of death, a feather.

TWENTY-EIGHT

Mathilda had slipped back into silence. Neither Anna nor I could make her say how a three-foot-long feather had found its way down her companion's throat, nor how they'd both come by their injuries. We couldn't make her say anything at all.

'They haven't been attacked equally,' Anna said, peering closely at Miss Franks' torn face. 'These wounds are far more severe than Mathilda's scratches.'

'But the same thing did them.'

'Possibly.'

'So Mathilda is a victim as much as Miss Franks,' I said.

Mathilda was once more staring into the fire without seeing. Her eyes were glazed. She swayed, even though she was seated. Her bloodied hand still drew the same strange shape.

'You might be right,' Anna said. 'She'd hardly have scratched her own hands. But until we know more . . .'

She limped into the next room, where the bed was, and returned with a large shawl of fine blue cloth, then she took up her knife and ripped the shawl in half.

'What are you doing?' I said.

'Tie her hands.'

'What?'

'It's too dark to go back out there now. Even if we managed not to fall in the river, we'd likely break our necks on tree roots.'

I saw that the windowpanes were indeed black. No curtains to hide us from those who might be spying still. With the candles lit we were easy to see from out there. As Miss Franks and Mathilda had been every night.

'So we're staying,' Anna said, 'and that being the case, I'd rather have one less thing to worry about. Tie her hands.'

'Anna, please. She's suffered enough. Look at the state she's in!'

'Something strange has happened here tonight, Shilly. I wouldn't say I understand it, and I daresay you won't, either. Until we know more, *please* tie this woman's hands. No conjuring knots, mind.'

Her voice betrayed her. She was afraid. I was none too strong-hearted myself, so I did as she asked, trying not to touch Mathilda's wounds as I did so. Even so, the silk was soon dark with her blood.

'We'll put her in the bedroom,' Anna said.

I wasn't sure we could lift Mathilda, even with the two of us, but when I pulled on the girl's arm she stood willingly, and let herself be guided to her bed. She lay down when Anna told her to. She has gone soft, I said to myself. A child-woman, her mind weakened by the shock. Oh for a drink for us all!

Anna still felt there to be threat even in such a mute, meek girl, and so she tied Mathilda's feet together with the other half of the ripped shawl. Then, for good measure she tied Mathilda's feet to the bedpost.

'Leave the door open,' Anna said. 'If she should somehow get free then I'd rather see her coming.'

As I turned to go I looked again at the poor figure on the bed. Her eyes were open but her lips were tightly closed. Her fingers were twitching. Trying, still, to draw.

In the main room was another poor soul, this one beyond pity. But still I felt it, for what a terrible way to die.

'Miss Franks might not have been talking to the Devil,' I said, 'but others could have been.'

'You believe the culprit to be of . . . otherworldly origins?' Anna said.

'You don't? What's your reasoning then, how it was done?'

She perched on the upturned box Miss Franks had sat on when we first visited, and I took Mathilda's chair. The wood still held the girl's warmth. Anna and I both looked at Miss Franks, as if we were paying her a call. Guests of a dead woman. She eyed us just as sourly as before.

Anna cleared her throat and turned so that she couldn't see Miss Franks.

'I do not believe the bird to whom that feather belongs is from the woods of Trethevy—'

'So you *do* think it's done by the Devil!'

'If you'd let me finish. I was going to say that the bird might be from further afield – *much* further. Collectors have access to specimens that you and I could only dream of, Shilly, exotic wildlife discovered far from these shores, shot and stuffed for posterity. Someone could have used the feather of such a thing to kill Miss Franks, safe in the knowledge it would be difficult to identify the weapon.'

'But that would cost money, wouldn't it? Having one of them foreign birds?'

'Undoubtedly,' Anna said.

'Well, I know who has money in *this* part of the world.'

'Your thoughts lead you to the squire again, Shilly.'

'They do, but . . .'

'But what?'

'I don't think a human hand ripped Miss Franks' face to rags, do you?' I said. 'That's a claw done that. Talons.'

'Using another part of the same stuffed creature?' Anna said. 'It's possible, I suppose. But putting to one side for a moment the means, let's consider motive. If both women were attacked by the same individual, why not kill Mathilda too?'

'Because it was only Miss Franks they wanted? And Mathilda's wounds, she got them fighting whatever it was. Trying to save her friend.'

We both looked at Miss Franks again. Anna shivered. I found a fire iron amongst the papers on the floor and stirred up the embers.

'The fire needs more wood,' I said. 'I could go out—'

'There's plenty to be burnt here.'

Anna snatched up sheets of paper, scrunched them and threw them into the hearth. Mathilda's drawings, but I didn't stop Anna burning them. I didn't want to go outside any more than she wanted me to go, and Mathilda now seemed beyond such fine work as was lying all around us. I looked at a few of her sketches before feeding them to the growing flames – the harbour walls at Boscastle. The springy green of the cliffs that looked over them. And then something else. The black lines she'd been drawing when we arrived.

'This shape Mathilda kept doing,' I said. 'What do you make of it?'

Anna took the page I held out to her. 'Not much. A boat?' She threw it into the fire before I could stop her.

'I don't think that's what it is.'

'Mathilda went on about them, didn't she? "Fish boats", she called them.'

'Yes,' I said, 'but . . . I don't know. They make me think of something else, but I can't catch on it.'

'You're likely right about the shock. The compulsion to produce that pattern – it's a symptom.'

I decided to put the shape in my pockets – my two pockets. I folded up one of Mathilda's drawings and put it in a pocket in my dress for things that could be touched. But I put it in a second pocket too, and that was a pocket in my head, for wonderings. Wonderings might be just as helpful as things that could be touched. I still had in this pocket of wonderings the fact that people in Trethevy weren't well – Lucy at the manor house, the poxed baby.

'I'm sure they must be connected,' Anna was saying.

A spark crackled from the flames and landed on Miss Franks' knee. Before I thought about what I was doing, I was patting it out. Her stiffening body wobbled, her torn face jounced, the blood and flesh glistening in the candlelight. I moved my chair away from her.

'Who is connected?' I said.

'Not "who" but "what", Shilly. The disappearance of Paul Haskell and the death of Miss Franks.'

'But Peter almost disappeared this afternoon as well, and if Miss Franks was here in the cottage at that moment, and Mathilda too, it can't have been either of them who tried to take him, and who might've taken Paul as well.'

'So where does that leave us? Back with the feather?'

I went over to it, glad to have a reason not to look at Miss Franks any longer, and picked up the weapon that had likely ended her life. It was dryer now than when Anna had first pulled it from the wetness of Miss Franks' throat, and so had fluffed out, as Anna fluffed her cropped yellow hair when she took off her wigs. The feather was three inches at its widest part, tapering to an inch at the tip. Apart from the touch of white at the bottom, where the sharp nib was, the feather was deep black.

'A connection,' I said, 'between the boys being taken and Miss Franks' death. I think I have one.'

'What is it?'

The fire crackled. Beyond the window, the sound of ferns and leaves moving as some animal stole past.

I held up the feather. 'The magpie tree.'

TWENTY-NINE

We left the cottage at first light, and mizzle was in the air. Anna eyed the scrap of dark cloud above the cottage, the only part of the sky the trees couldn't hide.

'If the rain worsens, then any evidence at the magpie tree might be lost,' she said.

'Then we must hurry.'

I handed her the stick she'd used the day before, and we set off.

Anna had refused to untie Mathilda before we left, and all I could do was tip a drop of water into the girl's mouth. She'd said nothing since telling us Miss Franks' throat was stoppered. Miss Franks herself I had covered with an old coat I found on the scullery floor. It was stiff with mud, and she wouldn't have liked it being anywhere near her, but I couldn't leave her looking out at the world with that one remaining eye. The blood on her face had darkened to near black.

'So do you believe in him now?' I asked Anna as we made our way to the river.

'In who?'

'St Nectan.'

Her foot was better able to bear weight than the day before so she hopped swiftly through the ferns and the fallen branches and all the traps the woods set for us.

'I believe there's a dead woman in the cottage we've just left,' Anna said, 'that yesterday you witnessed an attempted abduction, and another child remains missing. Each of these events were preceded by a bell ringing, which all and sundry in these parts attribute to a long-dead saint. Who might never have existed in the first place. Who very likely didn't.'

'But the bell did act as warning. It rang as Peter was being taken.'

'Shilly, I've already told you what the quarry captain said. It's a coincidence the blasting bell rang just as the figure tried to take Peter, and an unfortunate one at that. The superstition will only gain more credence.'

'But have you heard any blasting since we came to the woods?' I asked her. 'There wasn't any yesterday, after the bell had rung.'

'I doubt we'd have heard it near the summer house. The trees grow so close together, they would muffle the noise.'

'They're not so thick as all that,' I muttered.

'Are you an expert on blasting, Shilly? And the science of how sound travels?'

I didn't know what 'expert' was so I suspected I wasn't, and so I gave no answer to her peevishness.

'And besides,' she said, 'just because the alarm is sounded doesn't mean the charge will go off. Not everything goes to plan.'

We had come to the crossing stones and I lent her my arm, even though she was being teasy and I had little patience for it. There had been no blasting because the bell wasn't rung by the quarry. It was rung by the saint. I knew it, I knew it deep as the marrow of my bones.

I led the rest of the way, and when we began the climb up to the summer house I reached behind me to haul Anna when she needed help. The mizzle had made the going wet, and my boots slipped often as they sought purchase. At last we reached the top, where the ground flattened out again. We were muddy and panting. There was the summer house, our home, of sorts, looking out over the waterfall, and beyond it a little way, standing alone in the clearing, the magpie tree. One bird watched us from the branches.

'The magpies in these woods are certainly unnatural,' Anna said. 'But I haven't seen any with feathers three feet long and three inches wide. We've yet to find that bird.'

'There,' I said, and pointed to the summer house, the side furthest from the door. 'That's where I last saw the figure trying to take Peter.'

'Then that's where we'll start.'

We found marks where the ground was soft, six feet or so from the summer house. The print of a shoe, or the toe of it, at least, and next to it were others, those of a little boot, much clearer to see for it had scored the ground. Peter had struggled.

'From what you saw of the figure yesterday,' Anna said, 'have you any sense if it was male or female?'

'None,' I said. 'The cloak covered them. I saw only the face and that was . . . not as it should have been.'

'What of build, then?'

'Not tall.'

'That's it?' Anna said. 'You're no more use than Peter Haskell, and at least he had the excuse of taking a blow to the head.'

'It all happened so quickly!' I said.

Even to myself, this reason sounded poor. Anna would think my not knowing much was drink. I resolved to keep her thoughts on other things.

'Here's another part of a print, look,' I said.

This one was further from the summer house, towards the trees on the other side of the clearing.

'From the same shoe, I think, but see how it's turned the other way.' I hitched up my skirts to squat beside it. 'Not enough of a mark to know the size, though.'

'But what it does indicate,' Anna said, 'is that the wearer came to the clearing and left it again by the same means.'

I looked at the way the shoe prints were angled, and saw that there was a faint path that crossed the clearing, running from the summer house, past the magpie tree and into the woods. Anna and I walked it as far as the treeline.

'Where does this path go?' I said.

Anna squinted into the murk. 'The road. That's how the carrier brought my travelling case from Jamaica Inn. It takes longer than the way we've been going, down past the waterfall, but it's not so steep.'

I stood. 'If it leads to the road then it leads to the manor house, too.'

'And I'd hazard a guess that the squire visits the summer house by this route. I can't imagine he and Lady Phoebe climb up the path.'

'That's more suspicion on him, then, if whoever tried to take Peter came by this path from the manor house. And I'm certain it was the squire visiting Miss Franks and Mathilda in Boscastle. We still don't know why he went to see them.'

'Or if he did at all. Miss Franks didn't confirm it before throwing us out of the cottage, remember.'

'She's not likely to tell us any more now,' I said, unable to keep the gloom from my voice.

'What's that there?' Anna said. She went a few steps into the trees. Caught on a fern's soft coil was a scrag of white. She pulled it free and twisted it between her fingers. 'Silk.'

'From a dress?' I said.

'Or a shawl. Or a cravat. It's too little to be sure.' She tucked it into her pocket. 'But I wonder.'

I heard the tapping of her tongue against her teeth.

'You said the figure you saw was one of those things without eyes.'

'Yes,' I said, with great certainty for Anna was about to nonsense me again. I could see it coming clear as the rain.

'Well, I fancy this was how it was done. A stocking – a fine one, stretched across the face. The wearer's features would be hidden, including their eyes, but they would still be able to see.'

'So you don't believe me, then, about the blinded creatures?'

'I believe there are ways to achieve such an effect, Shilly. Ways of *this* world.'

'Yes, but—'

'You still think they're here, in these woods – the sisters who drowned Saint Nectan, who buried him beneath the river?'

I didn't need to look about me. I could feel, still, the hatred that stirred the trees, that made the very ground they grew from change its being.

'It's like an echo,' I said, and Anna frowned. 'You know, if you shout—'

'I know what an echo is, Shilly. What I *don't* know is why that sound phenomenon is relevant.'

'The sisters might not be here proper, flesh and blood as we are, as Miss Franks and Mathilda are. Or Miss Franks was. It's the hate that has come back, found bodies to carry it. To repeat their old work.'

'To grab children?'

'That I don't know.'

'Well, until such time as you *do* know the physical capabilities of these spirits, I suggest we concentrate on what we can see. Here. Now.'

'All right. I can see that magpie in the saint's tree.'

'And?'

'It was here yesterday, too.' I went over to the tree and Anna followed. 'There was a great gaggle of them at first, but when the cloaked figure had gone, when it was over, there was only one bird. And it was looking at the summer house. I wonder—'

'Well, it's got its eye on you now, Shilly.'

She was right. The bird hopped from foot to foot, threw its head from side to side. If it had been a person I would have said it was having fits. The blue-green of its tail flicked up and down. The orange

203

of its beak poked the air. I drew closer to the tree. My foot clunked something tucked between the roots. Before I could stop her, Anna was bending down.

'Ah! The figure left something else behind. I—wait.' Her hand closed on the bottle.

She held it out to me. A third left, sloshing brown and joyful wet. My knees went soft and I put my hand on the tree's damp trunk to keep myself steady. To keep myself from snatching the bottle and running into the trees.

'If it wasn't for Peter's testimony,' Anna said, holding the bottle by the neck and letting it swing this way and that, 'I might doubt there had even *been* a figure in a cloak, but all that nonsense about the rope blowing it away – you were insensible, admit it!'

'Anna, you don't understand. Without it I can't see such things, and they need to be seen, to know what's happening here.'

'I don't think you want to be without it, to get better.'

She smashed the bottle against the tree. The magpie shrieked and took to the air. The spirit stained the trunk, was trickling into the grass. So few drops. Not enough to be worth a quarrel.

'If I make you so angry, Anna, why don't you do without me? Go back to solving crimes by yourself, try to join the detective men when they don't want you.'

Her thin face had reddened with fury. The bottle's neck, broken off, was still in her hand. It shook in time with her panting breath. She could cut my throat if she wished.

'I have the answer for you, Anna. You don't turn me loose because you need me. And oh, the reasons.' I ran my fingers across the sticky, dripping tree trunk and then sucked them. Loudly.

As best her limp allowed her, she marched over to the summer house steps, climbed them, then leant over the shelf and threw the broken bottleneck into the river. It made no sound over the roar of the waterfall. She waited a moment to turn round, smoothing the stray hairs of her wig that were almost shining with the thin rain's gleam. This was to calm herself. She hated to give in to anger, I knew. To give in to her feelings for me.

A burst of black and white. The fat magpie was back, this time on the roof.

'To get back to the matter at hand,' Anna said. 'The cloaked figure surprised Peter while he was trying the summer house door.' She put her hand to it and pressed gently, as if to test it somehow.

The bird began to jump up and down, making the roof creak something terrible. Anna was speaking but I wasn't listening. I couldn't stop watching the magpie, because it was watching me, waggling its head and opening its wings and—

Coming for me.

I ducked, but not low enough. The talons grazed my scalp. I wheeled round, couldn't see where it had gone for my wig had fallen in front of my eyes and I was reeling as if I'd licked all the spirits from the tree. Would that I had.

A hand under my arm, Anna beside me, and I was steady. I pawed the hair from my face and saw that the bird was hovering in the air, not five feet from us, meeting our gaze.

'Whatever do you suppose . . .' Anna murmured.

Another magpie joined it, and another. Three of them, then more. Far more than I could count. They whirled in from the trees on all sides of the clearing, streaming across the river. All manner of birds, a blur of beating wings, of cries. I didn't dare move in case they should come at us. Who knew what drew them in such numbers? Who knew their desires? The air hummed with their held flight, beating the mizzle into our eyes.

Then they were leaving, flying away from us. But not far.

'The summer house,' I shouted over the noise. 'Look – they're trying to get in!'

But the foolish beasts hadn't chosen the weak point of the door. The birds were throwing themselves at the opposite side. One after another the birds flew straight into the slats just above where they met the stony outcrop on which the summer house was built. Flew into the *same* spot, fighting each other for their turn. The sound of their bodies hitting the wood was a dull crump, and most then fell to the ground where a heap of dead birds was building. Those who weren't killed outright, just stunned, flew again until they were broken in the attempt.

'Something has sent them mad,' Anna said.

'They're not mad – they're showing us.'

I picked my way between the bodies scattered across the clearing, some of them twitching. There were few left living now, but those that were still hurled themselves at the same spot on the summer house. A patch of the white wood was stained with blood, a rough circle, the edges of which ran into spatters. Two of the boards were splintered, thanks to the birds' efforts. I had to push aside the heap of bodies to get close. They were so soft I thought I'd be sick with the horror of touching their breasts, their wings. The breaking of their little bones as I knelt in the ruin of them. There were too many, sliding in my hands now the rain fell heavier, fell cold dripping down the back of my collar.

'Help me, Anna!'

She dropped to her knees beside me, in that pit of death, and for a moment could do nothing but gasp and then sob.

'I don't . . . Why . . . ?'

'These boards – help me get them out. Give me your knife.'

I slashed at the splinters while she used her walking stick to ram the broken boards. Cooler air blew from within, and the rain was falling heavier and heavier. I could hear its dripping loud in my ears. The last bit of broken board fell inwards and then I knew that the dripping wasn't the rain. I'd heard it before, on the edge of sleep in the summer house. Peter Haskell had heard it too. Now it was Anna's turn.

'A spring? Feeding the river?'

I bent myself small and stepped sideways through the hole we'd made, having to crouch for the roof was low. I was in a cave, the floor of the summer house above, I guessed. And before me was something I had seen before. The little pool set in the ground, ringed with moor stones and moss. I had seen the saint drowned here.

'It's a well,' I said. 'A holy well.'

Anna climbed in beside me and we were pressed together in that cramped space. I could barely turn my head to look about me. I took a few steps into the darkness of the cave but then my foot met something. Something soft. For a moment I thought it was another bird. A big one – a hawk. I reached down and found, not feathers, but cloth. Hair. Flesh.

It was Paul Haskell, lying face down in the water of the holy well.

THIRTY

We carried him out and laid him on the ground, away from the birds' bodies. His poor hands were bound. His sandy hair was dark with water and his cheeks were blue. We were too late.

'Wait, wait.' Anna was patting him as if trying to wake him from sleep. 'He's cold but . . . I don't understand. No discolouration.' She bent her ear to his mouth.

My own breath stopped. The likeness between the boys was so great, it was as if Peter lay before me. I wondered if it *was* Peter. If the blinded figure had come back in the night and taken the boy from his bed. Yesterday had come again and Paul was still missing.

Anna crowed. 'He's alive! Help me sit him up.'

His little body was chilled to the touch, his face and the top of his chest soaked from being in the well water. At his temple was a bruise, large as a shilling and dark as a sloe. He *looked* dead, but I could see now that his chest was lifting and falling. Slowly. Too slowly.

I ran to the summer house and fetched whatever clothing was nearest the door. It was only when I'd wrapped Paul in it that I saw it was Mrs Williams's best travelling coat. Anna was tapping the boy's cheeks, calling on him to wake.

He took a deeper breath, something more like a sob, and I gave a cheer.

Anna got hold of her walking stick again. 'We need to get him back to his family, Shilly, and in front of a fire, quick as we can. With my foot like this—'

'I'll carry him.'

'He's a dead weight, the state he's in. We should go upstream, see if we can find David Tonkin.'

She was shilly-shallying, her fingers fluttering near her lips.

'There's no time,' I said. 'I can do it. Have some faith in me for once, Anna Drake.'

I hefted the boy, and with Anna's help tipped him over my shoulder. She wasn't wrong about the weight of him, but my blood was coursing, my lungs were singing. We had found him, alive. The Haskells could stop their weeping.

I started to walk, carrying my burden, and after a few teetering steps, green as a new lamb, I was steady. Slow, but safe. Anna darted back to the hole in the boards.

'Go on, Shilly. I'll catch you up. I need to see . . .'

I heard no more. I was taking Paul Haskell home.

I carried him as far as the first of the cottages. There we were seen and people came running. He was taken from me. I fell to the ground without him, shaking from the labour, from the relief. Anna was with me when I slipped into darkness.

They brought me round with what was good for me, best for me. Gin. I sputtered fire and lurched into Anna's arms, and then the magpies were before me again, swooping low, their wings outstretched, coming for me. I cried out and covered my eyes.

'There now,' a voice said.

I forced myself to open my eyes. Mrs Haskell was offering me the cup again. Her dark shawl was as tightly wrapped around her as ever. Its cloth against my arm was coarse, but her voice held nothing but kindness.

'You're all right now, my bird.'

I grabbed the cup to tip down my throat all it held, but Anna took it from me.

'That's plenty for her, Mrs Haskell.'

The old woman patted my hand then moved away, chirping to the three girls clustered by the window.

Aches rang through my arms, my shoulders. I looked about me for the birds lying in wait. They might steal down the chimney. They might burst through the floorboards. The boards splintering. The water dripping. The child with his face in the well water.

'Paul. Is he—?'

'He'll be right enough soon,' Mrs Haskell said. 'We've warmed him, fed him. Bit of rest in his own bed and he'll be out trapping rabbits soon as you like.'

She stroked the littlest girl's hair, Esther's, but she was looking at me. I spoke to myself sternly. I was inside, beneath a roof. There were no birds to peer at me, to fly low with their talons out. There was glass in the window and slate on the roof. There was Anna beside me.

'That's twice in two days you've saved my grandsons, Mrs Williams. Whatever it was that brought you here, it has been well for us. For the woods.'

'Luck, merely,' Anna murmured, but without much heart. 'Our sketching holiday has held some . . . surprises.'

Mrs Haskell smiled and pulled her shawl tighter around her neck. 'Fair enough, Miss Drake. Not everything needs an answer.'

Answers . . . We had precious few of those. I thought of the ruined mill she'd said had burnt her, where there had been no fire. Of the thieving, and the coal left behind. Of poxed babies and scullery girls itching. Of women, without eyes, stealing children. Of Miss Franks, blinded, scratched and smothered. Of Mathilda drawing – that shape, over and over. I couldn't fathom what it was, though some cobwebbed bit of my thinking knew it. If I could only get hold of it. And still to discover – who was it that took Paul Haskell, that tried to take Peter?

Boards creaked overhead. The magpies jouncing. Mrs Haskell caught me looking up at the sound.

'His mother and father are with him, and his brother too. Couldn't keep Peter out! To see them side by side again, my nestle-birds.' Her hand on Esther's hair shook.

The girl ducked from her grandmother's touch. 'Can we go out now?'

'No, my sweet. We must all be here together, for your brother.'

Jenna, the eldest, kicked her heels against the wall. The room felt very crowded, and with the rain on the window I almost felt as if I was cramped back beneath the summer house and the holy well dripping. I reached for the gin bottle but Anna set it on the window ledge. The middle sister looked at me as if I was a worm or some-such that she had scraped from the bottom of her boot.

'Has he said how he came to be below the summer house?' I asked.

'Not yet,' Anna said, 'and he might not speak for some time. He had water but no food, not for days. He's very weak.'

There was the sound of a door opening above, then feet coming down the stairs. Anna got up to let Maria Haskell sit down, but Maria waved away the offer. She and James squeezed themselves next to the fireplace. They looked spent by the force of relief. They were stronger than they had been, now the boy was back, but that couldn't undo the strain.

'Peter still with him?' Mrs Haskell asked.

'Won't leave Paul's side,' Maria said. 'Couldn't bring myself to part them.'

'How is Paul?' I asked.

'He's awake, and he knows where he is,' James said. Maria put her arm around her husband's shoulder and he leant his head against hers. 'That's enough for us for now.'

'I'm afraid I must ask you,' Anna said, 'has Paul spoken of what happened? It's possible that whoever did this to him is still at large. Others might be at risk.'

'You've no cause to worry there,' Mrs Haskell said.

'Why?'

'The furriners,' Mrs Haskell said. 'Sarah was over there, saw the older one dead in her chair.'

'Spying still?' I said.

'Keeping watch. That pair weren't to be trusted. We're all better off now. The other one will leave, if she knows what's good for her, and then we'll be without worry. It was them that hid Paul, left him to die.'

'Is that what Paul said?' I asked.

James and Maria glanced at one another, then Maria said, 'He don't remember, but that don't mean it weren't the furrin pair.'

'What *does* he remember?' Anna said.

'He was setting his snare by the old gatepost, near their cottage. Something hit him. He came to in the dark, hearing water.'

'Beneath the summer house,' I said. 'So he remembers nothing between those places?'

Maria shook her head. 'A voice told Paul to go back to sleep, to wait. Said *he* would keep my boy safe.'

'He?' Anna said.

'Saint Nectan,' I said.

'Paul didn't see him,' Maria said, 'but he knows the saint was there.'

'And the saint has done what he promised, hasn't he?' James said. 'All that time Paul was locked in there and yet he lives. Nectan protects us from those who come to do us harm.'

'Forgive me, Mr Haskell,' Anna said, which I knew to be a sign she was going to say something these people would find rude, 'but how can Paul be sure it was the saint speaking to him?'

'Because this was in his pocket.'

We all turned to where the voice had come from. Peter was on the stairs. How long he'd been there, I didn't know. He came down, into the room, and held out his hand to Anna. She hesitated, then took what he was offering – some tiny, shining thing, so small it was almost lost between her fingers. The girls crowded round her, catching hold of her hand and trying to look at what it held.

'What is it?' their grandmother asked.

Tamsin, the middle girl, turned and grinned. 'A bell. Smaller than a thimble.'

Her elder sister snatched it from Anna and there was a faint ring, as if a church was calling its flock from fields away. We all heard it.

Anna, caught in the nest of children, looked like she might not be able to keep her scorn silent much longer. I said we would leave the Haskells to themselves. James saw us to the door.

Anna spoke to him in a low voice. 'If Paul should remember anything more about how he came to be under the summer house—'

'You heard Mother,' he said. 'The witch is dead. Throw her over the waterfall and let the sea have her.' He was smiling as he shut the door.

THIRTY-ONE

We found ourselves in the rain. Proper rain now. The kind that surprised the dry summer earth and turned it swiftly to mud. I caught sight of Jenna's face at the window and moved away from the shelter of the cottage walls, back under the trees and for once I was glad of their thickety ways. Anna followed me, slowly. Her thoughts were far from her feet.

Over the sound of rain dripping from the branches I heard the tap tap of Anna's tongue against her false teeth and knew that I should help her in her thinking.

'The bell in Paul's pocket—'

'Signifies nothing, Shilly. A trinket the boy found before he ended up in the summer house. He could have stolen it from Miss Franks and Mathilda.'

'Oh yes? And how do you explain the voice that told the boy he'd keep him safe?'

'A delusion brought on by the blow to the head. You saw the bruise. Whoever took Paul made sure he was insensible.'

'But they didn't kill him,' I said. 'They just left him in the summer house and then the saint kept him alive.'

'The *water* kept him alive. It's remarkable how long the body can go without food if water is in supply.'

'And if your head is stuck in it? Paul was *face down* in the well water, Anna. Drowned, and yet he lives. His face has no swelling. His flesh is firm. If not the saint's doing, how do you explain it?'

'Easily enough. Paul half-woke from thirst, moments before we found him, and drank from the well. While doing so he passed out again and fell into the water. It was him moving that alerted the birds.'

'And the reason for the birds doing as they did? Killing themselves like that to show us where Paul was? The birds who keep near the *saint's* tree?'

'Perhaps there is some poison in the tree, something that affects the birds' natural instincts to survive. Perhaps . . .'

I let her run out of certainty. I had learnt that was the best way. On the moor, in the woods, wherever we were in Cornwall, there were things she couldn't make sense of. Things she needed me for. She just didn't like to admit it.

'If the saint did ring the bell to warn of danger, if he kept Paul Haskell safe, if his birds were his way of showing us where the boy was hidden, then the sisters might be here too. The ones who buried the saint beneath the river. Who drowned him first.'

'Not this again, Shilly!' She stepped away from me, liking to be out in the rain rather than close to someone who countered her. 'Miss Franks and Mathilda are as sighted as you and me.' She saw my pained look, and added hastily, 'Yes all right. Miss Franks has been blinded in one eye, but they both *have* eyes. What you saw that first night we were here, the two women drowning the old man . . . It was just a dream. A nightmare.'

'You can believe that if you want, Anna. I believe different.'

'That they're back – the sisters who drowned the saint? On a sketching holiday, are they? Difficult when you can't see what you're meant to be drawing.'

216

'The woods aren't at peace,' I said. 'You've admitted you feel it. What if – and I'm not saying I know for sure.'

'Well that makes a refreshing change.'

'What if the woods have brought back the blinded women? Brought them back from the dead. Set them wandering here and causing pain.'

She laughed. 'I think you've been lying to me, Shilly.'

'What?'

'I think you can read, and you *have* been reading. The work of the poets. That's where these fanciful notions come from. Ghosts of the long-dead attendants of a saint. I ask you!'

'I . . .' Now it was my turn to run out of certainty.

Anna took her chance and was back to known things. 'There are two real women who need our attention. Miss Franks' body is still in the cottage.'

'And Mathilda is tied to the bedpost.'

'We must inform the authorities of the death. Fortunately, there's a magistrate within walking distance.'

She set out but I grabbed her back.

'You surely don't mean going to see the squire?'

'Of course I do,' she said. 'He'll want to know that Paul has been found, too.'

'But we still don't know why the squire went to see Miss Franks and Mathilda in Boscastle.'

'You mean, Shilly, that we still don't know if he even *did* go and see them.'

'Why does he want rid of them so badly, then? We can't trust him!'

Anna unshackled herself from me. 'You must think practically for once, forget these ill-founded fears. Even if we went further afield to report Miss Franks' death, to Boscastle, say, Squire Orton would still become involved because of his proximity to the place where she died. It's likely to be in his jurisdiction.'

'You're thinking about the reward, aren't you? Admit it, Anna! We've

217

found Paul so now we can go and collect. Except there's a problem, isn't there? One of the people the squire was so certain was guilty, it's them who's dead.'

'I am *not* thinking of the reward. I'm thinking of the stench of a body kept too long from the grave. One of us must be mindful of practical considerations, or would you rather do as James Haskell suggested, tip Miss Franks over the waterfall?'

'Of course not, it's just . . . I'm afraid, Anna.'

'Well, try and think of this as an opportunity to ease your fears. In reporting the death, we have a legitimate reason for calling on the squire. We can use this to ascertain what he knew of Miss Franks and Mathilda.'

'And if we should find out something bad, some reason for him wanting them dead, what then? To say a magistrate is guilty of a crime – who would believe us?'

Anna looked at me as if I was talking of the blinded sisters again, or some other thing she thought a kind of madness. 'Why, the law would believe us, Shilly.'

'Constables? They wouldn't help us, from what I know of them, and neither would other magistrates. They don't know what truth is.'

'*We* will know the truth when we find it. At the very least we can tell the squire that Paul is safe. What the squire tells us . . . Well. We shall see what happens.'

We set off.

Now that Paul was safely home, I had time to think about the way we'd found him. The birds wrecking themselves – that I was sure was the saint's doing, for all Anna's talk of poisons. But if she wouldn't – couldn't – make sense of that yet, then it was better to talk of firm, touchable things. Things like boards and nails.

'When you went back to the summer house,' I said, 'you were checking the boards that the birds broke through, weren't you?'

'I was.'

'Why?'

'Because there's no access to the cave, the cellar, whatever you want to call it, from the summer house's upper floor – our floor. Whoever took Paul had to have another means of getting in there.'

'And did you find it?' I said.

'I think so. Between the birds' efforts and our own we'd done a good job of ruining the boards, but I found a piece of wood that looked to have some kind of catch fitted. As best I could tell it was fitted on the underside – the side that faced the well. Nothing would be visible from the outside but if the board was pressed in just the right place, the catch would release and the board would pop free.'

'That's why his hands were bound,' I said, 'to stop him pushing out the boards himself. But he had his voice. I heard the water from the floor above. I would have heard him too if he'd shouted.'

'It is strange to put him in a place that risked discovery. It suggests that whoever took the boy might not have worried about him being found. It was the taking that mattered.'

'To cause pain to the Haskells?' I said.

'It was only their boys taken. A personal grievance?' Anna pulled her sleeve free of a bramble.

'The others, they only had belongings stolen – Richard Bray's spoon, Sarah's mirror.'

'Things of no importance.'

'Important to the people who own them, Anna. If you haven't much then—'

'What you do have is worth more. I understand that. You may not think it, but I do.'

We'd come to the small break in the trees that gave a glimpse of the quarry and the great open heart of it took my words from me. There we stopped and looked across the pit to the other side where a pony and cart stood waiting in the rain. The wheel atop the wooden struts, the poppet head, was still, was silent. No blocks hauled out today, and

I shared the quarry's quiet. The rushing I'd felt since we'd first come to Trethevy, the hurrying to find Paul while there was still a chance to save him, this had left me. In its place I felt the weight of my own bones.

I turned to go, then grabbed Anna.

'What is it?' she said.

'*Shh.* Look.'

Someone was coming through the trees. Softly. Not crashing through as we so often did. Someone who knew how to slip by. They were coming from the direction of the road, and making for the manor house, just as we were.

We stepped back, using the ferns to hide. He didn't see us. Crossed our path ten paces ahead.

Simon Proctor. Him of the horses, him of the card-playing. His hands—I gasped.

They were bruised blue with dye.

THIRTY-TWO

'Considering a change of career, Mr Proctor?'

He spun round at Anna's words. His lean face was beset by lines he wasn't old enough to have. Stubble darkened his chin and patches of his cheeks. Some need was pulling him away. His thin body, clad in muddied working clothes, was all but leaning in the direction of the manor house.

'Forgive me, I—'

'I'd have thought seeing to horses would be better work than dyeing cloth for David Tonkin,' I said. 'Them dye smells'll have you coughing day and night, and it stains, doesn't it? Hard to get yourself clean.'

Slowly, as if to make it seem like a very ordinary thing, he tucked his bluish hands behind his back. This made him stand like a gentleman, but he wasn't that. I had seen men like him before. Men pinched by worry. Eaten out by it.

'You're confusing me with someone else, miss,' he said, his voice harder now. He wore no coat and his shirt was sticking to his flesh in the rain. There was a blue stain near the collar.

'Oh, I don't think so,' I said. 'Why don't you come and sit on this bit of moor stone here and we'll have a little talk.'

Anna smiled at him, water dripping from her wig. 'Unless you'd rather take shelter in the cottages? Richard Bray will be glad to hear the fate of his christening spoon, I'm sure.'

'I don't know what you're talking about.' He started walking away.

'I think Simon would like us to go with him to the manor house,' I said loudly.

'An excellent idea, Shilly. We can tell the squire he has a magpie in his midst.'

Simon's shoulders slumped. Without turning round, he said, 'If it's money you want, I've nothing. Nothing but the shirt on my back and that mightn't be with me much longer.'

'We only want the truth,' Anna said. 'That shouldn't cost you anything. Come, sit.'

He did as she said, perching on a slab overlooking the quarry and looking very miserable and cold. Sold his coat for debts, I thought. I felt pity for him. I wasn't the only one in the woods with a weakness.

'You stole from Miss Franks and Miss Wolffs, didn't you?' Anna said. 'And from the cottages this side of the river.'

'Tried to get taken on down there,' he said, nodding towards the quarry pit. 'Better pay, but I don't know how to work slate. You can't tell the squire about my . . . about this.' He looked at his blue palms as if they were hateful to him.

'You should burn your cards,' I said. 'I'll do it for you, if you like.'

'Cards?'

'Isn't that why you took to stealing?' Anna said. 'You've run up debts?'

He laughed, which was not what I thought such a poor man would do at that moment.

'If it was only that,' he said. 'You have a debt, you pay it. Problem goes away, long as you don't pick up the cards again. But when someone's ill and the doctor says you must *keep* paying . . .'

Anna took a step back. 'What's wrong with you?'

And in that moment I knew I'd been right to wonder about the smaller parts of the lives around us.

'It's not him that's ill,' I said. 'It's Lucy.'

'The scullery maid?' Anna said.

I sat next to Simon on the moor stone. The deep cold crept into my flesh. 'I'm right, aren't I? You're courting.'

'Known her all my life. Played together in the woods, the old mill. I been waiting years for her to . . . Well. It'd all come good at last, I thought.'

'But now she's ill.'

Simon was gazing at the quarry again. 'She don't want anyone to know. If the squire should learn of it he'll turn her out. It's the child coming. He's that worried about Lady Phoebe.' Simon scored the wet ground with the toe of his boot. A wide slash, with the rain's softening.

'If it's catching, then the squire has a right to be concerned,' Anna said.

'It's not catching. Not in that way.'

'What do you mean?' I said.

He hesitated.

'We could ask Lucy ourselves,' I said, standing. 'I'm sure she'd be delighted at that.'

'It's in the blood,' Simon said. 'You either have it or you don't. Her mother did, and she kept it secret. Lucy thought she'd been spared, getting to her age and none of the marks. But then she found one. They came fast after that.'

'Cattle worms?' I said, knowing the red rings from the farm and thinking of Lucy scratching.

Simon shook his head. 'She knew what it was, her mother having had it. The marks come first, before the tips break the skin. They're coming now, that's why she's had to go to bed. The pain of the tips pushing.'

'Tips?' Anna said.

He looked at us both in turn, took a deep breath. 'The tips of the feathers.'

We none of us said anything for a moment. Anna couldn't speak for disbelief, and I thought best to let her find her voice in her own time. She did find it, of course, as she always did when she was scornful.

'You're telling us, Mr Proctor, that Lucy, the scullery maid at the manor house, has *feathers* growing from her skin.'

'You can't tell the squire. Please!'

'Oh, I won't, you've no cause to worry on that score. I have no wish to appear as if I've lost my wits.'

'Feathers?' I said, making sure I looked him in the eye, gave him faith that I believed him.

'That's what she says, and she would know. Paining her something terrible and I've got to help her, I've got to.'

'And what does the doctor make of this?' Anna said.

'He believes her pain and he's offering the salve—'

'You mean he's a quack, taking your money to treat flea bites caused by that wretched cat.'

'Anna!'

'If I had to suffer Mrs Carne I might try a similar ploy to evade work, but there have been consequences to Lucy's games, Simon. Serious ones. You've been stealing to pay the quack, haven't you?'

Simon hung his head. 'I didn't have a choice.'

'That's questionable,' Anna said, 'and so is the fact you took advantage of the suspicion already held against Miss Franks and Miss Wolffs to hide your own guilt. You left the coal to put the blame on them.'

'What harm could it do if people thought it just more of their tricks?'

'A great deal of harm,' I said. 'One of them is dead. Murdered.'

Simon's eyes widened and I thought of Miss Franks' staring eye, and the other one raked to water.

'Murdered? By who?'

'That is still to be determined,' Anna said. 'We were on our way to inform the squire in his capacity as magistrate when you appeared, a marked man.' She nodded at his blue hands.

'That's what you were doing at the cottage on the day Paul went missing,' I said. 'Stealing.'

'They could spare it,' he said. 'Just like the squire and Lady Phoebe. She keeps to her bed all day in the east wing when there's nothing wrong with her, no one to disturb her, while others are scrubbing and hauling pots and fighting spoilt pets from dawn 'til dusk.'

'Were you lying about not knowing who took Paul?' Anna said.

'All I saw was the boy by the gatepost on my way to the cottage. He's been found – did you hear? They're saying the saint kept him alive.'

'Are they indeed?' Anna said.

'The saint's bell,' I said. 'It made you leave the cottage in a hurry.'

'I worried the pair would come back because of it, if they thought bad things were coming. When I passed the gatepost on my way to the river, Paul was gone. I thought he must have run home, that he was frightened by the bell. I never guessed it was him being taken that caused the bell to ring in the first place.'

'Did you drop drawing charcoal on the way back to the river?' I said.

This confused him. 'Why would I take their coal? Plenty at the manor house. Are you going to tell the squire?'

Anna was about to answer but I got there first.

'Have you sold them, the things you took?'

'The shoes are ruined, but everything else cleaned up all right. I took them to Boscastle first thing.'

'Well I don't see the use in the squire knowing,' I said. 'But if anything else should be taken—'

'But what can I do, tell me that?' He held his stained hands out to us, palms up, as if begging. 'I don't want to be taking from people not much better off than me.'

'There must be some other way to pay for the doctor,' I said. 'What of Lucy's family?'

'She hasn't any. That's why the squire took her in, after what happened down there.'

Anna and I looked where he was looking. The quarry.

'Lost her mother and father same day. Crushed.' Simon shivered and wrapped his arms around himself. 'She weren't allowed to see them after. They were . . .' He got to his feet and spat.

'What happened?' Anna said.

'She weren't more than ten and she had no one, all because that pitman didn't take the time to blast the rock smaller. He had it hauled up too big, too heavy for the poppet. Head tipped over, into the pit, the block coming down with it. Lucy's parents were caught. Didn't have a chance.'

Anna moved towards him. 'Who, Simon? Who wasn't paying attention that day?'

'I don't say it was his fault. There's accidents all the time with the slate and there's many vouched for him afterwards, said the poppet was too close to the edge, that it was the captain's fault. Squire's, even, as owner. But if that pitman had just waited. Not been so quick to send that block up top. Everything might have been different.'

'Who was the pitman?' Anna said.

He spat again.

'James Haskell.'

THIRTY-THREE

Simon had nothing more to tell us than his own bitterness and that had told us enough. We watched him weave through the trees, slipping in and out of sight and then he was gone. Back to the manor house with money in his pocket, but for how long?

'We've had the wrong idea since we got here, haven't we?' I said. 'Thinking the person who took Paul was also the thief. Simon did the thieving, but I don't believe he took Paul.'

Anna sat down next to me on the slab of moor stone.

'Neither do I,' she said. 'He has no motive. But Lucy does.'

'But Simon said she was still a child when her parents died. She must be seventeen now. Why wait all this time to punish the Haskells?'

'These delusions of illness could have spurred her on, but speculation is no help to anyone. We need to speak to the maid herself.'

She got up and began walking in the direction of the manor house, but I called for her to stop.

'Lucy can wait,' I said. 'There's someone we must see first.'

'Who?'

'Mrs Haskell.'

'Why on earth would we need to do that? I've spent more than enough time in that strange woman's company today already.'

'It's her strangeness that matters,' I said. 'You said before, to find who took Paul we need to learn about Miss Franks and Mathilda. That them coming to the woods and the boy vanishing were part of the same thing. Now one of them women is dead – murdered, by something feathered. I think . . . Anna, I think a change comes over women in these woods.'

Her face was all bewilderment. She'd knocked her wig loose so I straightened it for her, and touched her cheek while I was close enough to do so. She didn't move away. I didn't know if she even felt my touch, such was her uncertainty.

'You believe what Simon Proctor said, that Lucy is some kind of . . . bird?'

'I believe she will be,' I said. 'The baby of the red-haired woman will be, too, in time.'

'And Mrs Haskell?'

'She's already changed. Won't show her skin, will she?'

'Her lie about being caught in the mill fire is still unexplained,' Anna said. 'But a *bird*?'

'That's how she reached Miss Franks and Mathilda so quickly after we stopped Peter being taken. She . . . she didn't have to walk.'

'But none of this is proof, Shilly. At best I might say it's a theory, and an outlandish one at that.'

'There's this too.'

I took from my pocket the scrap of paper I'd been carrying. It was crumpled and soggy but the shape it bore was still clear. Wretchedly so. It was the shape Mathilda kept drawing.

Anna took the paper from me. 'You believe this to be a representation of Mrs Haskell? In . . .'

'In her true form. Yes, I do. But I need help to see it. It's the only way, Anna.'

She looked longingly towards the manor house and the ordinariness

228

she had been seeking there. Informing a magistrate of a death. Asking questions about known things – stolen spoons and quarry accidents. And now there was something else. Something that lay hidden beneath women's skin and when it came to light, the world was different.

'It's a guess, Anna, but what if I'm right?'

She kicked the moor stone slab, and I knew then she'd follow my notion.

'We might as well put a stop to this nonsense now. Come on if you're coming, Shilly-shally.'

'I need money.'

'Now? Whatever for?'

'If I keep stealing from Richard Bray then I'm no better than Simon Proctor. You have to pay for what I need. It won't take much, I promise.'

She brushed past me. 'So be it, Shilly.'

I had half of what I wanted. Her trust, if not her love.

'Back again, my sweet?'

Mrs Haskell was in the doorway, smiling, her family safe and making a racket in the house behind her.

'We must speak to you,' I said. 'Away from here.' The words felt too big for my tongue. I steadied myself against the door frame. I hadn't had much but I'd had it quickly. Bolted it, and not just because it would help me see. Because I wanted it too.

'Now, my sweet? But I've the fire going and the pastry's made.'

'It's about the death of Miss Franks,' Anna said.

'I wouldn't know anything about that. Come in, if you're coming. There's plenty.' She turned away, chiding the girls to make room for the visitors.

'A feather,' I said. 'It choked her.'

Mrs Haskell ceased moving, ceased breathing I thought. As if she'd been changed to moor stone like the girls in the stories caught dancing on Sundays.

'Why're you letting the rain in, Mother?' James Haskell appeared

229

behind her. 'You don't have to worry any more, she's—oh.' He saw us and was surprised at our returning. 'What's the matter now?'

His presence made his mother come alive again and she was speaking brightly, taking a hat from the peg.

'This kind pair have come to tell me Sarah's poorly. She's asking for me. I'll not be long. Keep the fire hot.'

Before he could question her she'd shut the door and was walking towards the river.

'Lies come easy to you, Mrs Haskell,' Anna said as we followed.

'We all have our talents,' she muttered, and glanced at me askance. 'Though not all of us know them.'

I didn't like the look she was giving me, her so knowing with it, so I put the bottle to my lips again and rode the burn of what it held like others might ride a horse. Deep in the saddle and clenching. There was a flitter of black overhead. I didn't look up. I knew what it was. The birds were coming.

Mrs Haskell didn't stop until she'd reached the fallen oak, which she seemed to judge a good place for talking of death. As she sat down on its mossy back the branches of the trees nearby dipped. The leaves rustled as the birds took their places.

Anna looked about her. 'And so we are in session.'

'Are you acting judge, then, Miss Drake?'

'I'll make sure you're set before one, charged with the murder of Gertrud Franks.'

But this was all noise, as bad as the birds' chatter above, as the trees' muttering and tightening. I drank again and the noise dropped away. I stalked the fallen log. Made a circle of it to see the creature from all sides.

'And what proof have you that I harmed her?' Mrs Haskell said. 'A feather? There's no shortage of them here.'

At her words one fell to the ground before me. Tumbling, slower than was natural, the way the snow had fallen once in Blisland when

230

I was a child. She had called that feather down, as she called the birds to her.

'You can't deny your motive is clear,' Anna was saying. 'You believed the women had taken your grandson. When Peter was nearly taken too you sought revenge. You thought Paul was likely dead by then. There was no point waiting for them to give him up. You went to the cottage and you—'

'And I what, Miss Drake?'

'You let your true self be seen,' I said. 'We saved Peter, found Paul. In exchange we'll have the truth from you, Mrs Haskell. There was no fire at the mill. The reason you cover yourself like this, the reason you hide – it's not because of burns. It's because of who you are. *What* you are.'

The birds began to cry and then to scream. I covered my ears and fell to the ground. Anna rushed over to me.

'Shilly! What's wrong?'

'Can't you hear them?'

Anna's mouth was moving but I couldn't hear her. Then a voice came clearer through the birds' din.

She can't hear and she can't see. You know that, Shilly, my sweet. Why do you seek her agreement of what you know to be true?

Mrs Haskell stood. She drew her shawl from her shoulders. A corpse taking off a winding sheet. She let it fall. She unbuttoned her dress and drew her arms from the sleeves. She bared herself to us, her unclothed flesh. The rain still fell but I didn't think she'd feel the cold as the rest of us might.

Not with her skin the way it was.

Anna put her hand to her mouth, looked away.

I stepped forward, the drink making me slow and stumbling. Touched Mrs Haskell's arm. Felt the callouses, the whorls of hardened skin that covered her body. I stroked her, pressed and rubbed to know her and her strangeness. She watched me, her wide face, her dark eyes curious, as if she hadn't believed I would be so bold. But now the drink was in me.

I heard Anna's voice as if from far away, telling me not to touch that which might spread, might taint me. She was still in a world of ordinary sickness. I closed my ears to such talk and spoke in the language that Mrs Haskell used. That we shared. That I needed the drink to know. An unspoken language that waited in moor stone and magpies and roots reaching down into old water. Into well water.

Show me.

She closed her eyes. Twisted her mouth as if in pain. Beneath my hand still pressed against her breast I felt a stirring and jumped back. Broke our closeness for she had moved beyond me now. She was a different kind of beast.

You see me, Shilly-shally?

From the callouses came ticklish things reaching, flaring. Lengthening into the feathers I had known were there, within her. She crossed her arms over her chest and when she uncrossed them again, shadows hung from them. She lifted these shadows, these dark wings, opened them out, and before me was the shape Mathilda had been drawing. It had been a scrawl, made from fear, but the outline was the same. The tips of the wings, held up – two points. The curve of them below. And within that black shape, Mrs Haskell's face was her face, her hair was her hair, but her body was not her body and her hands—

Her hands were like blades.

I threw the bottle to the ground and it must have struck stone for there came a smash and I cried out and covered my head.

THIRTY-FOUR

When I could look again Mrs Haskell was buttoning her dress with swiftness that belied what had just been, as if she was cross to have found herself half-dressed in the woods in the rain, two strangers watching her. Anna was twitching, shaking her head like she was throwing off a wasp.

The power of the drink had left me, and left behind pain. My head was two slates struck together. I blinked until the blurriness before me was only that caused by the rain. Mrs Haskell's skin was the same as when she had first undone her dress – the whorls were there, the callouses. The feathers had gone.

'You . . . you call it into being?' I said.

'Another of my talents. Takes some learning, though. My mother taught me that.'

'I'm sorry – what are you talking about?' Anna was staring dumbly at us.

I knew then that she'd seen nothing but Mrs Haskell's strangely marked flesh. She hadn't seen the change. That was something that had passed only between me and the old woman who chose who was to see. Who was to be made fearful. Mathilda and I shared that.

'Simon Proctor told us it's in the blood,' I said.

'That's part of it.' Mrs Haskell picked up her shawl from where it lay across the fallen oak.

'And the other part?'

'The woods. They choose us. A day will come when I'll join the woods forever. Each time I push the other self away, it's harder to come back to skin.' She held out her hands and peered at them.

'Do people know? Your family?'

'There's some you can't hide from and there's no use trying.'

I glanced briefly at Anna who was looking furious with our secret talking. 'Why did you only kill Miss Franks?' I said.

'The eldest, she was full of hate. Her plots. Her schemes. The woods were stirred up by it. The path shifting. The birds driven mad. The other one, the girl, well. She's weaker. She'll go. And if she doesn't—'

'You'll kill her too,' Anna said.

'But Mrs Haskell,' I said, keeping my distance, keeping safely away now I knew what lay beneath her skin, 'the woods are still as they were before you killed Miss Franks. Nothing has been eased by her death. Can't you see, you made a mistake? Those women didn't take Paul.'

'They did it. I know they did it.'

'But they were seen at the manor house at the same time Paul disappeared,' Anna said. 'And when Peter was nearly taken, they were in the cottage.'

'Your own anger has blinded you,' I said. 'You know they aren't witches like the others think. You know that because . . . you know what that means.'

'She took them! My boys! I know she did and she paid for it.'

The birds rose in a frenzy of wings and screaming as Mrs Haskell bore down on me. I feared I'd be taken next. Would go in the ground with Miss Franks, my face raked beyond anyone knowing it was me beneath the blood and torn flesh.

'The other must go too,' Mrs Haskell said, shaking her shawl at me. 'We can't rest easy until then. None of us can. She doesn't belong here. Tell her. Tell her she's a stranger and she must go.'

'And us?' I said. 'We're strangers too. Will you smother everyone in the woods you don't know?'

She wrapped her shawl around her, once more sealing up her marked flesh beneath layers of cloth. She didn't speak until that task was done, and she looked more the kind, slow-moving woman I knew now that she was not.

'You did good here,' she said. 'Finding Paul, saving Peter. I'm grateful for that. The girl – she's not like either of you.'

'Because she's foreign?' Anna said. 'She's done you no harm, Mrs Haskell.'

'They should never have come here.' The old woman turned and began walking back to the cottages. 'You tell her. She has until the light goes. I'll grant her that, but only for you, Shilly. For what you did for my family.'

'So that's why she lied about the fire in the old mill,' Anna said, watching Mrs Haskell go. 'To cover her shame.'

'Shame?'

'She's clearly had some terrible affliction in the past. To be marked in such a way. It can't be leprosy or she'd have been turned out, but she must feel compelled to hide her disfigurement from those around her.'

'The marks on her skin,' I said, 'did you see what came out of them?'

'Came *out* of them? Shilly . . .' She shook her head. 'I shouldn't have given in to you. It's my fault. I just don't know the best way to help, what to do for you. If you keep on like this, the drink will kill you.'

'If you want me to help you, to do the things you can't, this is the only way. You *do* want me, don't you, Anna?'

She threw up her hands and I felt like doing likewise for I didn't know what to do for the best for *her*. How to make her see.

'Mrs Haskell had the means to choke Miss Franks with that feather,' I said. 'You might not have seen that, Anna, but I did.'

'For now, perhaps we can agree on what was said, if not shown? Mathilda is in danger.'

'But we'll keep her safe, won't we?' I said.

'We can try.'

I caught the smell at the doorway of the cottage – sweet and sharp, and I tasted bile.

'We should be grateful the heat has dropped or it'd be much worse,' Anna said.

She tucked her nose into her elbow then pushed open the door. The smell was terrible inside, but the place was as we'd left it. Miss Franks' body was still in the chair, the old coat over her face. But there was a new sound. A burring whirring sound coming from Miss Franks herself.

'Mathilda!' Anna called. 'Don't be afraid. It's only Shilly and me.'

She went into the bedroom and I heard her murmuring to Mathilda. I knew I should follow but the noise from Miss Franks drew me to her. Then I froze.

The coat was twitching.

A thought struck me – a thought so bad it sent me trembly and I thought I'd fall.

What if we'd been wrong about the two women?

What if they *could* make things do as they didn't ought to? To breathe again, when by rights Miss Franks' breath should be gone forever? The people of the woods had been so sure the Devil was helping them. Could it be that they were right?

I approached Miss Franks. The muddied coat I'd covered her with had slipped in its twitching, showing her crown and in it the first inch of the deep furrow I knew carved down her face. The rest of her was still. Her hand hung over the chair's arm, reaching for the handkerchief it would never get. Or so I had thought.

My shaking fingers closed on the coat. The wool was stiff with the old, dried mud. I took a deep breath, and wrenched the coat away.

My shrieks brought Anna from the other room.

'Whatever's the—oh. Well, what do you expect, Shilly? She's been dead a day.'

'But there's so many!'

'That's the nature of flies. Come and help me with Mathilda. There's nothing we can do for her companion right now.'

I scuttled from the writhing dark river that Miss Franks' wounds had become, and within the river the whiteness of maggots. None of the Devil's doings. Just the nastiness of death we all would face.

'She should be buried,' I told Anna as I followed her into the bedroom.

'I agree.'

'So?'

'So what's more important, the living or the dead?'

Mathilda was still on the bed, still tied up. She didn't appear to have moved since we'd left her. She was staring at the ceiling, her eyes glassy. A different smell was in this room, a sharper smell, and when I saw the dark patch on her dress I knew what it was and I felt wretched for leaving her that way. The poor girl. What had she done to be so ill used?

'We'll take her to the summer house,' Anna said.

'And then?'

'One step at a time, Shilly.'

We began to untie the knots, I at the girl's hands, Anna at her feet.

'She'll be safer with us than left here on her own,' Anna said. 'We can protect her.'

'But what if Mrs Haskell's spies see us take Mathilda to the summer house?'

'Her spies?'

'The birds.' I helped Mathilda sit up. Her head flopped, as if she had become a rag doll.

'Shilly,' Anna said sternly, 'whatever might have happened earlier, with Mrs Haskell, I can't believe that—'

Mathilda knocked her to the floor.

I was so taken aback that for a moment I could do nothing but watch the girl run from the room. She was no floppy rag doll now. She was a hare leaping from the hounds.

'Go after her!' Anna managed to croak.

I did – I ran, and I was faster than Mathilda who was not so lean as me. Who was stiff after being lashed to a bedframe for hours on end. I caught her at the old gatepost, got my arms around her waist and used the little weight I had to drag her to the ground.

She gabbled away in her German speak. I couldn't understand her words but her clawing my arms was loud enough. She wanted to be away. But the light was going. Mrs Haskell would soon come for her.

'It's not safe!' I said. 'She'll be back – the one who killed Gertrud. You're better off with me and Anna. You must believe me, Mathilda!'

'You leave me there! You tie me so I am trapped there, with Gertrud . . . Shilly, I thought you were my friend.'

'We are friends. I'm sorry we tied you up. That was Anna's idea, but we're going to look after you now, honest we are.'

Still she fought me. Her strength had returned to match her anger. She was going to get away, run into the woods and so to her death. I had one last means.

'You can trust us, Mathilda. Look – look at this.'

I held something before her, something I'd been carrying to make Miss Franks open the door to us, so long ago now. It was the framed picture I had found in the ruined mill. The picture of the woman who looked so much like Miss Franks herself.

'See what I found for you – saved for you. We won't hurt you, Mathilda. We won't, I promise.'

I held the picture close to Mathilda's face until she slackened in my arms. Her tears came then.

Anna reached us, holding her side and grey about the face. She'd taken so many knocks since we'd come to the woods. I had my own cuts and bruises, and had suffered much in my head. What a wretched pair we were. What a wretched place it was.

Anna leant against the gatepost. 'Is she going to fight us all the way?'

I looked at the weeping girl at my feet who stank of piss, was covered in dried blood.

'I doubt it.'

'Good.' She took hold of Mathilda by the elbow, but kindly. 'Up you come. We've a little way to go before we can rest easy.'

Mathilda kept hold of the picture and every so often murmured to it, but said nothing to Anna and me, and I couldn't blame her for that. She had lost her companion, in a terrible way, and just when she needed love, those she had thought friends had treated her badly. She had every reason to hate us, but that was the way of detection. It didn't allow for kindness. I didn't like that part of it.

The girl lagged. Anna and I waited for her to catch up, and as I caught the sound of her tears I wondered again at what Mathilda and Gertrud had been to one another, if Mathilda had felt for Gertrud as I felt for Anna. One thing I knew for certain, for I could see it, even in the last of the light, as Mathilda reached us. Her shaking hand shook no more. Had that to do with losing Gertrud? Had that to do with love? Or fear?

Dusk was all but fallen by the time we reached the summer house. Mathilda wasn't keen to follow me up the steps.

'You will tie me?' she said, and I felt so bad all I could do was shake my head.

Slowly, looking at me askance the whole while, she came inside, but then seated herself as close to the door as she could.

I gathered the few candles we had and set them on the window ledge amongst the things we had placed there – the lump of coal, the rabbit snare and the broken por-s'lain figure of the woman. Mathilda wouldn't look at me, but she murmured thanks to Anna for giving her a blanket, and I hoped that was the start of her making friends with us again.

I got the fire going, to help us forget the damp rather than for warmth, and Anna sat next to me on the floor, her knees creaking and her thin face drawn. It was easy to forget, when we were so busy with detecting, that she was older than me.

After a little time I spoke, and did so low, so that Mathilda shouldn't hear.

'You told Mrs Haskell you'd get her before a judge, have her tried for killing Gertrud. Did you mean it?'

'Of course I meant it,' Anna said. 'But what a judge would make of the case, let alone a jury, I can't begin to imagine. The squire might believe us. He thought Miss Franks and Mathilda were the guilty party. It might not be too hard to make him see that he was looking at the wrong women.'

'But Mrs Haskell has done what he wanted – gotten rid of them. She's killed one and is forcing the other to leave. He's hardly going to want to punish her.'

'Or pay us,' Anna said quietly, and pressed the heels of her hands into her eyes. 'If we can just get to the bottom of who took Paul, we might still be able to claim the reward. That was part of the agreement with the squire. If we manage that then we might convince him to bring Mrs Haskell to justice for the other crime.'

'But how will we do that?'

She stood and took from the window ledge the coal I'd found on the road to Boscastle. 'This is coal for burning, but it was drawing charcoal left where Paul was last seen, wasn't it? Outside Miss Franks and Mathilda's cottage.'

'And?'

'Well, it could have been left there on purpose, couldn't it? To put blame on them for Paul's disappearance, just as Simon Proctor did later when he left coal in place of what he stole.'

I took the charcoal from her and weighed it in my hand, as if that would tell me something of its secrets. 'So whoever took Paul wanted to make it look as if Miss Franks and Mathilda were responsible.'

240

'Yes,' Anna said, 'and I think it matters that they chose not to kill him. They wanted to cause his family pain. That's why they tried to take Peter too. And who do we know has reason to want to cause pain to the Haskells?'

'Lucy at the manor house,' I said.

I gave Anna back the charcoal and wiped its dust on my hands.

'Tomorrow, then,' Anna said. 'We'll go and see if we can't make this case come right after all.'

'What will become of Mathilda?' I looked over to the girl who had fallen asleep with her head against the door, the blanket heaped around her middle.

'We could take her to Boscastle,' Anna said. 'See her safely into a coach.'

'With money in her pocket? She hasn't anything, Anna. If we could help her . . .'

Anna groaned and went over to the sleeping Mathilda. 'This case has ended up *costing* us instead of earning.' She pulled up the blanket, tucked the poor girl in.

'The next work we get, that might pay,' I said.

'It'll have to. You'd better pray to Saint Nectan, Shilly. Ask him to grant us some vanishings, but tell him we want more deaths and fewer needy causes.'

I told her she was wicked, and then she let me kiss her.

THIRTY-FIVE

'You must keep it locked. Locked – you understand?'

Mathilda nodded.

'And the chair. When we go, you must put it like this.' I shoved the chair into place beneath the door handle. 'You see? Then no one can come in. Not until we come back, and we'll look after you then, I promise.'

She nodded again, but I wondered if she believed me.

When I had woken with the light, she was already awake, staring out of the window. Anna had given her something to wear, for the girl couldn't put her soiled clothes back on, but the only things in the travelling case that would fit were those belonging to Anna's men – the dresses were too snug for Mathilda's hips. I hadn't yet met the man who wore this loose shirt and trousers so strongly pattered with little black and white squares that my eyes strained to look at them, but I knew such a man could not be serious as Mr Williams was. Mr Williams wore only dark clothes, and them all neatness.

Anna called me from outside, told me off for shilly-shallying again. I stepped out, onto the top step, pulling the door to behind me. As soon as it met the frame, Mathilda locked it and then I heard the thump of the chair put in place. Her fear would keep her watchful. That was something, at least.

I followed Anna across the clearing. The magpie tree wasn't worthy of its name that morning for its branches bore only the last leaves of summer and no birds among them. I hoped with all my heart that Mrs Haskell believed Mathilda had left the woods. But it couldn't be true for there was anger, still, in that place. I felt it like cold rain beneath my collar. Both the Haskell boys were safe, so whose rage was it?

'Lucy's,' Anna said when I spoke aloud my feeling. 'She's the end point of this case. Our last chance for the reward.'

'And if she won't speak to us?'

The Dark River poured itself over the lip of the fall, tumbling to the pool far below. The air was wet with its spray. The pool was a nest of foam, the river fighting to escape and race to the sea. To freedom from the woods' brooding heart.

'Lucy will have to speak to us,' Anna said, 'because we know what lies beneath her clothes.'

'So you believe it now – her sickness?'

'She believes it. That's all that matters.'

The kitchen door was closed, as it had been before, to keep out Pigeon. Closed but not locked.

'What are *you* wanting in here?' a sour voice said. It was Mrs Carne, up to her elbows in potato peelings, a pail of dirty water beside her on the table.

'We need to speak to the scullery maid,' Anna said.

'I'd like a word with her too.' Mrs Carne slashed at a potato, taking half the flesh as well as the skin. 'She's taken to her bed *again.*'

'Well you'll have to get her out of it,' I said.

'Will I now?' Mrs Carne jabbed the knife at me and I was glad the table was between us. 'And why would I be going all the way up to the eaves when it's her fault I've got to get the dinner ready? As if I haven't enough to do.'

Anna took the knife from the housekeeper's hand as if it was nothing more threatening than a spoon. 'You'll fetch Lucy because otherwise the squire will hear that you stood in the way of justice, Mrs Carne. We've come about the disappearance of Paul Haskell.'

'Have you now?' Mrs Carne said, in a voice of wonder. 'So that's why the girl has been hiding upstairs.' She wiped her hands on her apron. 'I'll fetch her, but you can't be waiting in here.' And with that she shooed us into the passage, quite cheered by what Anna had said. 'The squire will have to turn her out now. The sooner he finds a new girl for the scullery, the better off we'll all be.'

And so grumbling cheerfully she went to drag Lucy from her bed. Had I not believed the girl had kidnapped Paul Haskell, I might have felt some pity for her.

The passage was dim for the doors on either side were closed. My foot brushed something. A clutch of soft grey feathers, and within them a lump, dark red and sticky. I pushed the feathers aside with the toe of my boot and saw the innards of some poor creature.

And then, very slowly, with a long, terrible creak, the door to my left began to open.

I clutched Anna's arm and felt her stiffen. An inch wider – two.

A thick, striped limb reached round the bottom of the door, and then a striped head appeared, forced it open.

Anna pressed herself against the wall as Pigeon stalked past, a low growl rolling from his fiendish body.

'I won't miss coming across this animal.'

'I will. Wait – where are you going?'

She had darted into the room Pigeon had just left, and I darted after her. It wasn't the room with all the tables and chairs where last we'd spoken to the squire. This room was smaller, with only one table – a desk, covered in papers and an inkpot in the corner. Anna snatched up something next to the inkpot and thrust it at me.

It was a figure made of por-s'lain. A man.

245

'Look, Shilly – his waistcoat. It's the same colour as the dress the broken woman wears.' She quickly turned him upside down. 'The maker's mark is the same as the one on the woman. And he's holding a birdcage.'

'To catch the birds at the broken woman's feet!'

'They're a pair, Shilly. Made to be together.'

'He won't like you touching that,' a voice said. Mrs Carne was in the doorway, arms folded across her chest and a look of great satisfaction on her tired old face.

'This belongs to the squire?' Anna said.

'Until he married there was no end to the things I was dusting. Crates of them, he brought back. Thankfully Lady Phoebe got rid of most of them. That was when she thought about the work it took to run this household.' Mrs Carne turned and was heading back to the kitchen. 'The girl's coming. I told her she was going to the gallows and that got her backside moving.'

'Mrs Carne, wait. What do you mean about the squire bringing back crates? Where had he been?'

'All over.'

'All over where?' Anna said.

'I don't know. Foreign places. Like all young gentlemen do.'

'Germany?' I asked.

'He wouldn't tell me, would he? And I wouldn't go asking him, either. He don't like talking about his trips. You've let the cat out, I see.'

'Mrs Carne?' I said.

'I told you, the girl's coming. Go up there yourself if you want her any faster.'

'Tell the squire we need to speak to him.'

She threw up her hands and went back down the passage, cursing us for not making up our minds.

Anna and I stared at each other.

'He didn't just meet them in Boscastle,' I whispered.

'He met them years before.'

'But he's a magistrate. Oh, Anna! A magistrate!' I had to lean on the desk to steady myself.

'Calm yourself, Shilly. We still don't know if he's done anything wrong.'

'He's lied to us!'

'Shh! We have to think—'

'He says he'll see you in the sitting room,' Mrs Carne said loudly.

Mrs Carne had decided she'd wasted enough time on us already so we found our own way back to the room with too many chairs and tables. The squire was facing the cold hearth, and when he turned at the sound of us coming in, his usually florid face was grey.

'Mrs Carne says you have made a discovery, and not before time. My wife grows more distressed by the hour.'

'Two discoveries,' I said. 'Paul Haskell is alive. We found him locked under the summer house.'

The squire clamped me round the shoulders and I near fell over. 'That is wonderful news, Mrs Williams! And Miss Drake! Wonderful! He is well, the boy?'

'Thankfully, yes,' Anna said. 'A little weak after being without food for some days, but he will soon recover.'

The squire sat down and gave a great sigh, of relief, I thought. 'Lady Phoebe will rest easier. All will be well. I have proof against them now.'

Anna and I shared a glance.

'That brings us to our second discovery,' Anna said. 'That of the person responsible.'

'Surely you mean *persons*, Miss Drake. There are two of the wretches!' He was smiling, as if Anna had made a joke.

'I'm afraid I don't, Sir Vivian. We believe there is just one person involved.'

'Really? Who?'

'Your little maid, Lucy,' I said. 'She took Paul Haskell.'

His mouth fell open and he pitched forward in his chair.

'Forgive me, Sir Vivian,' Anna said, 'but you don't appear pleased to hear we have solved the mystery. You wanted an answer to who had taken Paul Haskell. We believe that we have that answer.'

'But *Lucy*? I did not think . . .' His fat fingers had begun to fuss one another.

'You were sure it was Miss Franks and Miss Wolffs,' I said, 'but they don't talk to the Devil, you see. They talk German to themselves, for that's where they're from. That's their own talking. It was just that the people listening to them didn't know the words.'

The squire's fingers stopped fussing. 'Is that so?'

'It's something of a coincidence,' Anna said, her gaze never leaving the squire.

'What is, Miss Drake?'

'That a pair of German women should set up home in the woods of Trethevy, right on the doorstep of someone who has been to their native land.'

A high little laugh came from him. 'I'm not sure it's worth remarking on,' he said. 'Many people visit that country.'

We let him wait then before we spoke further. We needed no sign to know that we should do so. It was because we had learnt how to work together, for some things at least. It was as if the air had a heartbeat and we were counting it out. I knew when to speak again.

'I think it is worth saying, Sir Vivian. And it's worth saying that you met the pair of them in Boscastle. And that you chose not to tell us this when you asked us to find Paul Haskell.'

'You are mistaken, Mrs Williams.'

'You're saying you didn't visit the German women at a lodging house run by a Mrs Teague?' I said. 'She described a man much like you. He wore a patch over one eye, as if to hide an affliction. Or something that would make it clear who he was.'

'A mistake. The woman in Boscastle is mistaken, and at any rate, what does it matter now? Mrs Carne tells me the women have been driven from the woods after violence against them, so I don't see the need—'

'Ah, there *you* are mistaken, Sir Vivian,' Anna said. 'One of the women *is* still with us.'

His eyes widened. 'Which?'

'The younger of the two, Miss Wolffs,' I said. 'She's quite safe with us.'

Anna stiffened at my side and I saw my mistake at once. But the squire wasn't listening, for someone was knocking on the door. He crossed the room to open it and there was Lucy, her dress badly buttoned and a shawl wrapped tight around her neck.

She bobbed and mumbled, 'Mrs Carne said I was wanted.'

The squire pulled her into the room and she flinched at his touch, did her best not to cry out.

'These women wish to speak to you about the disappearance of Paul Haskell.'

'But they've found him, haven't they?'

'Miss Drake, Mrs Williams, I will leave you to your questioning. Good day to you.'

Anna started towards him. 'Sir Vivian, we haven't finished—'

But he was gone, the door shut behind him.

Lucy stood before us, bewildered and in pain. 'M-M-Mrs Carne said I'll be hanged. I've done nothing wrong, I swear it.'

I rushed to the door, but before I reached it I heard the key turn in the lock. Then another door slammed somewhere.

Anna was at the window. 'He's going into the woods! He must be after Mathilda.'

'What's happening?' Lucy cried.

And then the bell began to ring.

THIRTY-SIX

'Mrs Carne! Mrs Carne, open this door!'

Anna thumped the door, kicked it, wrenched the handle. No help came, and there wasn't any time. The bell was tolling the saint's warning and it was all my fault. I had let slip Mathilda was in the summer house and the squire had been a man undone.

I picked up a chair and threw it at the window that faced the woods. The glass cracked but didn't smash so I threw the chair again, and then Anna came and did likewise. Together we broke the window. Together we had an escape.

I made to climb out but Anna stopped me.

'Wait! You'll cut yourself.'

She got hold of Lucy who was cowering behind a table like a frightened rabbit, looking from the broken window to the door and all a tremble. Anna yanked her shawl away and Lucy screamed.

'No! You mustn't take—'

'We know all about you,' Anna said. 'Simon told us. And we've seen Mrs Haskell.'

Lucy made a choking sound and covered her mouth. Anna got the shawl free and threw it across the wicked-looking glass still attached to the window frame, and then we were free, running to the woods.

'It was the squire, not Lucy?' I said between gulps of air.

'He's revealed his true self at last.' Her words were almost lost in the bell's din. 'He took Paul to make everyone hate Gertrud and Mathilda, drive them out.'

'And Mrs Haskell did just as he wanted,' I said. And now I knew that I had to do as I *didn't* want to. Do what was needed.

I let my fingers catch the wide trunk of an oak as we ran.

Help us

A jolt ran through my arm, across my chest. I felt it flicker in my teeth.

Anna was turning it all over as we ran. 'But why he wanted them gone so badly, we still don't know. We have to hope we're in time. If the path should change—'

'It won't,' I said.

'How do you know?'

Even if I'd had the breath to spare the words, I couldn't have told her. I was speaking in a soundless tongue, the one Mrs Haskell had spoken to me.

Let us pass

I brushed another trunk, then a long-hanging branch. Still I felt the woods' anger but this time I didn't cower from it.

Take us to her

The roots made way for us. The path stayed true for us. And I hadn't touched a drop.

The cottages were shut up tight. If anyone was there to see us race past, there was no sign of them. The fallen oak passed in a blur. At the monks' wall I heard a scream from above.

'Anna, look!'

The squire was in the water, just shy of the falls. He was in up to his chest and struggled against the current wishing to drag him over, and against Mathilda. He had her by the hair. He was going to throw her over the waterfall.

I climbed up to the summer house, calling out to Mathilda as I went. The going was slick with the mud and my fear but I kept on. Nearly at the top. There was the summer house, there was the ledge. I faltered at the steep drop, the dark churning water below. But then I heard her, Mathilda, poor frightened Mathilda, screaming for help, and I found a scrap of courage. Enough to get down on my knees.

I lowered myself over the ledge but clung on with my fingers while I scrabbled to set my feet on the thin sapling that grew from the bank below. It bucked with my weight but if I could just drop down and grasp the branches—

'Shilly!' Anna's face above me was white.

I let go of the ledge with one hand and reached for the branches. And then I was falling.

The water hit me – a cold, hard slap. My feet were above my head. My fingers caught small stones. I had time to think how smooth they were before I realised I was choking. The current had me – was dragging me along the bottom. Towards the falls.

I fought it, lashed out. My dress had become huge as it snagged around me. Then my knees were on the stones, then my foot. I stumbled and there was light again. I was breathing. I could see.

The squire had Mathilda at the edge of the falls. She struggled to free herself but he was stronger and dragged her by the arm. He was shouting all the time – his words sounding like those Gertrud and Mathilda had used. German words.

The current raced me towards them but too fast. It wanted to carry me over, light as a fallen leaf. As the water whirled me to the falls, I slammed my feet into the squire's knees and he doubled over with a roar. Mathilda slipped below the water, her arms flailing. She didn't come up again. I tried to get hold of her shirt tail, which flapped behind her like a sail on a boat in Boscastle harbour, but sudden pain in my shoulder sent me limp. The squire hauled me up and shoved me against a moor stone slab. I felt the grind of its roughness on my back. Cold air beneath my neck. Fifty feet below me, the plunge pool surged. The Dark River, waiting.

The squire was shouting but all I could hear was the pounding of the water and a voice in my head saying, this is how you die. You will be drowned. It won't be the drink after all. Anna was wrong. Oh Anna, Anna. I felt myself lifted, rising up.

And then there was another voice, wordless, shrieking, and not only in my head for the squire looked around. I saw her before he did and my heart stopped, I would swear it. I died there, when her shadow fell across me, when her blades sliced into the squire's back.

He screamed and I was dumb. She lifted him from the water and his blood fell upon me like rain. His face was disbelief as he caught sight of the creature who had come to save me, as I had saved her grandsons. Some last strength came to him then and he grabbed her arm that was her wing and made her twist. They were a tumble of black and white then, and the red of his blood washing down his arms, turning his shirt pink. I scrambled to get away, get out from under them, and her feathers slipped across my cheek. Soft. Like the best of Anna's coats.

Mrs Haskell tilted for a moment, ungainly on the falls' lip, and then she gripped the squire more tightly in her shadowed arms, and they were gone.

I didn't look back. Ahead of me was what mattered. Mathilda, her head below the water, drifting near the bank. I fought the current with strength I didn't know I had, with hope I didn't know could find me. And there was the reason, a rope tied round her middle, reaching from the bank.

Anna Drake, reaching for me.

THIRTY-SEVEN

'There's no sign of him below,' Anna said, coming inside the summer house.

I was wrapped in half the clothes from her travelling chest. Mathilda was wrapped in the other half, Mrs Williams's fur hat low on her head, hiding her face. A fire burnt in the hearth and made the summer house's damp steam. All I could smell was the river as we huddled close to the warmth. Mathilda hadn't spoken since Anna had hauled us out of the water. I was just glad to see her breathing.

I threw a length of wood onto the flames. The sight of it burning gave me some comfort. I wished to burn the whole of Trethevy to the ground. That way we might get out. Burnt, likely, but gone. Mrs Haskell had talked to me of women who did such things. She had known that I was one of them.

Anna knelt beside me. 'I think the river must have taken him out to sea.'

'Both of them?'

She frowned. 'Both? What are you talking about?'

So she had only seen the squire. The truth of how he had died could wait. There were other things to speak of first.

'With him gone,' I said, 'we won't know why he wanted rid of Gertrud and Mathilda so badly.'

255

'Oh, I think we still might. I wouldn't claim my German was particularly good but I made out enough, I think, to piece it together.'

Anna plucked the hat from Mathilda's head, showing her face. The girl's plump cheeks were shiny with tears.

'One word in particular I was able to make out,' Anna said. 'A word you said quite often to the squire, Mathilda. A word you used to beg for your life.'

Mathilda let out a sob and buried her face in her hands.

'What was it?' I said.

'Father.'

'I think it's about time you told us the truth, Mathilda, before anyone else comes to harm.'

The girl shook her head and shuffled closer to the fire.

'There's nothing to be gained from your silence now,' Anna said. 'Gertrud is dead. The squire too, I should think.'

I put my arm around Mathilda. She felt lumpy as a tree beneath all her layers, but still I felt her flinch.

'You can trust us,' I said, and hoped she would believe me.

After a long pause, she spoke. 'He . . . he said we must not come.'

'The squire?' I said.

She nodded. 'My mother wrote him, he send her letters back. She was sad, of course, but she forgive him. He was young when they were married, she said. She love him too much, even though he took her money and we have nothing.'

'The woman in the picture – that's your mother?'

Mathilda nodded, and used the fur hat to wipe her tears.

'And you and Gertrud were sisters?' I said.

'Halfway sisters. Gertrud's father died and then our mother met him, Mr Orton. He was not a Sir then. He was a Mr but she falls in love with him at a ball. They marry and I am born and then after a little time he leave her. He take the money Gertrud's father left to our

256

mother. She have only an allowance, very small, from an uncle. When she . . . when she died . . .'

'The allowance stopped,' Anna said. 'And you had nothing.'

'Gertrud say we must act. The house – we have no house. No money. We must make him help us. Gertrud say, our mother was a fool.'

'So coming to England was Gertrud's idea?' Anna said.

Mathilda nodded. 'She says, he does not answer letters, we go ourselves. We have no money. We make him acknowledge me, his daughter. We go to Boscastle first, close to him but not too close. We will not beg, Gertrud say. We tell him we are there and he came then. Oh, he came at once!'

She laughed, but it was a hollow laugh. She sounded so much older than I knew her to be.

'He say then, we must go back to Germany. He owes us nothing. He has another wife, a title. He is man of law here. If people hear he marry this new wife when my mother was still living . . . Problems for him. *I* am problem. Not a daughter.' She sniffed. 'Gertrud offer him a bargain. If he give us money to live, we leave. But he say no, so Gertrud says, we come closer. We come to your house and we stay until you do what you must do.'

'That's why you stood outside the manor house most days,' I said. 'You were threatening him.'

Mathilda smiled. 'Gertrud, she very strong. She do not give up.'

'Because she loved you,' I said.

'Because Mathilda was her means to survive,' Anna said. 'I'm right, aren't I?'

The girl nodded, and there were no tears now. Only the cold, hard truth.

'What happen here, to Gertrud . . . No one deserves to die like that. Her screams, I will hear them always. But I will not miss her. She had no love for me because I am my father's daughter and she hate him. She did not want a sister. If my father had said yes, if he give her the money she ask for, what of me then, ah? She would leave me, like he left our mother? They are the same, though Gertrud could not see.'

'Well,' I said, 'you don't have to be part of her plans any more. I know that makes you happy because your hand has stopped shaking. It stopped when she died, didn't it?'

'You see things, Shilly. Small things that are important. And you are right. I am free now. Free and poor and alone. I have nothing.'

'That's not true,' I said. 'You have us. If you want us, that is?'

She gave a shy smile. 'You have been kind as well as cruel, and I know the cruelty was for reason. To find Paul, and you did find him. You are good at heart.'

I squeezed her hand, then turned to Anna. 'So, we'll leave this place together, won't we? The three of us?'

Anna said nothing for a moment, and I wondered at her cruelty in spurning poor Mathilda, in making the girl think she truly *was* alone. But then I saw that Anna's eyes were wet, and that I had been wrong to think her cruel.

'I was lost once,' she said, so quietly her words were almost lost themselves. 'If kindness hadn't been offered me then, I might not be here now.'

I thought of the scrap of felt, cut to make a duck, and tied to a little arm poking from a bundle of shawl. Of the butcher's wife opening the door. Making a choice.

'But you're not lost any more, are you, Anna Drake?' I said.

'Indeed I'm not, Shilly-shally. And neither are you pair.' She wiped her eyes. 'There's enough of a fug in here to pass out. Let's have some air.'

She opened the door and the sad song of the Trethevy birds came to us on the cool breeze. They were mourning one of their own, mourning she who had stirred them so, and in their cries was another loss, too. That of summer. The season had turned.

'We must inform Lady Phoebe of what's happened,' Anna said, back to herself and back to business.

I stood and gave Mathilda my hand to help her. 'Up you come, then. We'll go together—'

'I don't think that's wise, Shilly.'

'Why? Mathilda is safe now. She doesn't have to stay hidden.'

'It's not Mathilda I'm thinking of. News of the squire's death will be a great shock to Lady Phoebe, and we know she's a fragile soul.'

'The squire went on about it enough.'

'And there's the child to consider. The squire's *other* child, still to arrive in this world. If we should bring to Lady Phoebe's home the squire's legitimate daughter, who knows what damage we might do?'

'I will not hurt her,' Mathilda said. 'The badness – it was him. My father.' She found that last word difficult to say, and not because it wasn't in her own way of speaking, her German words. 'When he came to Boscastle, he was afraid. That his new wife would die, and the child. That I believed. Of all his talk. He loved her, as my poor mother had loved him. None of this is the new wife's fault.'

'That's settled, then,' Anna said. 'You'll be quite safe here until we return.'

Mathilda brightened. 'I pack! I pack the case and then you come back and we go.'

She began to take off the many layers Anna had wrapped her in, her broad cheeks once more flushed, a sheen of sweat above her plump lips from sitting so close to the fire. She wasn't unlike the squire in body, I thought, though that might have been my eyes agreeing with what my ears had heard. That she was his daughter.

'Where shall we go, Shilly?' she said now.

'Where indeed?' Anna said.

THIRTY-EIGHT

We didn't speak on setting out to the manor house, though there was much between us that needed saying. I let Anna find her own way to her questions, and by the time the monks' wall came in sight, she had it.

'Shilly, when you were in the water, when the squire had you.'

'Yes,' I murmured, and felt again the cold air at the back of my neck as he held me over the drop. I shook it away. It was autumn come to the woods, that was all. Such was the way of things now. The leaves would soon fall and the sky would be seen more often in Trethevy. 'What did you see?' I asked her.

'I . . . I'm not sure. It all happened so quickly. I was trying to find a way down, trying to keep sight of you in case you went under the water and didn't come up again.'

The fear was still with her. I could hear it in her voice. See it in her hand clutching and letting go her skirt. I took that hand in mine.

'I'm here now, though, aren't I? You got me out.'

She nodded, and cleared her throat. 'I saw a dark shape blown out of the trees. It fell on the squire.'

'You know what that darkness was, Anna. *Who* it was.'

'I . . .'

'That was her true self you were seeing. That she let you see, for the first and last time.'

'I can't believe that was Mrs Haskell, Shilly.'

'Then what do you think it was came out of the trees?'

'I think it must have been some covering from the quarry, blown free. A paulin. They use them to keep the slate-splitters from the rain. The captain told Mr Williams about it.'

'Did he now? And what about the blade that came out of it? That stuck the squire as if he was a pig?'

'I did see that. The light caught it, just before the squire began to scream. A knife.' She wouldn't look at me.

'Well, paulins don't come with knives, Anna, as I'm certain you know, you being so knowledgeable about them.'

'No, they don't. But I had a knife. One I can no longer find.'

She looked at me then, and I let go her hand.

'I didn't kill the squire, Anna.'

'He was trying to kill *you*, Shilly! I'm not condemning you.'

'Well it sounds like you are!'

'I just wanted you to know that I saw. I saw that knife go into the squire before he fell.'

'You don't know what you saw, Anna Drake, because you don't know how to look. I didn't put a knife in the squire's back. It was Mrs Haskell stabbed him. Mrs Haskell who is not a woman like you or I. Who is something else altogether.'

'But if it *was* Mrs Haskell—'

'Which it was.'

'Then why would she risk herself like that when she believed Gertrud and Mathilda took Paul? Why not let Mathilda be killed and so save her a job?'

'She risked herself for me. You and I saved Paul, and Peter too, so she came to save me in return. She told me, when she showed herself to me by the fallen oak, that one day she wouldn't go back to the skin she was born with. I think that day was today, and she knew it. She knew she'd be leaving her family so she saved me as she went.'

'And how did she know to come to the waterfall, just as you needed her?'

I thought for a moment, for it did no good to pretend Anna hadn't asked something. She would go after an answer like a terrier after rats.

'Because her friends told her to come,' I said.

'Her friends? You mean Sarah and all the rest of them, at the cottages?'

'Oh, there's many more of them than that, Anna. They fill the wood.'

'What are you talking about?'

'Surely even you can't miss them. They've been following us since we first came to Trethevy. They're here now.'

She looked around, then moaned with dread.

The magpies had come quietly, and now filled every branch in sight.

I took her arm, and took her from their gazing.

We didn't speak again until we had left the trees, the manor house before us, and this time it was me who ended the silence.

'How's best to tell Lady Phoebe of the squire's death, and of Mathilda? All out at once, do you think? Or piece by piece? I don't know which is the kinder.'

'Nor I. He troubles me.'

'The squire? He needn't. He's gone, Anna.'

'Something isn't right. Think back to when we told Sir Vivian we believed Lucy had taken Paul Haskell. What was his reaction?'

'He was surprised.'

'Exactly.'

'And he shouldn't have been,' I said.

'Exactly right again. If he *had* taken the boy, then surely he would have been delighted to have a scapegoat offered him? We've been working in the belief that he was happy to frame Gertrud and Mathilda for taking

263

Paul as a means to incite violence against them. If that supposition is correct, then why would he challenge Lucy's guilt when it offered him a way to hide his own?'

I had no answer for her, but I thought I saw a way to get one, and told Anna we should go to the stables before seeing Lady Phoebe.

We found Simon in the yard, holding steady a towering beast while the smith rasped its hooves. This was a good find. Simon had no chance to get away while the smith held the horse's leg bent at the knee.

Simon's face fell on seeing us, and I wondered if Anna and I would ever be liked by those we called on. To have people dread the sight of you – that was the lot of the detective.

'You've frightened Lucy half to death, telling her she'll hang.' He was whispering so the smith shouldn't hear, though he needn't have minded. The rasps were loud enough to hide his secrets. 'How can you think she'd harm Paul Haskell?'

'You told us yourself she had cause to hate Paul's father,' Anna said, 'given the quarry accident that took both her parents.'

'She don't blame James Haskell!' Simon said. His voice had risen and the horse started. He danced out of the way of her huge feet. 'Lucy's the most kind-hearted soul you'll find in these woods,' he said, once the horse was steady again. 'She wouldn't hurt people like you're saying – the boys or their family.'

'I believe you,' I said. 'If you help us, Lucy won't go to the gallows.'

'Anything. I'll do anything to keep her safe.'

'On the day Paul Haskell went missing, where was the squire?'

'What you asking about him for?'

'Just try and think back. Did he come into the woods?'

'Had no chance to. He was away to Truro that day, to speak to Mr Trunkett. Wanted Mr Trunkett to turn the furrin women out the cottage. That's why I was able to . . .' He fiddled with the rope across the horse's nose.

'That's why you were able to go and rob Gertrud and Mathilda,'

Anna finished for him. 'Because your employer was away from home and wouldn't notice your absence.'

The smith dropped the horse's rasped hoof to the ground. 'Soreness in the flesh here,' he said. 'Squire making you give 'em too much grass again, Proctor? He don't know how to look after his beasts.'

We hurried to the house.

THIRTY-NINE

Mrs Carne said Lady Phoebe would see us in her parlour.

'That's if she *is* seeing visitors today,' the housekeeper said, 'because she's worked herself up into a state. I've had the Devil of a job trying to keep that broken window from her. How she heard the glass smash in the east wing, with all the doors proper closed like she asks, that I don't know. Lucy wouldn't say a word about that window but I know it was something to do with you pair.'

'Tell your mistress our visit is of the utmost importance,' Anna said. 'We wouldn't disturb her otherwise.'

Mrs Carne nodded at a door a little way down the passage. 'In there. Watch that you don't break anything else, and don't you upset her. Sir Vivian will be spitting feathers otherwise.'

Neither Anna nor I said anything to that.

Lady Phoebe's parlour had two windows, and a long padded chair that was almost a bed. I thought of the little room with the desk, where we had found the por-s'lain figure of the man with the birdcage. The squire's room. So much smaller and poorer than this of his wife, when she was the littler of the two.

'We shouldn't tell her of Mrs Haskell,' Anna said. 'It will be too much for her, something so strange as that.'

'I agree. Learning of Mathilda will be shock enough.'

'We ought to have brought the doctor in readiness.'

'We'll send Mrs Carne if he's needed,' I said.

We didn't have to wait long before the door opened, only a crack, and the slight form of Lady Phoebe slipped inside on her tiny feet. She was clad in a pink dress that made her skin look even more pale than the few times I'd looked on her. I resolved to speak soft and low and kind, to give Lady Phoebe time to take in each surprise, but still I was fearful. I didn't want to cause her harm.

To my relief, Anna spoke first, thanking Lady Phoebe for seeing us.

'You have made some progress in your investigation?' Lady Phoebe said. Her voice was light and sweet as the tinkling of the tiny bell Saint Nectan had left with Paul Haskell.

Anna hesitated, then said, 'There has been a development.'

'Please, sit,' she said, and did likewise, taking the chair that was like a bed, her legs stretched out in front of her and a hand resting on the soft swell of her middle.

She smiled at us. Like a child, I thought, though she was so much older than me, closer to Anna's age. Perhaps that was why she had lost so many babies. Would that we didn't cause the loss of this one.

'Lady Phoebe,' I began.

'Ah, there you are!' she said, looking to the door.

I caught a glimpse of a striped tail weaving through the furniture. Anna tucked her feet under her chair. Lady Phoebe hauled him into her arms. I worried that she'd strain her poor, weak self, picking up such a fat beast, but I needn't have. She was stronger than she looked.

She fussed the cat, scratched behind his ears and smoothed his enormous whiskers. 'You've been out today, haven't you, my love? Chasing the birds. Did you catch any? Did you get them?'

His purr was a roaring fire.

Anna cleared her throat. 'Forgive me, Lady Phoebe, but we must speak to you about a delicate matter.'

'There now, my love. I must listen to these good women. I must! Sit quietly.'

Pigeon perched on his mistress's knees, his weight making them splay. He nestled in the space he'd made for himself, if such a beast could be said to do such a gentle thing as nestle.

Lady Phoebe smiled at us again, stroking Pigeon's rippling back. 'Now. What is it you must say to me? I'll be sure to tell Sir Vivian when he comes home.'

'That's what we've come to speak to you about, Lady Phoebe,' Anna said. 'He won't be coming home. Sir Vivian is dead.'

She ceased stroking Pigeon. He nosed her stilled fingers but she had forgotten him. Her hands fluttered to her belly.

'Dead?' she said, and her voice cracked.

'He went over the waterfall,' I said. 'Likely washed out to sea. You should alert them in Boscastle to keep watch, to catch him before the tide takes him out.'

'There must be some mistake.'

'I was there,' I said. 'I saw it with my own eyes.'

'I . . . I don't understand. What was he doing in the river? Had he fallen?'

I glanced at Anna.

'The squire was trying to hurt someone,' I said. 'Someone he wanted gone from the woods. From his life.'

'Lady Phoebe,' Anna said, 'I'm sorry to have to tell you this but Sir Vivian was already married when he wed you, and his first wife was still living at that time. She had borne him a child who now seeks recognition. She is one of the women in Mr Trunkett's cottage – the other was his stepdaughter, who has very recently died. But Mathilda, the squire's true daughter, she lives. It was *she* the squire was trying to throw over the waterfall.'

Lady Phoebe cried out, and the sound seemed to stave her in for she crumpled over her belly. Pigeon slid to the floor with his own noise of upset.

Anna was at her side in an instant. 'Calm yourself, Lady Phoebe, for the sake of your child!'

But still her cries came. Her hair tumbled across her face. I was afraid to see how red her cheeks were.

'Quick, Shilly – tell Mrs Carne to send for the doctor.'

I was halfway out the door when I heard Lady Phoebe's words swim free of her cries.

'The fool! The *utter* fool!'

Gone was her child's voice, its lightness. In its place, hate hissed from her twisted lips. She jerked her legs off the long chair and stood, her hands made claws with the anger running through her.

Anna slowly stepped away, her palms raised as if to ward off an attack from the creature before us. The frail woman the squire had so feared for, unable to bear shock, needing to be coddled. She was gone, if she had ever been real at all.

'If he had only waited,' Lady Phoebe spat. 'Another day and the wretched girl would have gone the way of her sister. To be so close—' She kicked a chair across the room.

And then I knew whose hatred had poisoned the woods of Trethevy, who had brought back the blinded sisters. It wasn't Mrs Haskell's. It wasn't Gertrud's.

The hatred was Lady Phoebe's.

'How long have you known about Mathilda?' Anna said.

At the mention of that name, Lady Phoebe made a face as if she'd sipped sour milk.

'Her! She would take what belongs to my child. I read the letters from the first – read of her greed. My husband is a sentimental fool. He keeps such mementoes of his mistakes when he should have burnt them.'

Pigeon had slunk to the door and now scratched and whined to be released. His mistress ignored him.

'*You* took Paul Haskell,' I said. 'You made it look like Gertrud and

270

Mathilda had done it, waiting until the boy went to their cottage and then leaving the drawing charcoal in his place.'

'And the squire knew nothing of your plans,' Anna said. 'He asked us to find Paul because he had no idea you were the one who'd hidden him.'

Lady Phoebe gave a scornful laugh. 'Vivian is a blunderer. I knew *that* when I married him.'

'But not that he was a bigamist, I'll warrant,' Anna said. 'A blunderer with an estate and a title – that's worth putting up with. It must have been quite a blow to discover the truth. With the death of his first wife, your place was assured. No one need know she'd ever existed, if not for the inconvenience of her daughter. The *squire's* daughter.'

Lady Phoebe's fingers tightened on the back of the chair as she glared at Anna.

'But you are a resourceful woman,' Anna said, 'making sure you were sequestered in the east wing so no one noticed your absence when you went into the woods. A strong woman, too. Stronger than your husband thought you to be, Lady Phoebe. Strong enough to carry Paul Haskell to the summer house, to drag his brother kicking and screaming.'

'You are a flatterer, Miss Drake. Paul needed no carrying. He was confused after the blow, but not incapacitated. He followed meekly enough. His brother put up a fight. A brave boy. Had you not conjured that trick, Mrs Williams . . . I thought there was only one woman in these woods who could do such things.'

Before that moment such a charge would have made my cheeks flame and my stomach pitch. My hand would have sought the bottle. But I didn't mind her words then. I didn't mind what I was.

'You knew Mrs Haskell's true self,' I said. 'You knew she'd attack Gertrud and Mathilda if you waited long enough because she's not like other people.' I carried on, the truth of it now so clear before me that my words poured from my mouth, swift and tumbling as the Dark River. 'And when Mrs Haskell didn't do as you wanted, after you'd

271

hidden Paul beneath the summer house, you tried to take Peter, to push her. You wore that stocking across your face to frighten him—'

'Stocking?'

'We found a little scrap of it,' Anna said. 'That's how you did it. How you hid your face. Your eyes. Isn't it?'

Her voice belied her words, because in that moment she felt doubt, and I could see why. Lady Phoebe was herself looking confused.

'I had no need of such tricks. My cloak gave me protection enough, and who would have believed the boy anyway, should it have slipped a touch? Now.' She moved to a fancy cabinet in the corner of the room. 'How much did my husband offer you?'

Her words took my own. Like a tree falling into the river, stopping its course. Like a feather forced down a throat.

'What?' I managed to say.

'To find the boy. How much?'

Anna licked her lips. 'Thirty pounds.'

'Anna! You can't take her money. She's the guilty one. We must send her to the magistrates.'

Without looking up from rootling in the cabinet, Lady Phoebe said, 'And what proof would you give them, Mrs Williams?' Her anger was gone. She saw that she was safe. That Anna was *letting* her be safe.

'I . . .' My mouth was dry. I looked to Anna for help but she wouldn't meet my eye.

'I would say you are without proof of any kind, Mrs Williams.'

'There's the Haskell boys,' I said. 'They would speak, be witnesses. You made a mistake not killing them.'

'I wondered that, Mrs Williams, I did. Those lonely afternoons in the east wing. What if Paul should wake and get free before anyone acted on their rage? Why did I give myself that fear? Weakness. I will own it. They are sweet boys. I could not harm them.'

I was sickened hearing her talk of Peter and Paul as if she cared for them, she who had taken them from their families, risked their lives even if she didn't outright kill them.

'But it mattered not in the end,' she said. 'I have heard tell that Paul Haskell remembers nothing, that Peter has no clue who tried to take him. It was you and Saint Nectan saved the boys, Mrs Williams, saved them from the evil intentions of those foreign witches, one of whom got what she deserved. The other has scuttled away, back to the Devil. That is the belief in these parts. I think you'll find it hard to make people think otherwise.'

There was a clank of metal and she withdrew a tin box from the cabinet.

'Now, Miss Drake. Your investigations are over, are they not?'

'They are,' Anna said quietly.

'Anna, no! What are you doing? This is wrong!'

'And they will not resume at any time,' Lady Phoebe said. 'You will assure me of that?'

Anna nodded.

'Good. Then the thirty pounds is—'

'Three hundred,' Anna said.

I nearly fell over. Lady Phoebe, however, remained quite calm, her hand steady on the tin box.

'For Mathilda to give up her claim on the squire's estate,' Anna said.

'You will ensure that? My child must be the undisputed heir.'

'I give you my word.'

Lady Phoebe smiled, sly and cold. 'It has been a pleasure to work with you, Miss Drake.'

FORTY

'How could you let her get away with it?' I said as soon as we left the manor house. I hoped never to see that wretched place again as long as I lived.

'You heard Lady Phoebe. We have no proof to condemn her in the eyes of the law. But there are other ways to punish those who deserve it.'

I stopped. 'What do you mean?'

'For all her bravado, her ladyship faces a future of uncertainty while Mathilda lives, and that is its own kind of prison. What's to say Mathilda *won't* make a claim on Trethevy? Not today, not next week, not even next month, but there is always the chance that she might.'

'That will hang over Lady Phoebe,' I said. 'Her worry that her child will stay the heir, it'll never leave her.'

'And if she should receive an anonymous letter every now and then to remind her of the threat Mathilda poses, well. That will help to keep the matter uppermost in her thoughts.'

'That will be us doing to Lady Phoebe what Gertrud did to the squire – threatening.'

'I suppose it will,' Anna said. 'There is a certain neatness there.'

Anna was grinning, but I was wary of her.

'You gave Lady Phoebe your word,' I said. 'Does it mean nothing?'

'Not to those who have done wrong.'

'It's a good thing the detectives didn't want you if you're not to be trusted.'

'Sometimes life is not so black and white as you think it, Shilly.'

I marched past her. 'That's all well and good for you to say, but you had no right to make such a bargain for Mathilda, to decide her future for her.'

'Shilly, you might be able to *see* what others can't, but you need to get better at listening to what people tell you. You'll be no help to me otherwise.'

'I heard what you just said to Lady Phoebe!'

'And what about what Mathilda told us in the summer house, after I'd dragged you both from the river? She never wanted to be part of Gertrud's scheme. She was used by Gertrud just as Mrs Haskell was used by Lady Phoebe. We've done Mathilda a good turn by getting her money to live on.'

'We? That was *you* bargaining with a criminal, Anna. I had no part in it.'

'You *are* part of this, Shilly. It's you Mathilda wants to be with, that's clear as day. And you're with me so there we are. Complicit, to a degree.'

Despite my anger, I felt a warm rush of pleasure. *You're with me.*

We had passed beneath the trees again, heading towards the quarry. Anna was speaking but her words flew by me and were gone, for I was listening to the trees. For the first time since we had come to Trethevy, there was peace. The trees were quiet. Wood, water, stone. Stillness in them all. No birds watched us pass.

'Come on, Shilly-shally,' Anna called. 'I have a proposition to put to Mathilda that might make you happier. Don't condemn me just yet.'

I caught her up but felt no need to hurry, now that the path wasn't going to change.

I felt no more need to hurry when we reached the cottages. One cottage in particular, with a stinking man, a singing man, covered in fish oil and leering as we passed.

'I've plenty today, my dears,' Richard Bray shouted. 'Come on in. Come on in for a sup.'

Anna took my hand. 'You mustn't, Shilly. Please. It'll kill you and I can't—'

'I know.'

'What?'

'You were right, Anna. I don't need it to see the strange parts of the world, to see things do as they didn't ought to. I might *want* a sup, but that's something different. When we were running to save Mathilda, I did what was needed and no drop had touched my lips.'

She pulled me closer, so that our hips pressed together as we walked on. Richard Bray's cries died away. My need didn't die likewise, but Anna's body next to mine would help me fight it. In time, it might leave me.

'It looks like I have a new task, then,' Anna said.

'Another case?'

'Of sorts. I can well imagine teaching you to read and write might prove to be mysterious.'

'There is another mystery we must speak of first, Anna. The silk scrap we found just off the clearing.'

'What of it?' she said, with wariness.

'You were sure it was Lady Phoebe's means of hiding her face, that it explained away the blinded women I have felt to be in the woods. But she told us she didn't use such a thing.'

'We only have her word for that, Shilly.'

'Why would she lie about it? What does she stand to gain when we know all the rest of it?'

'To toy with us, to leave us wondering? Her arrogance is the most likely explanation, because if she didn't wear that stocking as a mask, then . . .'

'Then there was strangeness at work when I caught sight of Lady Phoebe's face, when Peter saw it. She wasn't all herself at that moment. The sisters who drowned the saint – they were here, Anna. In some half-being way. They were with Lady Phoebe. *In* her. In Gertrud, too, I suppose.'

'You believe that Lady Phoebe and Gertrud were made a kind of sister to the other? Even though they weren't bound by blood?'

'It was the old story bound them,' I said, 'and their hate. Blood meant nothing to Gertrud – look at her meanness to Mathilda.'

'But it meant everything to Lady Phoebe, trying to secure the rights of her unborn child.'

'Well, that's often the way with sisters, isn't it? They fight. But the hate is done with now. That echo of the first pair, from the time of the saint, they're gone. Back to wherever it is we go when we leave this world.'

Anna shivered. 'I hope there's a better place when my time comes.'

'The people here had good fortune, having someone to save them from such wickedness.'

'When you say "someone", I take it you're not referring to my efforts in this case, or your own, Shilly?'

'I mean Saint Nectan.'

'I thought so. You still believe he was involved in what happened here? The bells. Paul's survival under the summer house.'

'Yes. And you believe different.'

She swiped at a fern by way of answer.

'Do you doubt he was ever here, in Trethevy?' I said. 'Even forever ago?'

'Forever ago? Who can possibly know anything about then?'

'You keep talking about these poets.'

Anna laughed. 'They have their part to play. Say there *was* a man here, in the distant past. Say he did good things in these woods, kindnesses, healing, and word spread, making those good deeds into something else, into miracles.'

'And that made others come,' I said. 'They turned his house into a chapel.'

'And built a monastery to worship in his name.'

'And at the end of his days he was drowned, by a pair of sisters who knew only hatred.'

'If any of it is true,' Anna said, 'then perhaps that last part is as likely as the rest of it. Which is to say unlikely. Saint Nectan is a myth, Shilly. A story.'

'Or the truth.'

'Or something in between.'

'Isn't that why I gave up milking cows,' I said, 'to help you with the in between?'

'Partly,' she said.

We found Mathilda on the shelf overlooking the waterfall. She was wearing Mr Williams's boxy black coat but the sleeves were a little short. I caught a glimpse of the scratches Mrs Haskell had given her. The flesh was beginning to heal, at last.

We sat down with her, and Anna told her what had passed between us and Lady Phoebe.

When Anna had finished, Mathilda said nothing for a little while. She stared out at the water where she had so nearly died. As had I.

'If he had known her better, his new wife,' Mathilda said, 'he might have got what he so wanted.'

'He certainly underestimated her,' Anna said.

'And paid for it with his life,' I added.

Mathilda stood. 'And now the wife has what she wants. The name, the land, the child.'

'You are not left with nothing, Mathilda. But there is a condition to the money. You must leave here.'

'That is what I want! I never want to be here. Is Gertrud's doing, all of it. I go. I take the money.'

'Three hundred pounds is a fine sum,' Anna said, 'but it won't last forever. It would be wise to invest the money to produce an income.'

I smiled. Here was Anna's talent.

'Yes,' Mathilda said. 'I must do that. To make the money last.'

'It just so happens that Shilly and I are looking for investors.'

Mathilda's eyes widened.

'We're setting up an enterprise,' Anna said. 'An agency, for detection. Do you know this word? De-tec-shun.'

I went inside and packed up the last of our things.

We were ready to leave the woods just after midday, deciding to take the longer way back to the road, it being the easier path with Anna's case. Our going was unnoticed by all but one.

From the magpie tree, a bird watched us cross the clearing. A large bird, with feathers of the deepest black. The most knowing of all Trethevy birds. I knew who it was, of course, because I knew her true self as well as I knew my own.

'Come on if you're coming, Shilly-shally,' Anna called.

'What is this, this "Shilly-shally"?' Mathilda asked her.

I didn't catch Anna's answer as they slipped beneath the trees and so to the road, the sea. The rest of our lives.

I looked back at the bird. Did she know where we were bound?

It was the going that mattered.

AUTHOR'S NOTE

The characters in *The Magpie Tree* are fictional. So is their story, but like the twisting roots of the trees of Trethevy, it goes deep into the earth of that place – earth that's rich with tales.

I first came across 'The Ladies of St Nectan's Glen' in Daphne du Maurier's book *Vanishing Cornwall*. I was fifteen and learning, for the first time, the stories that belonged to the part of the world in which I lived: north Cornwall. A place of bleak moorland and dangerous coasts. A place visitors drive through on their way to the softer, easier landscapes of the south. A place I loved, and continue to love to this day, though I haven't lived there for a good while now.

Du Maurier recounts the story of a mysterious pair of women who set up home in woodland near Boscastle. No one knows who they are. They speak a strange language. One day, someone spies through the window of the women's cottage and sees that one of them has died. Her companion is distraught but will not speak. The dead woman is taken away for burial, as is decent, and her companion remains in the cottage, wasting away, until one day she is found very still in her chair before the fire. Her hand hangs close to the floor, as if she is reaching for the handkerchief that has fallen there. But her hand will never reach the handkerchief: the poor creature is dead. And the cause? A broken heart. No one is any the wiser as to why the women came to the woods.

The image of the hand reaching for the handkerchief has stayed with me for almost twenty years. I have carried it around with me, trusting that, at some point, I would find the women's story. Along the way, a second image has joined it: a boy who traps rabbits, running into the trees. Where he came from, where he was running to, I didn't know. Until I came to know Anna and Shilly.

Following the trail of the story backwards from du Maurier made me feel, at times, as if I *was* that boy, but instead of snaring my prey I was instead falling down the rabbit hole, getting lost in a maze of tales and trees. Even the name of the place didn't stay the same. The spot now known as St Nectan's Glen has been, since the eighteenth century, Nathan's Cave, Trevillet Vale, St Knighton's Kieve, Glen Nectan, Glen Neot, St Kynance Keeve, and even the Haunted Valley, to name a few of its titles. It is a place that shifts about, and writers have had a hand in this shiftiness.

Trethevy has long been popular with visiting writers who have retold old stories about the place, and written new ones over them, into them. Anna isn't wrong when she claims that poets are responsible for the legends. A useful guide to the development of the stories, and the changing identity of the place as a result, is Sidney Joseph Madge who produced two excellent guides to the area: *Legends of Trevillet Glen and Waterfall* (1914) and *The 'Chapel', Kieve and Gorge of 'Saint Nectan', Trevillet Millcombe, Tintagel* (1950).

Madge makes clear that it's Robert Stephen Hawker, parson of nearby Morwenstow parish, famous eccentric and not-quite-so-famous poet, who has had the greatest influence on what is now known as St Nectan's Glen. Hawker first visited the area in 1823, on his honeymoon, and in 1832 he published *Records of the Western Shore*, which included the poem 'The Sisters of the Glen'. The opening line sets the action at 'Nathan's mossy steep', and the poem goes on to recount the story much as du Maurier tells it.

Hawker revised this poem several times during his lifetime, and the different versions he published changed the name Nathan to Neot and then to Nectan. But though Cornwall has plenty of early Christian saints of its own, Nectan isn't one of them. His home has always been Hartland in Devon, and I have drawn on the Reverend Gilbert H. Doble's work *St Nectan*, number 45 in his series on Cornish saints (1940), for the Nectan of *The Magpie Tree*.

St Nectan's lack of Cornish connections didn't stop Hawker's myth-making. In a note attached to the poem in the collection *The Quest of the Sangraal*, published in 1864, Hawker claimed that a pleasure house that overlooked the Trethevy waterfall, built in 1820 but by that time in disrepair, was in fact St Nectan's hermitage. Madge notes that the Ordnance Survey subsequently marked 'the hermitage' on the map, where it still appears today (see OS Explorer 111). The story has reshaped the land it sprang from, much like the River Duwy that has carved its way through the valley, fashioning and then destroying numerous 'kieves' (plunge pools or basins in Cornish) on its way to the sea.

And the stories run on likewise. Du Maurier's main source was Wilkie Collins' entertaining travelogue *Rambles Beyond Railways*, first published in 1851, which also informed my first novel, although on a very different subject: fishing. *The Magpie Tree* has had me circle back to old sources, old stories. Having been to Tintagel Castle, Collins decides to take in 'Nighton's Kieve' and the famous waterfall, but on arriving at the valley he finds 'one compact mass of vegetation entirely filling it'. The lack of a path means Collins has to fight his way through trees, which possess 'a living power of opposition', much like the enchanted woods of *Sleeping Beauty*. His antipathy for Trethevy's flora finds its way into Shilly's distrust of thicketyness. In his hunt for the waterfall, Collins stumbles across 'the damp, dismantled stone walls of a solitary cottage', and here he learns the tale of the former inhabitants who spoke 'a mysterious and diabolic language of their own'.

When du Maurier visited the Glen herself in the course of writing *Vanishing Cornwall*, the then-owner informed her that the ladies of the story were, in fact, St Nectan's sister-assistants, and this echoes Robert Hunt's retelling of the story in 'St Nectan's Kieve and the Lonely Sisters', first published in his *Popular Romances of the West of England* (1865). Du Maurier also draws on *A Londoner's Walk to the Land's End and a Trip to the Scilly Isles* by Walter White (1865), which I found very useful for descriptions of mid-nineteenth-century Boscastle.

Those familiar with St Nectan's Glen today will no doubt realise I have refashioned the landscape for my own purposes; the quarry, in particular, is a substantial addition to the woods. In this I'm following in the tradition of those who have gone before me. I like to think Hawker would approve.

ACKNOWLEDGEMENTS

Thanks to my agent, Sam Copeland at Rogers, Coleridge and White, for great faith.

Thanks to my editor extraordinaire, Lesley Crooks, and to Susie Dunlop, Daniel Scott, Kelly Smith and all at Allison & Busby.

Thanks to my mum and dad, who are always keen on research trips, even in the rain.

Thanks to my readers: Katy Birch, Tim Major, Hannah Ormerod and Kate Wright.

Thanks to Dave, without whom I'd still be at Lanlary Rock, wondering where to go next.

Today, Boscastle is home to the Museum of Witchcraft and Magic: an extraordinary treasure trove of materials relating to matters of the occult in Cornwall and further afield. The protection charms that feature in *The Magpie Tree* are based on objects held in the museum, and the novel also includes some of the practices of the Boscastle witches, which the museum displays explore.

In addition to the sources mentioned in the Author's Note, I have also drawn on Catherine Lorigan's book *Delabole: The History of the Slate Quarry and the Making of its Village Community*, William Taylor's *History of Tintagel*, and *The Parish of Tintagel: Some Historical Notes* by A. C. Canner.

KATHERINE STANSFIELD is a novelist and poet whose debut novel *The Visitor* won the Holyer an Gof Fiction Award. She grew up in the wilds of Bodmin Moor in Cornwall and now lives in Cardiff.

@K_Stansfield
katherinestansfield.blogspot.co.uk